OTHER BOOKS BY NICK GAITANO

Special Victims
Mr. X

NICK GAITANO

SIMON & SCHUSTER
New York   London   Toronto   Sydney   Tokyo   Singapore

NORTH COUNTRY LIBRARY SYSTEM
WATERTOWN, NEW YORK 13601

SIMON & SCHUSTER
Rockefeller Center
1230 Avenue of the Americas
New York, NY 10020

This book is a work of fiction. Names, characters,
places, and incidents either are products of the
author's imagination or are used fictitiously. Any
resemblance to actual events or locales or persons,
living or dead, is entirely coincidental.

Copyright © 1996 by Nick Gaitano
All rights reserved,
including the right of reproduction
in whole or in part in any form.

SIMON & SCHUSTER and colophon are registered trademarks
of Simon & Schuster Inc.

Designed by Irving Perkins Associates

Manufactured in the United States of America

1   3   5   7   9   10   8   6   4   2

Library of Congress Cataloging-in-Publication Data
Gaitano, Nick.
Jaded / Nick Gaitano.
p.   cm.
1. Police—Illinois—Chicago—Fiction.   2. Chicago (Ill.)—
Fiction.   I. Title.
PS3557.A3586J3   1996
813'.54—dc20   95-45709
CIP

ISBN 0-684-80750-5

As Always, for Theresa

JADED

Special Victims Bureau Detective Sergeant Jake Phillips sat nervously in the psychologist's office, fiddling with his gold Rolex, wondering if he was paranoid or if his estranged wife, Marsha, was really doing everything in her power to destroy any chance that their marriage could have to survive. Marsha hadn't arrived yet, which was fine with Jake. There were a number of things he wanted to get off his chest before she arrived.

"So, *you're* not going to be a part of this whole thing, right? You're not going to speak to this reporter?"

Dr. Evans—Florence—gave him a sour look. She was an attractive woman somewhere in her mid-thirties, a few years older than Jake. As always, she was dressed well, in a business suit of light summer colors. She was down-to-earth, never talked down her nose at him or pretended to be superior because she was a shrink and he was a cop. Usually they got along. For the most part, Jake liked her.

They were sitting in her office, which was a converted bedroom in a Streeterville high-rise apartment that had a killer view of Lake Michigan. Jake guessed it was easier to talk about your temporal problems when you were looking at something eternal. He watched a bunch of tall-masted sailboats cutting the water, puzzled as to how anyone could be so content, so carefree. The people who owned those boats thought they lived in a world that was mostly safe, a world that held little personal danger to themselves. Part of Jake's job was to allow them to live through the rest of their lives suffering under that delusion.

There was a touch of rebuke in her voice as Florence said, "I may not be an M.D., but I'm still a doctor, Jake, and I *do* believe in professional ethics."

Relieved, Jake hurried to cover himself. He said, "Listen, I don't know. I never thought Marsha would do anything like that, either." Florence didn't respond. "I just got off work. It's been a tough, tough day. I'm under a lot of . . . pressure . . . right now." Jake reluctantly looked away from the boats, over at the doctor.

"I go home to drop off my gun because it's intimidating to Marsha, and I understand that, I really do. I walk over here or take a taxi, you know. It's not like I can leave it locked in the trunk of the car or something."

Florence, as always, sat looking at him without expression. From time to time she'd make marks on the notebook in her lap. When he'd first started seeing her one-on-one, Florence had asked him if he wanted to lie down on the long black leather psychiatrist's couch. She'd explained to him in simple language that it would be easier for him to speak his thoughts more freely if he wasn't looking at her, if she was just a disembodied voice floating around somewhere behind him. He'd told her he'd prefer to sit facing her, in one of the two padded chairs. She'd told him that would be fine.

Six months later, he still hadn't laid his head down on that couch.

Jake said, "There was a message on my machine from that writer, and another one from Marsha, telling me she was going to talk with the woman. I felt sort of betrayed, I guess. I don't know. She—the reporter, not Marsha—said she's writing something about abused wives of Chicago cops, one of those bullshit stories that's so hot these days."

Although they often had heated discussions, Florence never judged him, never took sides, and Jake didn't often swear in front of her, mostly out of respect. Early on, he'd said "fuck" a few times, just to see how she'd react, and she hadn't. Since then, Jake had watched himself. He was here to try and put his marriage back together, not to make enemies. He had enough of those as it was.

Now Florence said, "Marsha's never claimed that you abused her, Jake."

"I never laid a hand on her."

"I don't know what she's told her private therapist."

That stopped Jake. Could this woman actually believe . . . ?

"I said I never laid a hand on her." Jake repeated it strongly.

"I didn't say you did. But I want you to think about what you just said to me. 'Bullshit stories that are so hot these days.' About spousal abuse, Jake? Particularly within a culture that traditionally protects its own *and* carries weapons legally? That's far from what you could call bullshit."

"That's not what I meant, Florence. That's not how I meant it."

"How *did* you mean it?"

"You know how the press can be, what they can do to someone. They could write a story about the Archangel Michael and make him look like a bad guy if they want to."

"The story's going to be about the high rate of divorce within the police department, not strictly about spousal abuse. Marsha is going to be just one of a number of subjects. The reporter did actually call me. I refused to even disclose to her whether you were a client, and she wouldn't tell me how she got my name."

"You don't have to be a trained investigator to figure *that* one out."

"No, you're wrong; I called Marsha, and I was angry. She assured me that she hadn't given the reporter my name or number, or even told her we were working together."

"And you believe her?"

"Come on, Jake. Marsha's one of the most honest people you've ever known."

He'd ever known? Jake had a psychiatrist's thought: What did she mean by that?

"Not to say that I'm not, right?"

"I'm not saying that at all. I think you've been as honest with me as you're capable of being, at least most of the time. You have . . . other issues, Jake."

"Could we talk about this at Wednesday's session, please? When it's one-on-one? Marsha'll be here any minute now, and I want to talk about—"

"Marsha won't be joining us for the first half hour today, Jake. When I spoke to her, I asked her to come at seven-thirty, instead of seven. I hope that's all right with you, but I wanted to speak with you about all this other business without Marsha present."

"Why?" Jake was angry. He was here to put things back together with Marsha; he was here to save his marriage. He had never been hot on the idea of coming here alone; in fact, he resented having to come twice a week at all. Once a week with Marsha, that was supposed to be the deal. Now they'd taken half of *that* away from him. He was already ten minutes into a session he would have trouble paying for. How he'd ever gotten talked into all of this . . .

Florence made a notation in her pad. He felt the sudden urge to tear it out of her hands and rip it to shreds.

"As far as you're concerned, the ultimate goal of our sessions is your reconciling with Marsha, correct?"

"Absolutely." What the hell else did this woman think he was doing here?

"Marsha's problems with reconciliation today are the same as they were six months ago."

"Trust, you mean."

"That's just part of it, Jake, but trust is still a problem, yes— your lack of openness with Marsha." Jake blew out his breath and threw his hands into the air. When he spoke now he spoke intently, leaning forward in his chair.

"Florence, I'm a *cop,* for God's sake. It's not like being a schoolteacher; you don't come home and talk about what happened that day at work." Jake leaned back in the chair, trying to gather his thoughts. He had a college degree; he could do better than this. "I mean, do *you* tell your"—Jake knew nothing about the doctor's personal life, whether she was married, engaged, straight, gay, nothing—"do you talk about your day with whoever *you're* with? You can't. And neither can I."

"Of course you can, Jake. You just chose not to."

"She doesn't want to hear it."

"Because you never gave her a chance."

"There are sometimes things I'm working on, Florence, that are confidential, that are strictly need-to-know. If I told even one person outside of my squad about that, I'd not only get bounced out of the Special Victims Bureau, I'd never be trusted in the department again."

Florence held a hand up, stopping him before he could say any more. She gave a slight negative shake of her head.

"This is something we'll want to discuss when Marsha gets here, Jake. I asked her to bypass the first half hour because of the reporter, the story. I want to know how you feel about it, how you're planning on dealing with it."

"Listen, it's Marsha's life. She wants to talk to reporters, it's her business. As long as she tells the truth."

"You won't try and stop her?"

"Stop her? How? What am I going to do, threaten her? Beat her up? I just don't think the problems in our marriage should be part of the public record, that's all. I don't like the idea of talking to reporters. I never have."

"You won't have a few drinks and call Marsha, try to convince her not to talk to the reporter?"

"I only did that two times—"

"Once is too many times."

"It was a mistake. I apologized. Both times I'd been drinking."

"Being drunk is never an excuse."

"I said I was drinking, not drunk. You remind me of some lawyers I know."

This won him a smile. Florence smiled a lot. Jake wondered who made her smile when she wasn't psychoanalyzing anyone. Whoever it was, Jake felt a little envy toward him. Or her.

Florence said, "It's odd how some people process resentment, isn't it?"

Jake smiled ruefully and shook his head. "You think I'm

insulting you? I just meant, lawyers always have a glib, easy, smart answer."

"Have you been doing anything about your drinking problem?"

"I don't have a—"

"Jake . . ."

Jake took several deep breaths, looked out the window, and calmed himself. After a minute, he said, "Listen, it's a sign of the times, I know. Every time a man argues with his wife, he's an abuser. Every time he gets mad, what's really happening is his inner child is crying out in pain. Every time someone fails in their lives, it's because they were abused as kids. Would you lighten up on me if a stroke of lightning hit me and I had a sudden realization that I'd been abused?"

"Not one ounce. And you're veering way off course here."

"That's because a woman I love moved out on me, Florence. We don't live together. We don't have relations. We hardly know each other anymore; she doesn't have the right to judge me." Jake realized he was raising his voice. He wondered if Florence made a mark in her pad every time he did, with the goal of making him pay for it later. Add six sessions for each outburst.

More calmly, Jake said, "I go over to pick up my daughter and my mother-in-law *smirks* at me. The woman never did a real day's work in her life, and she smirks at *me*. Can you imagine what she tells my kid? I work with a group of people who are the best and the brightest the department has, and you know what? They respect me, respect my work. And I've got an ex-Las-Vegas-showgirl grandma bad-mouthing me to my kid."

Jake paused, but Florence just patiently looked at him, as if she somehow knew he wasn't finished. He waved a hand in the air in frustration, then put it on his lowered brow and kneaded his forehead. Florence remained silent.

"Telling my daughter I'm a lush." He looked up at Florence. "They don't live with me; they don't know anything about me anymore. None of them has any evidence that I have a drinking problem, but now, all of a sudden, out of a clear blue sky, I do."

"Evidence? Now who sounds like a lawyer?" Jake shook his head. He wasn't in the mood for jokes. Florence said, "You and Marsha have both told me that you started drinking heavily right after she left you. And we've discussed the fact—several times before—that you've been binge drinking on your days off since Marsha left you, haven't we?"

"I never said 'binge drinking.' "

"It's what you described. On the days you can't have your daughter, you drink."

"What the hell else is there for me to do!"

"You've been separated almost a year, yet you haven't dated anyone." Jake looked up at her. Was she telling him that Marsha was going out with other men? No, that couldn't be. Florence was *his* counselor; she didn't see Marsha alone.

Did she consult with Marsha's doctor? Jake thought these doctors were supposed to make you feel better, not worse. Now he had a whole other set of problems to worry about.

"You admit you don't socialize with other officers, that you don't have any real friends. You're either working, or with your daughter, or here, or out drinking, correct?"

"I blow off steam, Florence. I'm a big boy."

"You're a man. A big man, with the legal authority to carry a gun. You're living out a long-established pattern here, Jake. First the wife leaves, then the friends avoid you, then you lose the job. It's classic."

"My job's not in any jeopardy. And I don't *want* a lot of friends. Marsha was all I needed."

"But she's not with you anymore, is she?"

"What are you saying here?"

"I'm saying it's easy to understand why Marsha fears you."

"*Fears* me—"

"You've admitted that you're growing increasingly paranoid—"

"I said I've gotten *cau*tious—"

"You used the term yourself, Jake, more than once. You said paranoid, not cautious."

"You don't have any idea what I'm involved with, with what I'm doing." Jake stopped himself before he blurted out things that were none of the woman's business. "*All* cops are paranoid! It's what keeps them alive, for God's sake!"

"Jake . . . "

"Maybe you'd understand if you'd seen the things I've seen."

Florence looked at him, puzzled. "Why do you act differently when it's just you and me together than you do when Marsha's in the room? Can you answer that?" Florence continued without waiting for an answer. "And you have to do me a favor, Jake. You've always been more or less straight with me. Don't try to pull that sort of thing with me again, all right? I spend half my days working with the sort of kids you spend your career locking up; let's not pretend that you've cornered the market on witnessing life's ugliness."

"Tony Tulio used to send kids to you, didn't he?"

"An assistant state's attorney assigned to work with him did, yes. Now, you want to stop changing the subject?"

"You want to talk about my drinking some more."

"No, I don't. What I want is your word that when Marsha gets here, you'll behave like the mature adult that you are. I want your word that you won't try to tell her what to do, that you won't try to control her, that you won't even *ask* her not to do whatever she wants to do with her life."

"She's a full-grown woman, and I've never tried to tell her what to do." Jake paused purposely before he said, "Not even when I'm drinking."

Florence shook her head. "Your drinking, your"—she gave him that small smile again—"*caution,* your separation from Marsha, these are all symptoms, Jake. What I want to talk about is the problem."

"Problem?"

"What's really wrong, Jake? What's wrong with you—that's what we need to talk about."

Jake looked at her oddly as a muted bong sounded. Florence smiled at him reassuringly. "Marsha's here." She rose and stood over Jake, looking down at him. "Don't worry, though, we're closer than you think to finding out what it is. We'll get into it more deeply on Wednesday."

"Wait." Jake looked up at her, and she held his eyes steadily.

"Wednesday, when I come here. What I want to know, Florence—I mean, I don't want to end up like Mark Fuhrman here. I don't want to tell you things and have them come back to haunt me in court ten years from now." Florence didn't move toward the door. The intensity of her gaze told Jake that she was paying strict attention.

She said very softly, "That was a different situation, Jake. I can explain it if you'd like."

"I'd appreciate it. Marsha's outside, and I don't want to keep her waiting, but let me ask you this: What I tell you, it stays inside this room, right? Within certain boundaries. I know I can't tell you about breaking the law, anything like that. I mean, if I talk about my childhood or, say, about an investigation, *anything*, it stays between the two of us, doesn't it?"

"It does."

Jake nodded, scratched briefly at his cheek, then looked out the windows at the sailboats floating peacefully on Lake Michigan's calm blue waters.

———

The man was tied securely to the heavy wooden chair. He'd been beaten beyond recognition. Using the eye that hadn't been smashed, he looked at the little black box, then closed the good eye in terror. The bulky man who was holding the box saw this, and he smiled. He looked at his slender companion, who was also grinning, and nodded. They figured they had Jimmy cold, that he'd finally tell them where the money was stashed.

The name of the man in the chair was Jimmy (Jimbolaya) Duette. His good eyeball was burning from the double, salt-sting attack of sweat and his own blood, which had flowed into it from the wide gash the bulky man had opened on his forehead when he was slapping Jimmy around with the flat leather sap. It was at that point that Jimmy's spirit had been broken— he'd lost his stoic, tough-guy facade and had begun to scream. Working together, the men had managed to gag him.

Jimmy had lost most of his teeth—white, well-kept teeth of which he'd been inordinately proud. He'd swallowed half a dozen. Most of the rest of his teeth were now on his chest, in his lap, and on the concrete floor beside the chair. The teeth that hadn't been knocked out had been broken and were still in his jaw, their jagged edges tearing into the inside of his cheeks and his sensitive tongue.

Jimmy no longer felt any pain in the ruined eye; it had been enucleated; he would never see from it again, even were he to survive. He couldn't feel the jellylike fluid that had dripped down onto his cheek, nor could he hear anything in his right ear, with the exception of a loud, constant ringing. Several of his joints had been avulsed, particularly in his fingers. The centralized pain deep within his chest told him that at least two of his ribs had been broken. He believed that one of the broken ribs had punctured a lung, because it hurt to breathe. His nose was shattered, and with his mouth gagged, he was having a terrible time breathing at all. The leather belt they'd used to secure the handkerchief gag inside his mouth prevented him from spitting, was forcing him to swallow down great gobs of blood. He was nauseated and aware that if he vomited, he would die, which made the nausea grow worse. Before he'd closed his one good eye, concussion had caused him to see two metal boxes, swimming in and out of focus. One box would have been enough. One box would have been way more than enough.

The only thing that had given Duette a slender thread of hope for his survival was his knowledge that he had something that these men wanted—money, and a lot of it—and he therefore didn't believe that they would kill him until they had it. But Duette knew what the box was and what they were going to do with it. Neither of the men in the room with him knew anything about gentility. The thought of what was about to occur made Duette lose all hope.

Two slender wires extended from the front end of the box. The wires had alligator clips attached at their ends. There was a crank handle around in back.

An animal noise escaped from somewhere deep down in Duette's chest. He opened his good eye and looked wildly around, as if seeking some sign—even the smallest sign—of hope. But nothing had changed; no one had come to rescue him. With a sinking feeling he understood that no one would be coming to do so.

The room they were in was small, and looked like some sort of bomb shelter. The ceiling and the floor were constructed of concrete and the walls were made of cinder block, which in effect soundproofed the room. The blocks were painted light blue. There was an old, worn little card table leaning against one wall. Next to it was another chair identical to the one that Duette was tied to. The slender man had settled down into the second chair and was now breathing raggedly from his exertions, gently rubbing the knuckles of one leather-gloved hand with the fingers of the other.

The bulky man disgustedly said, "Get up and bring that table over here." He never took his eyes off Duette. Duette heard the slender man sigh.

"You better put some gloves on, man; you're gonna touch that hillbilly piece of shit now." He grunted heavily as he lifted the light table. "All that blood on him, he's a candidate for the AIDS if I ever heard of one, and you been pounding on him all

night without nothing on your hands." There was a hint of
jocularity in his tone that the bigger man didn't care for.

"What makes you so all-of-a-sudden concerned about my
welfare?" The bulky man was still glaring at Duette. He, too,
was breathing heavily. There were great round sweat stains
under the armpits of his white short-sleeve shirt. Duette was
hyperventilating. "Come on, hurry it up, for Christ's sake,
would you? This thing ain't getting any lighter."

The slender man dropped the table to the floor, and the bulky
man put the black box on top. He grabbed the wires, then
pulled them toward Duette, making sure they'd reach. They
did. When they touched Duette's chest, he tried to leap out of
the chair. The bulky man grinned again. Duette couldn't help
himself; he was now crying uncontrollably.

"You could make it easy on yourself," the bulky man said. He
wiped blood off his knuckles, onto his dark pants. He frowned
suddenly and turned to his partner. "Where's them gloves?"

"Little late to worry about it now."

The bulky man snapped his fingers. "Come on!"

The slender man took off one glove, reached into the back
pocket of his navy blue suit pants and took out a pair of latex
surgeon's gloves and handed them to the other man. "Can't hit
him with those; they'll split."

"I'm through bruising my knuckles on this country asshole,"
the man said, as he pulled the gloves on over large, bloody fists.
He snapped them at the wrists, and grunted. Duette was brutally shaking his head, tossing it from one shoulder to the other.
The two men thought he was trying to deny what was about to
occur, but they were wrong. Duette was trying to snap his own
neck, trying to commit suicide before these men could finish
killing him.

The bulky man leaned down until he was looking Duette in
the eye.

"Jimma?" The man who had been born and raised on Chicago's Southwest Side now spoke with an exaggerated South-
ern drawl. "Hey, Jimma?" Duette stopped shaking his head and

looked into the bulky man's smiling eyes. "Now, you should know, Jimma, you're prolly three-quarters dead already. Least half. And you know why that is? 'Course you do. 'Cause you cursed me, boy. I coulda had you talkin' without all this pain, but the thing is, I don't let punks like you curse me, Jimma. I wouldn't last long in my business if I did." The man paused and gravely nodded his head before he continued, confirming his words to both himself and his captive.

"Now, you brought this on yourself, Jimma, by acting like a jagoff, by cussing when you should have been talking. But I'm a reasonable man, and I'm willing to let bygones be bygones, all right?" He smiled now as he nodded. Duette could control neither his weeping nor his hyperventilation. It appeared that he might die of suffocation soon, even if the men left him alone. He wished that he would. Now that he was trying to, he couldn't force himself to vomit.

"Fact is, you're prolly more dead than alive at this point. Can you feel the life slipping right out of you? I've seen it enough times to know when a man's near his death. The good news is, son, if we get you to a hospital right quick, the docs, with all the good shit they got today, well, they might just be able to save you."

The bulky man's voice was suddenly pure Chicago as he said, "What I need to know is, if I take off the belt, Jimmy, take out the gag, are you gonna tell us where that money is? Or are you just gonna cuss at me some more? See, I'll get real mad this time if I got to touch all your sweat and snot and spit and blood, just to get cussed at. So I'm gonna leave it up to you, give you what we call in Chicago a *ca-reer* choice. Should I take the gag out? Or should I put that machine on your titties and give it a crank or two, see if you want to talk to me then." Duette was nodding his head up and down, rapidly.

"You don't like the machine? All right. You gonna talk to me, right, Jimmy?" He walked around behind Duette and began to loosen the strap. "Me, I gotta admit it, I admire you, I respect what you did tonight. I really do, Jimmy. I want you to know that. Shit, stood up to us like that, for, what now, forty-five minutes, an hour? You know how much balls that takes?'' The strap came free, and a hand carefully removed the gag. Duette sucked in grateful lungfuls of air, gasping, choking, spitting thick strings of blood down onto what was left of his shirt.

"I want to cut you loose, Jimmy, and stop this all right now. I really do. Your face looks like raw hamburger. Me, I get paid whether you talk to me or not; I don't want to do any more of this to you. Just tell me where the money is. All right? Tell me, and my partner here goes and finds it. Soon as he does, well, then, buddy, we drop you off at the emergency room. When you get out of the hospital, you head on back down to Shreveport, or New Orleans, or wherever the fuck you're from, and you keep your ass down there this time. Swim in the swamps, barbecue tarantulas, wrestle alligators, I don't give a shit what you do. As long as you don't never try to come back up here to Chicago, try to play with the big boys again, you'll be all right by us, okay?''

The man was bending over again now, in front of Duette, their faces close. The slender man had moved in closer so he could hear what Duette said. When the man spoke now, his voice was friendly, cajoling, manipulative. He knew that he'd won, and he didn't see himself as the type to rub it in.

Duette said, "Law-ahd fah-gi me . . . " The bulky man leaned forward, his eyes alert, straining to hear.

"What? What's that, Jimmy?"

The slender man said, "Shit, he's praying in hillbilly."

"What?" The bulky man looked at his partner, puzzled.

"He said, 'Lord forgive me.' " The big man shook his head and chuckled, then turned back to Duette.

"The Lord can't help you now, Jimmy; only *I* can help you. And I will, just as soon as you tell me where the *money* is!" He forced himself to calm down. "Only, you're missing them pretty teeth, so it's gonna be hard for you to talk. But give it a shot, come on, Jimmy. Where's the money, son? Come on, stop crying now and tell me. Where's the money?''

Duette lifted his head, gulped in one last, long breath of air, then spat as hard as he could into the man's open eyes and mouth. The man jumped back as if he'd been shot, screaming, hands going to his eyes, rubbing at them as he spit harshly and repeatedly onto the floor. The slender man gave out with a little laugh before he caught himself. The bulky man moved toward him, stopped, rubbing at his eyes still, not believing what had occurred.

He tore what was left of Duette's shirt off his back and jammed it into his mouth. Duette closed his eyes, fatalistically waiting. Seconds later, he felt the alligator clips clamping down on the sensitive skin of his nipples. Then his entire body began to quake involuntarily; his back arched and bowed as the voltage flowed into him. Duette was fighting and struggling, his mouth open in a silent scream, until the force of his struggle caused the heavy chair to fall over sideways to the floor. The alligator clip that was attached to his left nipple took a little bit of skin with it as it tore free from his chest. The clip on the right nipple stayed attached. The black box fell to the floor.

The bulky man was screaming now, cursing Duette at the top of his lungs. He turned to the slender man and shouted: "Get that jagoff upright. Now, goddamn you! Get those clips on his balls!" Then, to Duette, unconscious on the floor: "You mother-fucker, you cocksucker! You want to spit on me. You want to spit in *my* eyes!" He was still cursing when the slender man informed him that Duette was dead.

The bulky man was sitting in the second chair, smoking a cigarette and thinking. The cigarette was dangling from his lips. He was rubbing the swollen knuckles of one hand with the other, and he was trembling, and every few seconds he turned his head to spit hard on the concrete floor. The slender man had untied Duette, taken off the clips, and picked his belt up off the floor. He held the belt up in front of him, then looked at it in disgust. "Goddamnit, how'm I gonna get this clean?" He shook his head in disgust. "Just as well. I'd never be able to wear the goddamn thing again without thinking the AIDS was floating around my waist."

"Why don't you shut your goddamn mouth up about that AIDS shit!"

"Hey, don't start in on me. *I* didn't kill him; you did."

The bulky man sat smoking. At last he wiped his forehead with his hand. "If this son of a slob of a prick of a bitch gimme AIDS, I swear to Christ, I'll go down to Louisiana and find everyone he ever loved, I swear to God I will, and I'll kill every one of them."

"He give you the AIDS, you'll never live it down. We got enough enemies tell anybody who'll listen that you got it out on the street." The slender man paused for effect, then added, "From little boys."

"That shit ain't funny."

"Neither is this mess. Who's supposed to clean it up? You want me to do it, right?"

"You're damn right I do. I did all the work."

"Shit."

"There's a pail and a mop in the utility closet down the hall. Go and get it. Let me think for a minute in peace. And tell that punk at the door to get lost; I don't need another witness."

"He's my sister's kid; he's all right."

"Retardation runs in the family. You trust him, that don't mean I got to."

"What do you mean by that?" The slender man bristled.

"Goddamnit, will you shut up and let me think?"

"He's a good kid, solid." The slender man waited, but his familial loyalties weren't challenged this time, so he said, "How we gonna get the stiff out of here?"

"That ain't the problem. Same way we came in. Pull his car to the alley door, carry him out, and pile it in the trunk, either now or we wait until the shift change at eleven, while everybody else in the building's getting ready to go to work or get off for the night. And we got to move it; it's almost nine already. What I got to figure out is what we're gonna do about the money. How we gonna get it now?"

"Word is his partner's that shithead Kevin Wrisberg."

"Wrisberg, right." The man's voice betrayed his emotions. "Somehow I doubt that." The bulky man's brow furrowed. "I heard that bullshit too, but I don't believe it. Wrisberg's shit is weak; that's known all over the street."

"Still, we ought to have our guy check it out."

"Wrisberg's day is over; maybe his life, too, from what I hear. Gangs ran him out of business when they got smart enough to figure out how much money he was making. Besides, even down on his luck, Wrisberg's too smart to ever rip off an outfit honcho like Lemelli. Nobody would back him; he wouldn't pull a suicide play."

"Wrisberg? Shit, all those people ever think about is money. Down or not, those people don't respect the outfit, or Lemelli. All they respect is cash. And that's all that was stolen."

"What would a KKK redneck asshole like this be doing with a guy like Wrisberg? You want to tell me that?"

"I don't know."

"Goddamn right, you don't know."

"What are we paying the Special Victims guy for if we ain't gonna use him?"

"He'll pay off for us in spades in the long run. Do me a favor, let me do the thinking, all right? Just go and do what I tell you, would you? We got to get this guy out of here before somebody comes around."

The slender man walked to the door, then opened it just enough so he could slip his body through. He stepped into the hall and closed the door behind him. He heard it lock behind him. He reflected that the big son of a bitch could move fast and quiet enough when he wanted to.

A uniformed police officer was standing next to the door.

"The guy do the right thing, Uncle Mike?" the cop asked the slender man. He said, "Jesus, I heard him screaming all the way out here, right through the cinder-block walls, man. Right through the steel door." It was obvious that the young man's heart wasn't in his statements. His eyes were darting back and forth; there was a dark sweat stain around the collar of his blouse. He was nervous, wanting no part of what was going on.

The slender man looked at him, sensing his fear, then said, "I think he's about to. We're gonna take him for a ride, see if his information's straight. You go ahead now; we got to get him out of here. And your sergeant's gonna be wondering where you are before too much longer."

"You and the lieutenant gonna be all right? I could change into civvies and come back."

"That's all right. We got it under control, Billy. Now go ahead. And thanks," said the slender man, Homicide Detective Sergeant Michael Anson, as he quickly walked down the precinct basement hallway, heading for the utility room to get the mop and bucket.

There was a time, not all that long ago, when he would sit in this same chair and look out this same window and feel happiness as he looked out at the twin blinking beacons high atop Sears Tower. His mind would be at rest; he'd be content.

But that was before Marsha had left him, left him and taken their daughter, Lynne, with her.

Detective Sergeant Jake Phillips was sitting in a wooden chair that had once been bolted to the concrete foundation of the bleacher section at the old Comiskey Park. He'd bought it when they'd torn the old place down. He and Marsha used to go to a lot of White Sox games at the old place back when they'd been dating, almost ten years ago. Just thinking her name made him wince in pain today, even after having lived these past ten months without her. Jake started at the thought, not believing that they'd already been separated for that long.

What had Florence been trying to tell him this afternoon? That it was time to forget about Marsha? To move on with his life? He couldn't do that; he *adored* Marsha; even now, he adored her.

Jake took a long sip from the long-necked bottle of beer in his hand, held it to his lips until he was sure that it wouldn't fizz over. When he was sure it wouldn't, he put it back between his legs. It was only his second beer of the night, since he'd awakened at midnight. That was happening more frequently now. Jake would have nightmares so real they drove him from bed; other nights he just couldn't sleep at all, no matter how physically exhausted he was.

He'd been under a great deal of stress just lately. He wondered if he had gotten himself in over his head. He wondered if he would drown. He lowered his head, shut his eyes tight, and tried to figure out what was happening in his life. He couldn't. So he took another sip of his beer, wishing it was something stronger.

Experience had taught him that after the second or third beer he'd be able to go back into the bedroom and fall into a fitful sleep until it was time to get up for work. Experience had also taught him to stick to beer, to never drink hard liquor on a work night. Once he started in on the scotch, fell prey to its mind-numbing magic, he couldn't stop himself from pouring it down his throat until he passed out.

He believed that drinking made him forget about Marsha, and the pressures of his work. He was wrong on both counts.

He was careful to never drink on the job; he'd seen far too many coppers go down the tubes that way. What he did on his own time was his own business. Still, it niggled at him, what the counselor had told him: first you lose your wife; then you lose your friends; the job was usually last.

Jake thought about that now as he stared blankly out at the clear hot summer night, paying no attention to the sounds of the horns and stereos that were blasting through the open windows of cars cruising more than a hundred feet below him. He was oblivious to the smell of diesel fumes from the buses, which wafted in to him through the screens of the open bay windows. From time to time the apartment would shake as the subway passed close by, almost directly underneath the old, solid apartment building. The building would tremble, as if suffering through a minor earthquake. He'd spent most of his childhood living in a two-story house. After he'd gotten married, before moving here, he and Marsha had lived in a second-floor apartment in East Rogers Park. The trembling on the eleventh floor of this building had taken some time to get used to.

It hadn't bothered Marsha, though; she'd even seemed to enjoy it. She'd liked the apartment. They'd had some good times here.

Jake took another drink of his beer, thinking about the slump he was in. The counseling didn't seem to be going too well, what with Marsha expressing her opinion that Jake had become a secretive, controlling man. Jake, on the other hand, tried to convince the counselor that married couples didn't need to know everything about each other, that there were times when partners in even the best of relationships needed their space and some isolation. Florence wasn't buying that part; she wasn't even renting it.

He thought about the phone messages left on his machine earlier that day, all three of them still unanswered. He wondered if Marsha was intentionally trying to hurt him or if she was just another innocent pawn being manipulated by the press.

The first and last messages were from a woman named Dabney Delaney-Hinckle, who said she was a contributing editor for *Chicago Alive!* magazine. Jake knew her name; he had even seen her work. He could barely read the sort of crap a woman like that called writing. And now she was after him, seeking an interview and acting as if he should be flattered to hear from her.

The tone of her voice warned him right away; he'd heard it from media representatives plenty of times before—sweetness and light. She was planning to do a piece called "Cops' Wives," about the high divorce rate among coppers, focusing on his marriage to Marsha. When would it be convenient to meet so he could tell his side? She was savvy and had experience; Jake had to give her that. She didn't want to know if he *could* meet with her; rather, she wanted to know *when*. It was a cop's trick she'd picked up somewhere, or maybe the cops had stolen it from a journalism school textbook. No, Jake didn't think that was the case. The journalists he'd met over the years had been the dumbest people he'd ever met, with the exception of your average criminal . . .

In any event, Jake knew what the woman's statement meant. He'd talk; she'd tape and scribble; then she'd improvise, not bothering to write a word he'd really said; and he and the rest of the male cops in the story would come off looking like the misanthropes of the century, maybe even as wife beaters. If the reporter spoke to his mother-in-law, that could be a real concern for Jake.

The second message was from Marsha, telling him that she'd decided to go public and tell her story and she hoped he understood that she was doing it for Jake's own good. After his initial resentment at her condescension, he'd realized that the mere sound of Marsha's voice had been enough to choke him up. She would not discuss it when they'd met together at Florence's, and he had been too glad to see her to press the issue. He always tried to stay on his best behavior when Marsha was there with him.

Jake took another long pull on his beer and looked around the living room with something approaching despair. There were tiny holes in the white walls, evidence of nails that had once supported prints from various Chicago artists, artwork that somehow called out Marsha's name. Jake had to look away. The only safe place was outside. The street below him was the only thing that didn't remind Jake of his wife, and he had to work hard to achieve even that level of denial.

How many times had they sat here, side by side, in their matching Comiskey Park chairs, holding hands and laughing as they looked out at the city? These past ten months Jake saw only one thing down there: desperation. In the behavior of the winos as they smashed their bottles on the sidewalk or the street, shouted and kicked out at cars as they passed quickly by on Dearborn. Jake often heard the throbbing beat of the bass of some rap artist, the music turned up past the point of eardrum damage, as the car's owner gassed up in the Standard station across the street.

How often had he sat here, drunkenly thinking about throwing something down at one of the cars? He'd even played with the fantasy of tearing a hole in the screen, popping a quick round or two down at some ignorant bastard who felt that his own personal taste in music had to be shared with the rest of Chicago. He'd thought about it often.

Thinking about such behavior at all would once have disturbed Jake Phillips; he hadn't even noticed the music until after Marsha and Lynne were gone.

The phone rang and Jake jumped, pulled out of his venomous musing. He looked at his watch and cursed in surprise; it was already after two.

He'd awakened just before midnight, had looked at the large digital clock in the bedroom before crawling out of bed. It was almost getting to be a habit; midnight struck and *wham,* he'd awaken, and the nightly jitters fell over him. He'd done what he'd been doing for the last several weeks: grabbed a beer out of the fridge, sat down, and begun to drink. Twice he'd gotten up to use the bathroom. He'd gotten up again just a minute ago to get the second beer. Still, if he'd been asked, he'd have thought that at the most, maybe half an hour had passed since he'd dragged himself out of bed.

Had he sat here staring off into space for two full hours? The thought gave Jake pause. And who could be calling him at this hour of the morning? It wouldn't be Marsha; she never called him anymore unless it was to discuss something about Lynne.

He reached a hand out and grabbed the phone, hoping it was the reporter. It was late enough and his thoughts were dark enough that he'd feel comfortable expressing his personal, heartfelt opinions concerning the media.

"Phillips."

"Jake, it's Mondo."

It was neither the reporter nor his wife; it was Jake's boss. Newly appointed Lieutenant Alex Mondello, commander of the Special Victims Bureau—the title officially made Mondo the third-highest-ranking member of the department, as far as the detectives in the bureau were concerned, right under the captain and the superintendent of police. Many other officers outranked him, but these were the only two men to whom Mondello had to report. Unofficially, and for all practical purposes, Mondo was number one, the only man any of the bulls ever had to account for themselves to.

Jake made certain that his voice was level when he said, "I'm just fine tonight, Mondo."

"I doubt that, Jake, but I'm not calling to inquire about your mental health."

"For a change."

Mondo ignored him. "We got a bad one, and it starts with a busted-up body."

"I got court in the morning." Mondo didn't respond. "I'm not on call . . . " It took Jake a second to realize that Mondo wasn't on call, either. So why was an administrator calling him out on a job? "And you're supposed to be in bed." Still, Mondo didn't answer. Jake said, "What do we got?"

Mondo was suspicious, his tone sober and grave. "Jake . . . I didn't wake you up?" Jake didn't answer. Mondo didn't equivocate. "You been drinking tonight?" he asked, in a harsh voice that Jake had heard a lot of lately. The tone, along with the implications of the question, annoyed him.

"Oh, for Christ's sake, I only had one beer. Just opened my second."

There was a pause, then, "All right. Now listen to me. Couple of winos watched two guys trying to dump a body in that bullshit yuppie golf course on Lower Columbus. You know what I mean? The one just west of the lake and just north from Grant Park."

"Grant *Park*?" Jake was alert now, surprised at what he'd heard.

He said, "OC hit, had to be, right? Outfit or gangbangers, leaving the stiff right there downtown to send a message, probably to whoever might have been skimming with him." What he couldn't figure out right away was what any of that had to do with him. There were detectives on call to handle uncommon late-night homicides.

"We got an ID on the guy; his wallet was right in his pocket, money in there, driver's license. Hell, they left his *car*. He was beat all to hell; his own mother wouldn't recognize him."

"It's outfit, then," Jake said. "The *paisans* still like to do that, to show their disrespect. Gangbangers don't go in for beatings, dusting up their knuckles. They just shoot their prey." Jake thought a second, then smiled into the phone.

"And besides that, we're in the middle of Taste of Chicago, for Christ's sake; off-duty cops are *every*where in the park, all night long. It's OC, Mondo; they left the stiff there as a message." Jake chuckled. "We haven't heard from them in a while. But it's their style, out front, bold like that, the outfit."

"Maybe."

There was another long pause as Mondo waited for Jake to ask: "Who was it?"

"Jimbolaya Duette." Mondo spoke the words and let them hang in the air between them as Jake took in a deep breath, then slowly let it out.

"Brass think a gang war's coming? What do they want us to do, put surveillance on every asshole on the outfit's payroll? They need the National Guard for that, not us."

"Duette was freelance, but he had serious backing; we know that much. Guys down South *loved* him. But up here, he wasn't covered."

"I heard they think he pulled that Lemelli score. I heard a whole lot more got stolen than what was reported to the Lake Forest police."

"I've heard everything from a hundred grand to a half a million. That's the word."

"What's this got to do with Special Victims? I could see the bosses wanting Homicide to close this out fast, what with Taste going on." Jake grunted. "Can't have stiffs popping up across from Grant Park now, can we? Make all those hungry folks from Naperville and Schaumburg nervous about coming into the big, bad city."

"Taste of Chicago? Are you hearing what I'm saying? Jake, there's a probe, an Internal Affairs investigation into the Homicide department as it is. Do you understand what I'm talking about here?"

Jake was silent; he had no idea.

"Jake . . . You only had one beer?"

Jake calmed himself. "Just opened the second."

"Well, pour it down the sink. Or if you want, I could call someone else."

"You called the right number." Jake didn't bother to ask why he was being called out over the murder of a generally small-time thief. In Special Victims, your coworkers were the only real friends you had, the only members of the department who weren't jealous of your status, and you learned real quick not to question Mondo's orders. Special Victims had become, since being reactivated, the most prestigious unit in the Chicago Police Department, with even more celebrity coppers than that other newly reactivated department, Homicide. When you were invited to join Special Victims, you were joining up with the best.

"You want to meet me at the murder scene? Where'd they try to dump him?" Jake asked.

"It's not a murder scene yet, Jake."

"What?"

"Paramedics found a pulse. Duette's right there on the edge.

He's not gonna make the hour—they aren't even going to work on him. They just gave him something to kill the pain—but for the moment, he's still alive."

"Jesus Christ." Jake sat straight up, spilling beer onto his groin. It poured off the seat of the chair onto the cream shag carpet. Below him, outside the window, an ambulance siren began to blare. He saw colored lights racing toward him, up Congress Parkway. Jake waited until its wailing passed before he whispered, "Is he conscious?"

Mondo said, "He doesn't have any teeth left. His lungs were perforated by broken ribs; they've both collapsed. His skull's been fractured in a dozen different places; there's swelling on the brain. Both his eardrums are broken. His balls are crushed. One leg's busted so bad that if it looked like he'd make the night, they'd amputate the damn thing. He's been blinded in one eye, and there are small burn marks on both nipples, next to what they first thought were bites, but now figured out were caused by small clamps."

"Clamps?" There was a touch of disbelief in Jake's voice. Disbelief and panic.

"You heard me. Like alligator clips."

"Oh, no, don't tell me this, Mondo." He hadn't been thinking clearly. The pressure must have been getting to him. Jake knew with a sudden clarity why this was a case for Special Victims.

"The same sort of marks that were on the guys—"

"I remember. Shit, every copper and half the citizens in this city still remember." Jake paused, not wanting to ask his next question, but having to.

At last he said, "Mondo, they think it's cops who did it, don't they?" Jake suddenly knew what Mondo had been talking about earlier, when he'd mentioned the IAD probe into the Homicide department.

Mondo said, "Nobody's come out and said it straight out yet, but the press'll get it all soon; they might even have it already. Soon as they do, they'll put it together, if IAD doesn't call a press conference first. It doesn't look good. A career criminal gets pinched after a major score, and then he gets tortured. Just like the Wilson brothers. And it gets worse."

Mondo paused, and Jake heard his lighter click to life. He heard Mondo suck in smoke, heard him blow it out. Jake remembered the exact moment that Mondo had started smoking again. It was right after they'd moved him out of Intensive Care at Rush Presbyterian St. Luke's Hospital, after the last time he'd been shot. By a sexual psychopath who called himself Mr. X. Mondo took another drag and inhaled again before he spoke.

"The derelicts who saw it were two male blacks, ages twenty-one and thirty-three years old. They had begged enough for a bottle and they were drinking it under the viaduct when two pair of headlights passed over them and scared the living shit out of them. They claim two middle-aged white males pulled Duette's body out of a car trunk—drove two vehicles off LSD and right onto the Illinois Center golf course. Both bums swear one of the vehicles was an unmarked police squad, with the spotlight on the driver's door. That's about all they saw before the two men spotted them, pulled pistols, and screamed and yelled threats until they ran off."

"Didn't fire any shots?" Mondo didn't bother to answer. "God*damnit*, this sounds wrong. If it was a mob thing, they'd have killed those guys in a second; they wouldn't leave any witnesses." Jake thought for a moment. "The witnesses get a decent look?"

"They're working on a composite now, and they're being very cooperative. They're drunks; they're not reliable; but what else can we do, ignore them? Imagine the firestorm *that* would bring when the press got ahold of it. And God only knows what they'll tell the press the second we cut them loose, anyway. Hell, this is the first time in either of their lives that anyone thought they were important. Maybe we'll try forcible protective custody, but I don't think that'll work, particularly if the press gets wind of it." Mondo paused and took another deep drag off his cigarette.

Jake said, "Drunks, Mondo, come on. Who's gonna believe them? What kind of witnesses will they be?"

"That's the state's attorney's problem, not ours, thank God."

"Still, Mondo, they're *winos.*"

"Drunks or not, from what they said, the way the two men acted, it looks like coppers, Jake. Or two guys pretending to be coppers."

"The second the press gets ahold of this, there won't be any 'looks like'; they'll blame us right away." Jake felt a stab of discomfort when he spoke the word "us." He knew damn well that there was no "us" anymore, at least not for them. He knew, too, what his job would be, and he dreaded it. He knew what happened when cops accused other cops of high-profile crimes. Blaming a headline crime like this on one of his fellow officers could get him a bullet in the back of his head just as quickly as another commendation, whether he solved it or not.

But he voiced none of his misgivings to his boss. Jake was feeling too good about being on the inside again, about being called out by the boss for a big one. He'd been worried for some time now that his tenure with Special Victims was, like his personal life, on the teetering edge of extinction. So he only said to Mondo, "Where do you want to meet?"

"Three of our guys are at the scene, observing the processing of the crime scene. The car was registered in Duette's name, but there might be other prints in it; the winos didn't say anything about the men wearing gloves. I got another guy working with the Violent Crimes dicks, who are out looking for all known associates of Duette's." Jake did not envy any of those men their jobs. "They'll do a roust and question them hard, but I'm not expecting a lot to come of that." Mondo paused. Jake didn't bother him while he was thinking. "We've got the Rat Patrol working it, too, naturally, from their own end." "Rat Patrol" was slang for the Internal Affairs Department. Mondo grunted. Jake wondered if the conversation was being monitored.

"And they're working it without any cooperation with us; right now, we're all under suspicion. They'll wind up doing all of the inside questioning, if it comes down to that. At least we won't have to carry *that* weight."

Mondo paused, as if thinking things over, then said, "Get dressed and meet me at Northwestern Memorial. Duette's been beaten so badly he should have died halfway through it, or before he got to the hospital. But to answer your question . . . yeah, that ignorant, redneck, murderous swamp bastard's somehow still conscious and hanging on. In fact, he wouldn't allow the doctors to touch him; but he was calling for someone—they couldn't make out the name. If we can catch him at the final moment, maybe with a priest? If there's a God, he might say one name. We could call it a deathbed confession and clear this up before it gets ugly."

Mondo hung up, and Jake did, too, left his hand on the phone for a second, thinking, then picked it up and dialed a number he'd committed to memory over six months before.

"**W**hen's this guy supposed to show up?" Tommy Malardi said angrily. The music in the bar was starting to get under his skin, that rap bullshit, one song after another. It got on his nerves pretty quick. And to top it all off, it was a white guy doing the DJ chores. The DJ was a whigger—a white nigger— who was wearing long baggy multicolored shorts, a black leather vest over an orange-and-black striped oversized shirt, with a Chicago White Sox baseball cap with the brim turned backwards. He looked like every second asshole you saw these days walking on the streets of Chicago. The DJ was biting his lower lip and bopping his shaved head along with the music, mixing it, scratching it, acting like being a Caucasian male was something to be ashamed of. Tommy chain-smoked Salems and tried to ignore his feelings; not doing so had gotten him into enough trouble in his life.

Tommy's disposition wasn't improved a bit by all the pretty young white girls out there on the dance floor, rubbing their groins against the nigger boys they were with and calling it dancing. Add that to the facts that he was half drunk, it was getting late, and his hotshot cousin next to him hadn't even told him who they were waiting for, and you might say that Tommy Malardi was having a rough night.

Partly this was caused by his cousin, by the way he always acted like Tommy was the retard of the family. *Every*one in the family treated him this way, but Rick seemed to do it more often, and with intent. Rick was always messing with Tommy, making fun of him, never even giving him a taste of any of his action. Tommy often wondered about what he might have ever done to earn such disrespect. He thought about that now, with resentment, as he watched the pretty young white girls dancing.

He'd done his time, and he'd kept his mouth shut, and he'd gotten out alive; by general standards, all of the above should have earned him respect, rather than disdain. A quick stab of shame coursed through him as he thought of some of the things he'd had to do inside to survive. Rick wouldn't know about that. Jesus, he couldn't have found out about that. With an effort, Tommy calmed himself down. If Rick had known, he would have busted Tommy on it, called him an undercover jailhouse faggot. Rick was very proud of the fact that he himself had never done time.

Not that he didn't deserve to. He'd just never gotten caught. Something he credited his intelligence for, rather than pure dumb luck.

As for Tommy, he believed that he'd been born under a dark, pregnant cloud.

He'd done two years once for simply having the bad luck of being on an airplane that was on its way to Vegas when it was caught in a crosswind and dropped a couple of thousand feet.

Although everyone aboard, including Tommy, had been filled with terror, the guy in the seat next to him wouldn't stop screaming and crying and praying, even after the craft had stabilized. So Tommy had kicked the shit out of him, and had gone away to Terre Haute for two years. His lawyer had told him he'd gotten off easy; he could have gotten fifteen years. The air, Tommy was told, was considered to be federal property. The lawyer had taken the money Tommy had been planning to gamble with as a down payment on what Tommy owed him for his services. Tommy had stiffed him for the rest.

Now Tommy looked into the highly polished glass of the mirror behind the bar and tried to give his cousin a dirty look, but as usual, Rick wasn't paying much attention to Tommy tonight. Rick was looking at the dancing girls, ogling them, shaking his leg to the music, chair-dancing. In spite of the intense heat outside, Rick was wearing a leather sport coat. Tommy knew he wore it only so that he could carry his gun around with him.

"You at least going to tell me this guy we're meeting with's name?" Tommy asked, and Rick turned to look at him, surprised, as if he'd forgotten that Tommy had been sitting right there next to him for over two hours.

"I don't want you to prejudge."

"Prejudge?" Tommy said. "Who the fuck are you, Oprah Winfrey?"

They had to raise their voices to hear each other over the pounding beat of the music. It seemed to Tommy that they were the only people in the packed bar who were talking to each other. Rick turned and waved a hand until he caught the bartender's eye. He pointed his finger at their glasses, made a swirling motion as he silently ordered a round.

Tommy tried again.

"I'm gonna be doing business with a guy, I want to at least know his name."

"You still don't get it, do you?" Rick shook his head. "You

ain't here to do business with, *or* to approve this guy—he's coming here to look *you* over. If he likes what he sees, you might get lucky; he might have something for you."

Tommy's festering resentment boiled over on the spot.

"You drag me out here, to the middle of some jig"—Rick flinched and shook his head—"gin mill so some son of a bitch can come in here and see if *I'm* good enough to work with?" Rick didn't reply. He didn't have to. His expression told Tommy more than Tommy wanted to know. Tommy decided to press his point home.

"I done time and stood up before, man, didn't rat nobody out, and all of a sudden I got to be checked out, like I'm some rookie? What are you, *nuts*?" Rick sat there watching him, now blank faced, giving Tommy nothing to work with. His anger was slowly ebbing. Rick looked away.

The bartender was picking up Rick's glass and putting down a fresh drink for him. He put another bottle of Budweiser down next to Tommy's half-full bottle. He took their cardboard tab out of the bar well, walked over and shoved it into a slot on top of the cash register, touched a few keys, then brought the check back to them. The bartender ignored Tommy's glare. The DJ was playing a long mix, dancing full-out now, with his hands clasped together, held way above his head, the man thrusting his groin out as far as he could, slowly, then snapping it back. Like he was fucking the stereo equipment in front of him. Tommy tapped Rick's shoulder and waited until his cousin acknowledged his presence.

"You tell me this guy's name, or I'm out of here, I swear to Christ." He stared at Rick, who sighed, shook his head again, and gave Tommy a disgusted look.

"Wrisberg."

"Who?"

"Wrisberg. The guy we're meeting. His name's Kevin Wrisberg."

"Oh, for Christ's sake!" Tommy picked up his warm Budweiser and drank it down. He slammed the bottle down onto the bar. He picked up his cigarettes, shoved them into his shirt pocket. He was a weight lifter, and he now tightened his muscles as he moved, knowing how impressive he looked in a short-sleeve shirt. Tommy didn't do it to impress the girls, though. He tightened his muscles at every opportunity, even when he was alone; it was just the way he was. He'd look into glass on the street and flex. He stood up now and stared down at his cousin.

"You think I'm gonna sit in this shithouse and wait for some *Jew* . . . !"

All Rick did was shake his head a third time. Tommy closed his eyes tight until the urge to punch Rick passed. When he opened them again, Rick seemed to have once again forgotten that Tommy was even there. Rick was watching the dance floor, nodding his head to the beat, tapping his thigh with the fingers of his right hand. He looked over, noticed Tommy, then sadly lowered his head.

"All I ever hear from you is your begging"—Rick lowered his voice and did a passable Stallone imitation—" 'Rick-y, you got to help me out, Rick-y. My probation officer's mad at me, Rick-y; I ain't give him nuttin' in munts.' " Rick saw the offended look on his cousin's face and smiled. "Finally, after all this time, I decide to try and help you out, to hand you a golden opportunity, and what do you do, how do you pay me back? How do you act? Like a cell-block asshole, that's how you act, Tommy."

"I don't sound like that, anyway," Tommy said, and Rick just kept shaking his head. It made Tommy want to knock it right off his shoulders.

Rick said, "Do you have any idea who this guy is, Tommy? What he controls? You name it: gambling, drugs; he sets up scores; he fences. The guy, he's younger than you are, and he damn near controls the entire South Side. And *you* don't want him to look you over. You small-time goof. Go on, get out of here. Go back to boosting cars. See how long you're on the street this time."

"Come on, Rick, don't be like that." Tommy had had a sudden change of heart. He was sniveling now, acting ashamed of himself. He wondered if Rick was fooled.

Rick didn't seem to be. He said, "No, really, I go out of my way for you, and you're gonna pull some white-man Farrakhan shit on me. 'A Jew, a *Hebrew*? I don't work for no Jew!' What if this guy can make more money in a week than you can in a year? Does that change your mind about things?"

"He's good, huh? Solid?" Tommy sat back down on the bar stool, leaned in close to his cousin, acting eager now. The thought of money went a long way toward soothing Tommy's many and varied bigotries.

Rick said, "And the music, since we walked in here, all I hear about is the fuckin' music. Your problem is, Tommy, you're stuck in the seventies. They started playing 'Love to Love You, Baby' or 'Disco Inferno,' you'd be out there on the dance floor, gamboling like a disco fool." Tommy smiled, relieved that Rick was kidding around and wasn't mad at him anymore. He'd never heard anyone say the word "gamboling" before, not even in the joint.

"So what is this Jew, you say, a thief or a fence?"

"I got a news flash for you, hotshot, he's not—" Rick cut his statement off as a tall slender black man approached them. He must have just come in the door; at least Tommy hadn't noticed him until just this moment, and he was the sort of man Tommy made it his business to always notice, a player.

The man was dressed in a sharply cut electric blue suit over a formfitting dago tee—what color was it, yellow? Gold. His long, handsome face glowed with a light sheen of sweat. He walked toward them with purpose, staring directly at Rick, solemn but not in too much of a hurry to forget about putting the ditty-bop in his step. He had a trimmed little goatee, and his hair was cut in a modified Afro. Talk about the seventies? Tommy thought this guy had watched too many episodes of *Good Times* on the television.

Rick had leaned back on his stool, giving the man room, and the man walked directly to the bar and stood between them. In spite of his fear, Tommy was getting ready to ask the guy where his manners were when the man turned full toward him and glared at Tommy, hard. Tommy had seen that look before, more than once, in the penitentiary. Usually right before somebody took a shank in the chest. He closed his mouth and waited. Tommy's pistol was in Rick's new Buick, shoved under the front seat; Rick had insisted Tommy leave his shit in the car, even though Rick was carrying his own under the leather sport coat.

He decided to let the man get his drink and hoped that he'd leave them alone.

"You want something?" the black man said, looking directly at Tommy. "You been staring at me since I walked in the door. We know each other, steroid?" Tommy turned to face the mirror, twisting his face into an insolent, hate-filled expression. Sometimes, inside, it had worked; other times it hadn't. He slouched, leaned forward on the stool. He put his forearms on the bar and did what he could to pretend that he hadn't heard the man's comments.

The black man turned to face the bar, then ordered a drink, looking not at the bartender but into the mirror, so he could see if any sudden angry movements went down on either side of him. The bartender handed the man his drink and didn't give him a tab.

The man nodded to himself in the mirror, seeming somehow satisfied with an inner judgment. He turned to Rick, leaning on the bar, showing Tommy his back. Tommy wouldn't have felt more disrespected if the man had slapped his face. He looked at the back, saw the broad shoulders straining the fabric of the suit, the tightness of the bunched neck muscles. He may have misjudged this man just a little; the guy looked skinny but strong. Tommy could almost smell the scent of violence emanating from him. He leaned in a little closer so he could hear what the man said to Rick.

"We got some problems."

Rick turned to look at him. "I figured that out, Kevin, I really did, right after the first two hours. But what do you mean by 'we'?" Rick asked, and the black man nodded calmly, as if he'd expected denial.

"I just heard it on the radio. Duette's dead, man; they found his ass in the park. Word is, the cops did it."

Rick was suddenly half off his stool. "You got to be shitting me."

How did Rick know this player? And who was Duette? And why would his death cause Rick such surprise? When Rick's *father* had died, he'd gotten angry when his own mother had called him up in the middle of the night to break the news to him, had wanted to know why she hadn't waited until a decent hour to call. Tommy didn't have any answers, so he just sat there, intrigued, listening in as well as he could.

The black man seemed to sense that Tommy was crowding him, and slowly turned to face him.

"I asked you before, you want something, motherfucker?" The words were spoken soft and low, but the man's eyes were *ablaze.* Tommy looked away quickly, then back at the man. He hadn't moved a muscle. He continued to glare. Slowly, the man straightened up, and Tommy was suddenly afraid. The man didn't even flinch when Rick touched his arm.

"That's my cousin, man; that's my cousin, Tommy." Rick was anxious now, sounding frightened himself. "He gets a little too wrapped up in his jailhouse bullshit, is all, listening to other people's business, you know." Rick gave a nervous little laugh. "He's used to sticking a hand mirror through the bars, trying to read your lips. I mean, you never know when they might be talking about *you.* Don't mind him."

The man's expression slowly changed, lightening a little with each word that Rick had quickly spoken, until he was smiling, just slightly, his head cocked to one side, eyeing Tommy quizzically. Tommy felt himself relax. The man put out his hand.

"Didn't see no family resemblance. What with that mustache, those gym muscles, all them gold chains tangled in the hair on your chest, I thought you might be an undercover de-*tec*-tive." It was an explanation, not an insult, but still, Tommy was offended. He took the black man's hand, tried to squeeze it hard.

Tommy said, "I know what you mean." Then paused and smiled back at the man. He said, "I seen you in that suit, with the facial hair, the tight 'Fro? I thought you might be a pimp." The man stopped smiling.

"Rick tell you I was a man you could play around with?" He was squeezing Tommy's hand back now, and squeezing very hard. Tommy tried to pull away and was held as if he were a child. Thin, strong biceps muscles jumped under the electric blue suit. Tommy thought that his fingers were about to break into pieces. "He tell you that?" the man said, right into Tommy's face. His breath smelled of booze and lemons.

"No . . . " Tommy grimaced as he spoke. "I didn't mean nothin' by it." The man let him go suddenly, and Tommy fell into the man on the other side of him. He, too, was black, and tall and strong and wide. Built more like Tommy than like the slim man with the powerful hands and deceptive strength. The man said, "God*damn* . . . " and turned to face Tommy. Tommy quickly apologized, feeling ashamed, and the large man turned back to his date. She was white. The thin man had squeezed his hand so hard that Tommy didn't think he could hit anyone now if they called his mother a ten-dollar Halsted Street whore; if he did, he felt that his hand might break right off his wrist. He nursed it, held the hand close to his chest with his left hand. He rubbed it gently with his fingers. The slender man had turned his back on Tommy again. Tommy thought about hitting him on the back of the skull with the full bottle of Budweiser, but as he thought it the man turned back to him and put out his hand again.

"You want to try that one more time, Rick's cousin?" Slowly, tentatively, Tommy reached out his throbbing right hand. The man watched him closely as they shook, as if expecting Tommy to try and save face by making another comment.

As if to reassure him, Tommy quickly said, "My name's Tommy. Same last name as Rick."

"Kevin Wrisberg," the black man said, then paused as if in thought. "You can just call me Kev. Tell me, Tommy, what you know about talk radio celebrities?"

"Talk radio . . . ? All I know is, the dumber the disc jockey, the higher the ratings."

Wrisberg said, "My man," then turned to Rick and said, "I think he do just fine, Ricky."

T he Emergency waiting room at Northwestern Memorial Hospital was full to overflowing at twelve-thirty on this Tuesday morning. Set in the heart of the ritzy Gold Coast, with scores of multimillionaires living within a stone's throw of the door, the place still couldn't escape the problems of any other big city hospital.

Jake pulled back the hem of his jacket so his belt badge could be observed as he nodded to the armed security guard at the door and entered the room, moving quickly, wearing the Special Victims uniform, a sport coat and tie. He strode to the admitting desk, ignoring the waiting patients and their angry family members. The man he was here to see wouldn't be sitting in one of the chairs, or standing with the overflow crowd. Jake flashed his badge at the admitting nurse, spoke to him quietly, and was pointed toward a door set unobtrusively in the back of the room. He heard resentful whispers as he walked through it, into ER.

In there, all was chaos.

There was loud moaning and shouts for salvation, mixed with curses coming from behind pulled curtains. Doctors, nurses, and paramedics rushed from one cubicle to another, their voices raised in command, speaking over the din of the badly maimed and the merely wounded. Jake looked around nervously, saw that several people dressed in scrub outfits were standing and sitting inside a squared-off little island of a medical station that was built right in the center of the room. The counter was waist high. There was a variety of chairs and tables and computers in that section. No one back there was wearing name tags, and they all had stethoscopes hanging from their necks. Jake couldn't tell the doctors from the nurses, or the nurses from the orderlies. He walked over to the station and flashed his badge at a group of medical personnel, who didn't seem impressed to find a detective in their midst.

He said, "Jimmy Duette—where you got him?" That made them sit up and take notice. One of them, a young woman with shoulder-length hair that had been permed, and a no-nonsense attitude, nodded at him and walked around the counter, waving a hand for him to follow, and he did so, following her down a corridor that led out of the Emergency Room and into a long straight hallway that was wide enough to accommodate wheelchairs, gurneys, and hospital beds. Jake wondered if she was a doctor and, if she was, how a doctor could be younger than he was himself. There was a large bloody handprint on the backside of her green doctor's gown. Had some stabbing or shooting victim grabbed her ass? Jake, looking, wondered about the man who had done it; it wasn't a smart move, alienating a woman who was there to help save your life.

The woman said, "He's had only a few moments of lucidity; he's in and out. When they first brought him in he was alert and screaming for what we later figured out was Jesus—his words aren't clear; you'll see what I mean. He refused any treatment, wouldn't let us near him. He was calling for someone else, too, it was hard to tell who; his teeth are gone, and his tongue's

chewed almost in half. Anyway, he's out now. They've got a
police guard with him. A priest was in there earlier. Duette
wouldn't let go of his hand, but he wouldn't say anything to
him; at least he didn't while there was hospital personnel in the
room. The priest gave him the last rites."

"We can't talk to the priest," Jake said, without further explanation. "He as bad as the initial report?"

"Worse." She spoke without turning to look at Jake, walking
rapidly down a corridor that had a highly polished, stonelike
floor. She stepped aside so that a black orderly pushing an
elderly man on a gurney could pass, and Jake took his cue from
her and moved back against the wall. The man on the gurney
looked at Jake with anger over the fact that he was being
watched; the expression seemed to be mixed with what looked
to Jake like guilt. Jake averted his eyes uneasily as the man was
pushed hurriedly past him.

Hospitals always reminded him of the day his father had
died.

Face-to-face with the woman now, as they waited for room,
Jake asked, "How long do you think he has?"

She gave Jake an appraising look before she answered. "He'll
be dead before morning; I'm amazed he lasted as long as he
has." Jake nodded, admiring her professionalism, her cool
look, the direct, frank way she held his eyes with her own. He
wondered if perhaps it *was* time to begin dating again. The
woman took off again, and Jake followed closely behind her,
trying to think of something to say. Words failed him.

They walked through a door that led down another hallway,
and Jake spotted the uniformed officer standing at attention
outside the last door of the hall. The woman stopped before
they reached it. "He's over there," she said, and waited, as if
allowing Jake time to respond in some personal manner. When
he didn't, she smiled and walked past him, heading back toward ER.

The officer was grossly overweight and at least twenty years
older than Jake. Jake could almost feel the man's anger at his

station in life oozing from his pores. Jake suspected that the
word "sir" wasn't in the man's vocabulary, probably not even
for Mondo, probably not even for the police superintendent
himself. He was right. The man nodded at him guardedly, and
Jake nodded back just as curtly. He heard the click of heels
rounding the corner behind him, moving fast. Had the woman
forgotten something?

It wasn't his escort coming toward him, though; it was another woman entirely. A youngish woman, tall, attractive, and
fashionably dressed. Short skirt, silk blouse, and Reeboks on
her sockless feet. She had a large briefcase purse hanging over
her shoulder. She had the thick leather strap of the purse
around her neck, bandolier style, so that it crossed between her
breasts, and she was holding the strap tightly in her right hand;
no mugger was going to get that purse without a fight. Jake
looked at her breasts stealthily, then looked back up at her face.
The woman had shortish light brown hair, cut in a masculine
style. As she came up to him he noticed that she was wearing a
minimum of makeup, if she was wearing any makeup at all.

She stopped right in front of him and held out her hand, and
he took it automatically, thinking she was a detective. The
woman smiled, as if she'd won something because of his action.

"Sergeant Jake Phillips?"

"Yes."

"I'm Dabney Delaney-Hinckle." Jake started, pulled his hand
away. "Ooh, touchy," Delaney-Hinckle said, and laughed. "Is it
me, or the profession?"

"I have no respect for either, and I have nothing to say to
you."

"You'd best have, partner."

"Is that a threat, lady?"

"Not at all." Delaney-Hinckle shot a sideways glance at
the uniformed officer, whose beefy veteran face betrayed nothing but his boredom. He wouldn't get involved unless she
tried to enter the room. "It's just that—let me phrase this as

delicately as I can—I've heard a lot about you, Jake, and none of it's good so far. You might want to tell me your side of what's going on."

"My marriage and my life is none of your business. Go bother somebody else; I'm working here."

"I hear you're a drunk." The cop at the door grunted with humor at her audacity. "I hear the Internal Affairs Division and the Office of Professional Standards are both looking into your . . . uh . . . *problems*." What? Where had she heard *that*? It had to be a trick, lies she'd invented to try to get Jake to talk to her. Anyone with any sort of police contacts could have found out about the Rat Patrol's investigation into the Homicide department. She was just singling him out.

"I hear you're a racist, too." Jake glared at her. "That you slap around homeless black people from the shelter all the time, cleansing your neighborhood, keeping it free from the— ahem—bad element."

Jake was incensed. "You print those lies and I'll sue the shit out of you and that rag you work for, and I'll win."

"I'm just repeating what a former neighbor told me. I've got the interview on tape."

"Whoever told you that's a liar."

"I'm just telling you what your family, friends, and neighbors have been saying about you, Jake. In fact, I've heard so much that I'm thinking about just writing the story about *you*. About you and Marsha."

"Listen, you want my lawyer's name? I don't have any more time for this."

She shrugged. "It's opinion, Joe Stalin. Protected speech." The woman looked at him directly, then softened just a bit. "I want to be fair. I want to talk with you. I want to hear your response to what I've been told, Jake."

"You call me Sergeant Phillips, detective, or sir." Jake's voice was glacial. Delaney-Hinckle merely smiled.

"I've been sitting out in that waiting room since they brought

Duette in here, *hours* ago. I suspected someone from your unit might be arriving, and I wanted an interview, at the very least a quote about you from a fellow Special Victims officer. I'm surprised to see you, though; my sources said you weren't on call tonight. It *is* a Special Victims case, isn't it? And you used to be their bright-eyed superstar." She smiled at him now in a friendly, calculated manner.

"You gonna pay my perseverance back with spite, Detective *Sergeant* Phillips, sir? Or are you gonna grant me an interview. If you're busy, I can go back out there and wait for you, no problem."

"Lady, I got work to do."

"I'll be waiting."

"Don't bother." Jake saw Mondo and two other Special Victims detectives turn the corner, and he glared at the woman, lowered his voice to a whisper.

"You get out of here before I have you arrested for impeding an investigation."

"Tough talk for a man who lets a woman pay his rent."

"I mean now, lady."

Delaney-Hinckle turned and smiled at Mondo and the other detectives. "Lieutenant Mondello, Sergeant Lynch, how nice to see both of you again." She held her hand out to the female detective who was now standing between Mondo and Kenny Lynch, holding a microcassette recording device in her left hand. Mondo was looking curiously at Jake. "I don't believe we've met. Dabney Delaney-Hinckle." Delaney-Hinckle held out her hand, and the detective, Elaine Hoffman, stared down at it, made a disbelieving face, then looked with undisguised disappointment at the uniformed officer, who for the first time showed discomfort.

"This is a secure area," Mondo said, speaking to the officer. "Get her out of here, *now*." Without another word he walked past the cop and into the room, and Jake waited, not going inside until Lynch and Hoffman had entered. Lynch walked by with a nod; Hoffman glared at him. It had been obvious for some time that she didn't care much for Jake.

"I'll be waiting, Jake," the reporter called out to him as he entered the hospital room. Jake knew, if he spoke, it would be words of anger, so he kept his mouth shut and let the door close gently behind him. He heard the uniformed officer take his anger at Mondo out on the woman, harshly ordering her away from the door under penalty of arrest. If Jake could have, he would have smiled.

Mondo took command the second they entered the private room. He dismissed the two uniformed officers who were guarding the body on the bed, then addressed the exhausted-looking orderly who was sitting in a molded plastic chair at the side of the bed, reading a well-thumbed paperback novel.

"We need to speak to him alone."

"Yeah? And why's that, Kojak? You guys ain't beat him bad enough already? You here to finish the job?" Jake moved toward the young man, but Mondo stopped him with a glare. Hoffman and Lynch just looked at each other in surprise.

Mondo quietly said, "Get out of here, son, I mean it. I won't ask nicely again."

The young man stood, squared his shoulders, looking at Mondo with a near smirk on his face.

"Yeah, right, just what you guys need tonight, another brutality case." He walked toward the door, speaking over his shoulder. "Someone got to tell the doctor when this guy dies. You sent me out of here. He dies and you don't tell no one, it ain't my fault." He spoke the last words as the door closed behind him.

Jake knew that if word had gotten around the hospital that the police had done this, then it was a cinch the press had it, too. But if so, where were they? The reporter, Delaney-Hinckle, hadn't said a word about the rumor. Maybe she'd been too busy trying to get a rise out of him. Jake looked at the body on the bed. It was nearly unrecognizable as a human form at all. He closed his eyes and shook his head in disgust at the inhumanity of what had been done to the man. Maybe Marsha had been right; maybe he was too sensitive to look upon sights such as this.

But she had made that remark a long time ago, when he'd first joined the department. She hadn't accused him of being sensitive anytime lately.

He sensed the buzz of activity in the room, opened his eyes, and stood there feeling like a fifth wheel because he didn't have anything to do.

The rest of them surely did, the three of them performing their well-thought-out professional roles. Hoffman was securing a small supersensitive microphone onto the sheet that covered Duette up to what was left of his chin. Jake looked at it, then shifted his gaze to Duette's muscular chest. He was damned if he could see the man breathing. Lynch was pulling a chair over, his notepad and pen out, ready to take down and further document anything Duette might say. On the other side of the bed, sitting in the chair the orderly had abandoned, Mondo was leaning far forward, his left hand on the nightstand for stability. His mouth was inches away from Duette's right ear. He began to speak softly.

"You hear me? Jimmy Duette! Jimbolaya, can you hear me?" Mondo used his free hand to cradle Duette's fingers. "Try and squeeze my fingers if you can hear me, all right, Jimbolaya?" Jake watched. There was no response from the body on the bed. Mondo didn't show impatience.

"You know you're dying, Duette? It's over for you, son. There's nothing the doctors, nothing *anyone* can do. Tell me who did this to you, and I'll see that you get justice, Jimmy. Come on, talk to me."

Again there was no response. Mondo looked over at Jake, who was wondering about something. He stepped around Kenny Lynch's chair and moved around the bed, closer to Mondo, leaned in right next to him so that he wouldn't appear

to be showboating, wouldn't be embarrassing Mondo on purpose when he whispered: "Tell him we're with Special Victims. He knows you're a cop. He might think you're one of the
people who did this to him." Mondo nodded without looking
at Jake.

"Jimmy? Can you hear me? We're with the Special Victims
Bureau. You know what that is, don't you? We're here to help
you, Duette. We're here to bring you justice."

Jake stood back against the wall, looking around. He did not
want to look at Duette. The intensity in Elaine Hoffman's voice
made him look back at the bed.

She said, "Mondo—Mondo, look at his mouth! I think he's
trying to say something!"

T ommy Malardi sat in his cousin's car, parked just around
the corner from the radio station. He was reading the latest
issue of *Chicago Alive!* magazine, squinting in the soft glow of
the dome light, trying to read and listen to the radio at the same
time, which was hard. But educational.

Tommy had learned more about this mark in the last half
hour than he'd even known before about anyone he'd had to
work over. Wrisberg had just handed him a magazine, said a
few words, and he'd figured everything else out on his own.
Tommy was proud of himself, of how quickly he'd reacted. But
he'd never been much of a planner, so all he could think of to do
was to sit here, wait for the guy, then play it by ear when the guy
came out of the building.

The guy, this Ray McCauley, who worked eleven to three
talking on the radio, had a serious gambling problem, and he
was stupid enough to admit it. Not only on the air, but also in
print; it was right there in front of Tommy. In a little gray box

filled with words that were in larger print than the rest of the article, the sort of thing magazines do when they want to point out an important quote.

McCauley was quoted as saying, "Sure, I got a gambling problem. And I smoke and I drink and I fuck way too much," Tommy read. "Artists have compulsions, man . . . " Tommy looked out his windshield, smiling and shaking his head.

The car was parked and running on Lake Street, the air conditioner on full blast. Tommy could smell his own cologne, and he was glad. The smell covered the stench of the garbage that was coming out of the car's radio speakers. It was the talk show host's last hour of the night, what he'd referred to as the Dis Ray Hour.

Jesus, what a lightweight. Tommy was looking forward to the evening's work.

At the moment, a woman was berating McCauley for the foul language that had filled the magazine piece, telling him that he had no right to have a talk radio show. At this point, McCauley cut her off.

"No right! No right! I have a *First Amendment right* to speak anyway I please, ma'am." The tone of his voice made it clear that Ray was not saying "ma'am" with respect. "Or haven't you ever heard of the First Amendment?"

"I have indeed heard of the First Amendment. And along with all the other amendments, it was designed to be a *shield* for protection, sir, rather than a sword used to carve up the rest of society."

"*What?*"

"And one more thing. You spoke about the difficulty of 'raising' your 'kid' when he doesn't live with you. May I remind you that one *raises* cattle; one *rears* children. And a kid, Mr. McCauley, is a goat."

"Oh my God, I've got an English teacher on the line." Tommy sat back, still smiling, and lit a Salem from the Buick's lighter. This guy would fold in a minute. All Tommy would have to do is look at him.

"Blow me, all right, lady?" McCauley said, shouting. He paused for effect, then added, in a fake English accent, "Oh, forgive me; 'blow's' not the proper term. You 'blow' out a candle, you 'suck' a man." He reverted back to his own voice to shout, "So *suck* me, all right?" Ray chuckled at his own witticism, then went to a commercial.

Tommy looked at the dashboard clock. Ten minutes to three. Thank God. He wouldn't have to listen to but a few more minutes of this. He looked down at the article in his lap, squinted, and read a few more paragraphs while he waited.

The lady reporter hadn't pulled any punches. In the part Tommy was reading now, she had just pointed out to Ray McCauley that he regularly claims to have been a professional fighter and that he'd often declared on his radio show that he'd done time in the county jail. She pointed out that he brags about one or the other almost every night on the air, yet she could find no evidence that he'd ever fought a single amateur or professional bout or that he'd ever been arrested for anything.

In fact, no boxing license had ever been issued to him— under his real name, at least. She'd checked.

As for the long thin scar on McCauley's neck—one he claimed he'd received in a knife fight when he was a kid—the lady reporter had scrounged up medical records from some suburban hospital that proved the scar had come from a failed suicide attempt; it was a hesitation mark, a tryout.

When confronted with his own lies, McCauley had blown up at her, and she'd gotten down every word he'd said. He'd gone berserk, cursed her, then had stormed out of the room, leaving her alone with her tape recorder and notepad. For Tommy, the best part of the article was the last sentence in the piece: "I watched his quivering fat backside waddle out of the room in a fit of self-righteous raving."

Oooh, did she kick this guy's ass. It was almost enough to compel Tommy to order a subscription to *Chicago Alive!*

Ray was back now, taking another call. He'd be easy, Tommy

thought again. He'd met plenty of fat, mouthy profilers in the pen. Loudmouths who equated fat with physical strength. Tommy wished that Rick's car was equipped with a cellular phone so he could call this McCauley himself, set the rest of the night's action up with an early threat, throw a little fear into this fat bag of wind, right there on the airwaves.

Ray said, "Jerome from Hegewisch, wuzup, my man?"

"Funky article about you in that magazine, Ray babe."

"Jerome, I'm disappointed in you. You are the last person I ever expected to call during the Dis Ray Hour. And let me tell you, I never said *any* of those things that woman—and I use the term loosely to describe her—said I did. Bitch, I might have called her"—Jerome and Ray shared a giggle at this—"but the rest of it, the things I can't say over the air without the FCC thinking I'm Howard Stern and fining me, Jerome, she made it all *up*! Can you believe that? She made it all up, word for word, out of thin air!" From their discussion Tommy could tell that this Jerome was a regular caller, one whom McCauley obviously got along with.

"Don't surprise me. Still, I got to tell you, the woman was on a different radio station earlier tonight? She said she had it all on tape, man."

Ray seemed to figure out that the caller might not be as sympathetic as he'd at first thought.

"Are you calling me a liar, Jerome? Are you taking that bitch's side against me on *my* radio show?"

Jerome backed off. "No, no, come on, man, you know me better than that. I've been waiting for an hour to get on the air. My brother's on the extension, man; I want you to indoctrinate him into the kingdom."

The what? Tommy leaned forward, smiling and puzzled, and turned the radio up.

"What's your brother's name?"

"Mal."

In a self-important, regal tone, Ray McCauley said, "Mal from

Hegewisch, brother to Jerome the Greater, you are the knight in charge of the far South Side, in the fiefdom known as the Tenth Ward."

"All *right!*" Jerome said, and a younger-sounding voice said, "Cool!"

"Now let me hear that secret password, Mal." Mal mumbled something that sounded like, "Mmmppfffscabbibble."

"You're *in*, Mal," Ray said, then cut him off. He immediately said, "Eleanor from Lake Forest, you're on the air with big, bad Ray McCauley. Come on, dis me, baby!"

"I certainly will."

"Good!"

"My daughter was on the movie set with you when you did *The Runner*? She said that for a bit player, you had a bigger ego than the star, Harrison Snipes."

"Your daughter said that, did she?"

"And I wanted to ask you, why do you constantly suck up to all these movie people, Ray? Is it the only way you can get roles, through your connections?"

"Suck up! Suck *up!*" Ray's outrage sounded phony to even a first-time listener like Tommy.

"Yes, suck up. The fact is—and this was in the article in *Chicago Alive!* magazine, too—that if you didn't bring your knee pads, you couldn't buy a part in a movie."

"Lady, I get paid, and paid well, to act."

"Oh, really."

"Really. And it's obvious that your daughter is a stuck-up little rich-bitch snob from a filthy-rich, lily white suburb who spends too much time staring at herself in mirrors and reading sickening glossy North Shore rags like *Chicago Alive!* magazine instead of working to perfect her craft."

"How *dare* you!"

Did people always end their sentences with exclamation points on the radio? Tommy didn't know; he'd never listened to it before. He looked at the dashboard clock. Thank God. At last, it was a minute before three.

"I dare because I have the radio show and you don't, honey; that's how I dare!" Ray cut her off.

He said, "There's only about a minute left in the show. I don't think I'll take another call. There's something I want to say." Tommy heard the man sigh, as if the weight of the world were on his shoulders. If only he knew, Tommy thought, what was in store for him later tonight.

"I'm the only talk show host in this country who lays his soul on the line, puts it out there until it's raw, every night on the air, you hear me? In the entire damn *country,* nobody else does what I do. I admit to my failings. I admit that I'm divorced, that I've got emotional problems, that I'm on lithium and Prozac, that I had open heart surgery at twenty-nine, for God's sake! I admit that I've got compulsions—that I drink too much, that I smoke too much, that I gamble every day of my miserable life.

"I don't sit here and pretend to be perfect, like the other radio hosts, even some of the other hosts on this same radio station! Not me. I invite callers to ring me up and disrespect me for a full hour every night on the air. I know it's too much to ask to expect one of you to call in with a compliment. But you know something? *Every single damn one of you, with your complaints? You're listening in,* aren't you! And I'll tell you something else: there isn't a single damn thing any one of you can do to me that hasn't been done before."

Ray paused, and Tommy thought, No shit? They'd be seeing about that real soon.

McCauley said, "You can claim to hate me, you can call me arrogant and egotistical, and you can say that you hate my show. But you're *listening,* aren't you, America? You're listening to me. Think about it. Good night."

A commercial came on, and Tommy shut off the radio. He turned off the dome light, too, then sat there in the dark, waiting. Within five minutes a grotesquely overweight figure came waddling around the corner. He had a light brown leather backpack slung over one shoulder, hanging down to his ample hip. The backpack appeared to be empty. Tommy shut off the

car and was reaching for the door handle when a second figure
turned the same corner just a moment later.

A cop. A Chicago cop, in uniform, who was now looking at
Tommy. Tommy looked away quickly, working to put a benign,
aloof expression on his face. He put the car in gear and pulled
slowly away from the curb. As he passed them, he saw that the
cop was no longer eyeing him.

Shit. What now?

Tommy had to drive up Lake Street to Wabash, because State
didn't allow private vehicles on the street, only cabs, buses,
police squad cars, fire trucks, and other emergency vehicles. He
ran the light on Wabash, raced down a block, barely skidded
around onto Randolph right in front of a taxi that was coming
from the east with the right of way. Tommy ignored the shriek
of brakes, the blaring horn, and tore down to Dearborn, shutting
off his lights just as he made the turn. He pulled to the curb in
front of a closed restaurant, directly across the street from a
long-abandoned movie house, and waited.

What had the woman with two last names written? Mc-
Cauley had been a spoiled, beat-up wimp as a child. An overly
protected, suburban-raised kid who a year ago moved into one
of the most exclusive neighborhoods in the city, drove a new
Lincoln to work in the Loop every night, and thought that
somehow made him streetwise. Whatever would have made
him think such a thing? Tommy wondered. The scary walk to
the indoor parking garage in the heart of the Loop after three in
the morning with an armed on-duty cop as an escort? That
would make you streetwise, all right. Tommy was hoping to
teach the fat boy something about the street this very morning,
but he didn't know what he'd do if the cop escorted McCauley
home.

Tommy watched the entrance of the garage, breathing
heavily, thinking about what he had to lose here, and to gain.
The nigger with the Jew name had been suddenly distracted as
he'd spoken to Rick about somebody dying, then he got mad as
hell; but he'd had the presence of mind to go to his car, get a

package with the magazine in it off the front seat, and hand it to Tommy, had given it to him along with three short sentences of conversation.

"This man owes me twenty-two thousand dollars. You collect it tonight, Rick's cuz, you get to keep every dime for yourself. But I need proof that you collected it," he'd said, then he and Tommy's cousin Rick had gotten into Wrisberg's brand-new shiny Mitsubishi 3000 and had driven off into the night. As the car started up, the underside of the Mitsu had come alive with purple neon. Tommy had looked down at the magazine in his hand, frowning.

Twenty-two grand? And he got to keep it all? Tommy couldn't believe his good luck. If he still believed in God, he'd have said a prayer of thanks. For that kind of money, there wasn't anything Tommy wasn't willing to do. Even if it meant reading a goddamn magazine.

Even if it meant beating the shit out of a cop in order to collect it. The concept of waiting wasn't one that Tommy could grasp.

Tommy heard the short warning blast of the car's horn before he saw the front end of the Lincoln nose its way out slowly onto the sidewalk, then pull quickly onto Dearborn Street. He watched the car turn onto the late-night empty street, saw through the rear window that there was only one body in the front. Tommy breathed a sigh of relief, slipped Rick's Buick into gear, and began to follow the Lincoln, maintaining a discreet distance behind.

The four Homicide detectives watched the dying man's lips, all of them leaning forward, breathing through their mouths so they wouldn't have to smell his horrid breath or his body's stench, the death scent that surrounded Jimmy Duette. They strained to hear if he was talking or if the lip movement was simply reflexive. Although Duette certainly seemed to be trying, no intelligible sound passed across his lips, just moans, cries, mumbo jumbo that was picked up by the recorder and would be listened to later by a series of officers with specialized training in deciphering not only regional accents but foreign languages.

After a half hour of pleading and cajoling, Mondo turned to Jake and said, "Let me talk to you a minute alone, outside." He looked at Hoffman. "Stay here, maybe he'll say something." She looked over at him. Elaine's eyebrows were raised, but she didn't reply.

There was something in Mondo's voice that made Jake suddenly afraid. He felt as if someone had taken a hammer to his hamstrings; there was a weakness in the back of his legs; he had trouble standing straight.

It wasn't a new problem for him; Jake had felt this before. He thought it was a mixture of cowardice and a lack of confidence, although the fear never came at him like it used to, through his spine, rippling. These days it came through his legs first, made them all weak and rubbery.

As for his confidence, Jake thought that he had lost that sometime back.

He knew that he could keep his face straight and that he could play the game by rote, shout the words and command the respect; only he himself knew how afraid he always was. He had thought that no one would suspect it, but now he wasn't so sure. Mondo looked at him as if smelling the fear, a puzzled look on his face.

"Outside in the hallway, all right?" His words spurred Jake to nod, as if he'd been so wrapped up in watching Duette that he was hearing Mondo for the first time. He walked to the door, opened it, then waited, but Mondo was saying something to Lynch and Hoffman, speaking in a low, soft voice, excluding

Jake. His paranoia grew. He walked out the door and let it close behind him, stood directly in front of it at parade rest.

The cop standing beside him seemed to detect Jake's terror without a whole lot of trouble. Jake believed he sensed the man's amusement as strongly as if he'd been laughing out loud, right in Jake's face.

The door opened, and Jake willed himself to stand as tall as he could. He stepped away from the door, keeping his hands clasped behind his back. Mondo came out first, followed by Lynch. Hoffman had stayed in the room.

"He say anything?" Goddamnit, that was a stupid thing to say; how much could the man have said in the last sixty seconds? Jake heard the tremor in his voice. He coughed, trying to cover it up, then loudly cleared his throat.

"Not yet." Mondo took Jake's arm and began to lead him toward the far end of the corridor. "Just the usual spastic movement and groans. That's your assignment in there, Jake." Lynch left them alone, walked in the other direction, back toward the Emergency Room. Jake felt the uniformed officer's eyes boring into his back.

When they reached the end of the hallway, Mondo said, "I know you've got court in the morning, but go in there and pay attention. Don't leave until he dies. Try to talk to him. Maybe he'll sense your compassion." Mondo spoke in a normal tone, but it held a touch of something Jake couldn't understand. Was Mondo worried about him? Jake hoped that was all it was.

Mondo leaned in close to Jake, watching him, studying him closely. "Listen, Jake . . . Are you all right? I mean, you've been under a lot of strain, what with the separation. And I know I've been piling a lot on your plate. I've been doing that on purpose. I thought keeping you busy, you know . . . "

"I know, Mondo." Jake tried to act surprised, remembering what the psychologist had said to him earlier. "What's the matter? Are you telling me you think my performance has been slipping?"

"No, it's not that at all. It's just that you haven't seemed . . .
yourself lately. Your personality, Jake." Both men knew they
shared a bond that Mondo didn't have with any other detective
in the bureau. Jake had been the only officer who'd believed in
Mondo last year, when Mondo had needed a friend.

Watching Mondo study him, Jake felt, more than anything,
relieved. Which caused a flush of shame. In a very real sense, he
was betraying Mondo, deceiving a friend. But Jake couldn't
think about that now.

He said, "Everything's fine, Mondo. It's just a funk, that's all. I
can't see Lynne as often as I'd like. I can't seem to even talk to
Marsha anymore without some nonsense coming up."

Mondo nodded thoughtfully. His own divorce had been
painful; he'd been publicly cuckolded. Elaine Hoffman had
helped him get through it; Jake, on the other hand, had no one.

"You didn't seem to want to come out tonight. When I called,
you got into all this about court, you weren't on call, I was
supposed to be sleeping. And you acted like I had a hidden
agenda in calling you; you acted very defensive." Mondo stood
close to Jake. Mondo leaned one hand against the wall and
stood there, holding Jake's eyes. Jake fought to keep his face
from showing his pain. Mondo seemed to be feeling the discomfort men often feel while discussing things of an emotional
nature.

"It's going all right with Florence, isn't it?"

"She's gonna break my bank account, but it's going all right, I
guess," Jake said. "I can't always figure out what she's trying to
say to me. I think she feels I should start seeing other women."

"Not a bad suggestion. Florence knows what she's doing. She
told me the same thing, and I know it helped me." Mondo was
plainly embarrassed now. Jake was one of the few people who
knew that Mondo had sought counseling, and that he was
living with one of the detectives under his command.

"If there's something bothering you, Jake, if there's anything
wrong, you *do* understand that you can bring it to me, don't
you?"

Jake nodded. He didn't trust himself to speak. The sincerity in Mondo's voice, his unbridled trust in Jake, was as heartening as it was heartbreaking. He felt an urge to talk to Mondo, to tell him what he'd gotten himself into. If anyone would understand, it would be Mondo.

Then again, he might not. Rather than understanding and trying to help, he might see it as the duplicity it truly was and, at the very least, bounce Jake out of Special Victims. Jake would save it for Florence. On Wednesday. Maybe.

Mondo lowered his voice and said, "You and the captain have been talking a lot, Jake." Mondo waited, but Jake didn't reply. "Is there someone in the bureau you suspect, Jake? Has this Internal Affairs thing gotten close to home? If there is, for the sake of the entire unit, you have to let me know. If someone's dirty, or if you even suspect there is, we can cut out the bad seed, even if there's no evidence yet. I can transfer whoever it is; we're autonomous. I don't need excuses to appease the union."

"It's not that, Mondo."

"In other words, you don't want to tell me. What's going on between the captain and you. That's none of my business." Mondo didn't act as if he were hurt, or even confused. There could be a thousand reasonable explanations for what Jake and the captain had been doing together in the captain's office. Jake looked at Mondo with an expression he hoped seemed one that pleaded for understanding.

Mondo looked down the hallway with a pained expression on his face. He looked back at Jake and softly said, "Jake, level with me." He paused and stared directly into Jake's eyes. Jake had to fight a strong desire to look away. "Is anyone investigating me? My relationship with Elaine?"

Jake let his breath out in relief. "No, Mondo. As far as I know, nobody even knows about that."

Mondo seemed to make a decision, nodded again, and patted Jake on the arm. "Do me a favor, get that hillbilly to say something, would you please?" Mondo smiled. "We've got enough problems with the internal investigation without the city thinking that we're all a bunch of psychopathic killers. Let's wrap this up and get back to business, without the media glare." Mondo waited a few seconds, then added, "This investigation has me paranoid, I guess. I'm sorry."

Jake nodded acceptance. He gave Mondo a weak smile. He said, "You had me worried there for a minute. I thought you were seeing things about my performance that I couldn't. I thought maybe I was slipping up."

"You?" Mondo grunted good-naturedly. "Detective Goody Two-Shoes?" Jake forced a laugh, and Mondo dropped his smile. "So as far as you know, Jake, everything's all right within Special Victims, right?"

"Mondo, if I suspected anyone in Special Victims of being crooked, I'd come to you; that's a no-brainer." Mondo nodded.

"Good. Relieve Elaine, then take care of the death watch. If Duette says anything, I'll be home; call me right away. If he doesn't, try to grab a few hours' sleep. You don't have to come in after court; just go home and get some rest. I'll see you in the afternoon, if you're up to it."

"Mondo?"

"Yeah?"

Jake hesitated, then said, "I don't care how long court lasts, I want to come in tomorrow. I want to be a part of this investigation, this Duette thing."

"I didn't call you at midnight to cut you out of it, partner," Mondo said, smiling, before he turned and walked down the hall, back toward the hospital room.

Jake felt the tension drain from him. At first he'd thought that Mondo had been onto him. Jake leaned against the wall, bowed his head, lifted a hand to his eyes, and rubbed them. He took several deep breaths, letting them out slowly. When he was sure that he was in control of himself, he pushed off the wall and proceeded down the hallway, in a hurry to get rid of Hoffman—there was a phone call he had to make, and he needed total privacy.

————

Kevin Wrisberg knew that there was only one single loose end left that could tie him to Duette and the robbery of the dago's drug money, and that loose end was sitting right beside him in the West Side safe-house apartment. At least he thought it was safe; neither the dagos nor the cops had come around kicking the door down yet.

It was something that could happen at any time, though. He had to worry about that. Especially since they'd been in this apartment, talking, for a long time. It was something for him to think about. Wrisberg sighed. There was *always* something for him to think about.

In his ever-increasingly irrational, self-pitying, drug-induced moments, Wrisberg would think that that was always the way it was, that he himself always had to carry all of the weight. Until recently, there had been a lot of people who worked for him, and a very few who worked *with* him, but what it came down to was, Wrisberg was always the brains. He had to figure everything out, scheme out the plans, by himself.

He was in fact scheming right this very minute, although Rick Malardi could never tell. Beside the fact that Rick was too messed up over his rap partner, Duette's, death, Wrisberg had made all the right moves, said the appropriate things, given the proper responses to Rick's statements and questions as they'd discussed their situation, but he could do all of that with half his brain tied behind his back—the rest of what he thought of as his computerlike mind had been plotting, sneaking sideways glances Rick's way, weighing benefits against risks, sitting on Italian leather with his jacket off, a gold silk tank top showing off his well-defined upper body muscles.

Thinking.

Rick seemed to have gotten over his partner's death. That, or he'd finally figured out that his whining made him look like a pussy.

"You're something else, Kev, I gotta hand it to you," Rick said, shaking his head in admiration. Whenever they were alone, smoking dope and drinking, as they were now, Rick would allow his speech to drift into a mellow, slurred, ghetto manner of talking. Wrisberg always instantly resented this, but he'd never said anything before, so he wouldn't this time, either. He had to be careful to behave in a manner consistent with the way he'd acted in all his past dealings with this man.

And besides, he had other things on his mind. Such as making sure that this ignorant Italian boy didn't ever find out how far down Wrisberg's fortunes had fallen.

So he smiled rather than frowned, then innocently asked, "What'd I do?"

Rick grunted a laugh, as if they both knew exactly what he'd been thinking about. "Man, giving that half-retarded cousin of mine all the money, if he collected it . . . That's a work of genius, brother, the way to do it, Kev. I really gotta hand it to you, you're pure class."

Wrisberg took a sip of his drink, put the glass back down on the table. "What was I s'posed to do? Tell him to keep half? I don't give a shit about twenty-two grand; it's the *point*."

"The principle, you mean."

"The *point,* motherfucker, the *point* is what I said, and what I *meant!*" Rick looked over at him, wounded. Wrisberg controlled his mounting anger. He hated it when some high school dropout white motherfucker tried to correct him in any way.

He calmed himself down and said, "I got guys owe me ten times that; no problem, 'cause I know they're gonna pay. Now this fat guy, this McCauley motherfucker, he tells my boy Ingram he ain't paying, uh-uh, no way. He's famous; he'll go on the air and tell the whole wide world that Ingram threatened his ass. Problem with that is twofold, Rick."

Wrisberg was now affecting a laid-back attitude he wasn't

feeling. He reached over and picked up a ready-rolled joint from the polished clear-glass end table. He leaned back, put his stockinged feet up on the table, and fired it up.

Rick didn't say anything, even when Wrisberg handed over the joint. Wrisberg knew that the boy was still smarting from being yelled at just a few seconds ago. The joint was as much a peace offering as it was a part of the plan to get Rick good and relaxed. To get the man to let his guard down.

Wrisberg said, "First, the problem is that the white boy—the fat one, I mean—he could do it and get away with it. Go on over the damn airwaves live and talk about Ingram's threats. Brag about how he ain't paying no gambling debts. People hear him in—what?—something like forty-six states every night? Forty-five and most of the forty-sixth I don't give a shit about. What I give a shit about's Chicago and the south suburbs; that's my area.

"Fact is, McCauley wouldn't know my name if it got shouted in his ear, but there's plenty of others know Ingram's my boy, and some of them are police, and that wouldn't be good for business. I can hear my other gamblers crying already: 'Shit, I ain't paying you nothin'. That white radio man didn't have to pay you, why should a brother?' " Wrisberg gave a lazy shrug of his wide shoulders, as if the first problem was obvious to any thinking man.

"Second problem is, I don't know how Ingram'd hold up under po-lice interrogation. It's why the boy's twenty years old—been with me four years and still only collecting my bets. He ain't been arrested for nothing but gambling, ain't never did no real time, so I ain't never been able to test him."

"Tommy, on the other hand, has."

"More important, Rick, he did time and kept his mouth shut . . . right?"

Rick waved an impatient hand; the topic wasn't worthy of discussion. "Rick's natural enemies is the po-lice; he hates them all. Boy wouldn't rat no one out if they put a loaded gun to his head."

"So, twenty-two's a small price to pay to maintain the in-*teg*-rity of my business, to keep everything flowing smoothly. Now someone owes me money balks? I just point out to them that even a famous motherfucker such as Ray McCauley paid up what he owed me. Me, I don't discriminate. I'm equal opportunity, and now I can prove it."

"Can I ax you a question?" Rick said, then took another puff on the joint.

"Shoot." Wrisberg held up one hand, and laughed. Rick snorted a little smoke through his nostrils. "Wait, scratch that, don't take that one seriously. Go ahead, ask."

Rick spoke while exhaling marijuana smoke.

"Why use a dummy like Rick? Why go through me to get someone?" His voice was tight and rough, Rick consciously expelling as little oxygen as he had to from his smoke-filled lungs. Wrisberg just looked at him, as if he didn't understand the question. Rick waved his hand around, and his voice, when he spoke now, was normal.

"I mean, look at the way you live, dude. You got it *all*. We're in one lousy hideout apartment you act like you don't even care about, and you got it laid out like a mansion, like some kind of castle. You're rich, man; everybody be knowin' that. Shit, a titan of crime, a Mount Olympus." He patted the sofa beneath him. "My ass is sitting on more money that Tommy'll make this year."

"Yeah? So what? All this talking got a point?"

"Well, yeah." Rick, looking slightly wounded again, said, "You got to have three hundred men working for you, who'd stand up for you no matter what the po-lice did to them. So why use Tommy to collect this money?"

"That's simple. Number one, if Tommy can scare this asshole into paying off, then everyone's happy and I write off a small bit of cash. He *can't* scare the guy off—if this McCauley shows up on the air crying about what happened—hell, think about it, Rick."

"So why you need the money collected tonight, man? What

was the hurry? If you're giving it all to Tommy, why you need it done tonight, and why you need proof it was collected?"

"Figure the man too dumb to make a ca-reer out of it, might forget about it, what with all else he's got going on in his head. Far as proof, shit, think about it."

"Makes sense to me."

"You should be grateful I give the boy a job in the first place, Rick."

"You just did it so it'll never get back to you."

"Cops connect me to a dago leg breaker? Never in a million years."

"Hey, watch it, *I'm* a dago."

"I heard that." Something in Wrisberg's voice made Rick look over at him warily.

"Well, I mean, you wouldn't like it if I said something about niggers."

"No, you're right about that." Wrisberg was staring at him now.

Slowly, Rick said, "So why should you be able to talk about dagos?"

" 'Cause I can," Wrisberg said, the scheming over, his mind made up, and his plan set in stone. Wrisberg took his feet off the table, slipped them into his loafers.

"Wait a minute, wait a fuckin' minute . . . " Rick sat up straight, looking off into space, thinking. Wrisberg looked at him, pitying the white boy all that hard work. He stabbed the joint out in the ashtray, debated eating the roach, then changed his mind; that thing had been inside a white man's lying lips. Rick at last seemed to make a connection, and he looked over at Wrisberg.

"You're using Tommy, and man, I got to tell you, when you told me the cops killed Duette, you didn't seem too broken up over the loss." Rick swallowed hard, then pressed ahead. "Were you using *us*?"

"You? *You?* Are you crazy? You and Duette were my two favorite white boys." Rick forced a small smile. He patted his leg in amusement. "See here now, Ricky, listen to what I'm saying. I told you all this before. You and Duette were the best men for the *job*! You ran with him when he came up here, and—I got to hand it to the boy—Jimmy was the best safe-cracker ever to come out of the swamp. You worked with him, you know it. There wasn't a box made that boy couldn't smoke!"

"Yeah." Rick drew the word out. Wrisberg knew that he had to stop showing off, knock off all that "dago" stuff, stop giving Rick glimpses of his fine mind at work, such as the way he'd used Rick's cuz. It had started the boy thinking, and it was never a good sign for him when a white man got to thinking.

Keeping it simple, Wrisberg said, "I needed two good men I could trust to cultivate my plan. And guys who'd done it before. I spent months making that plan. I didn't need some big-mouth pimp I got working for me, some bet taker, some numbers runner or crack seller, even a stone killer—someone ain't never done anything *but* those things—to be going around town running their mouths about how they're all of a sudden professional burglars, ripping off the dag—ripping off the outfit. Some of these guys, they can't take what they do at its true worth, either; they got to make everything political. Go to the temple and brag about how they took down the white o-pressor to further the brother's cause."

Wrisberg's words were bitter, but he grinned and Rick responded, the two of them laughing behind their hands at the silly niggers Wrisberg employed.

"I needed a good solid working crew, and I found it in you and Jimmy."

"And now one of us is dead."

"That's right. You said I wasn't too broken up, and you were right. I was too worried about warning your ass, saving you from the same shit. Cops connect me to Duette? Never in a million years. Radio announcer say, 'Police suspected in thieve's death,' what's the first thing I do? Go find and try to save the ass of the man who's connected to the dead man."

Rick seemed to be thinking this over. He slowly nodded his head. "Yeah, I guess you did. Cops *can* connect me to Jimmy. I been pinched with his ass a time or two; they know we's a team."

Wrisberg winced, then caught himself. Let the fool talk. Rick smiled. "The buddha we be smoking making me paranoid." Wrisberg forced his smile to remain immobile.

Rick said, "So what do we do with his piece of the action, Kev? We talked about everything else, about the lawyers, the crooked cops, what we got to do. All that shit, I'm clear about. But you didn't tell me what we're gonna do with Jimbolaya's share."

Was that a sly look on Ricky's pretty dago face? Wrisberg thought it was.

He said, "We did the work, we split the money."

"He got a wife and five kids, did you know that?" Wrisberg listened, then slowly shook his head back and forth until Rick got the point.

"You ain't givin' them nothin'?"

"You want to give them a cut out of your end, that's none of my business; you go ahead on, Rick. I did the work, you and me and Jimmy. Not his old lady, not his five kids. That mean I *take* the money."

"*We* take the money."

"Fifty-fifty, right down the middle."

"That's cold."

"It's a cold, cruel world, my man," Wrisberg said, then stood, stretched, and reached down for his electric blue jacket. "You got a place to stay until you get your lawyer and we can get this all straightened out? Like you say, cops can put you together with Jimmy; you two been buddies a long time."

"I'll be with—a friend. And I'm waking my lawyer up right now, soon as I get to her crib. He can go to the TV news with what the cops did to Jimbolaya. Claim they're going to kill mo, too. After that, they'll assign me bodyguards, make sure no harm be-falls me."

"Befalls you." Wrisberg chuckled at the words. "I like a man knows how to properly frame a sentence." He patted his jacket, as if checking to see if he had everything he needed.

Rick took the hint and stood himself, grabbed his leather sport coat from the arm of the couch, where he'd tossed it. He put it on, casually adjusted the shoulders, then reached inside the jacket, as if his left shirtsleeve had gotten bunched up and had to be pulled down.

He casually said, "Where's the dough, Kev? The hundred grand, where'd you stash it?"

"Need lawyer fees?" Wrisberg smiled. His eyes went dreamy. He issued a gentle, almost contented sigh. If Rick had been paying close attention, he might have felt as if he were being seduced.

Wrisberg reached into his pocket, as if looking for his keys. He said, "We go over to get it right now. Two weeks is long enough to sit on it. And let's face it, with Duette gone, there's a serious trust problem seems to be arising between the two of us."

"We split it up tonight?" Rick made an angry face and looked at his shoulder, his hand still inside his leather jacket, pulling at his shirt. "Goddamn lining gets caught up every time."

"Half of a hundred thousand dollars buys you a whole lot of new leather coats."

Rick began to pull his hand out of his coat and Wrisberg shot him twice before Rick's fingers could clear the fabric. The bullets tore holes through the pocket of his jazzy blue suit coat. The impact twisted his wrist; the noise had been incredible. Wrisberg took his hand out of his jacket, let the .22 Derringer with the Magnum loads drop to the floor. He shook his pained hand, then jumped, startled—the front of his jacket was smoldering; what was left of the pocket was afire.

Doing a little dance of fear, Wrisberg tore the jacket off and angrily threw it at Rick's corpse. It fell on top of Rick, covered the butt of the pistol that Rick had been trying to pull out of his inside jacket pocket.

"Son of a bitch," Wrisberg shouted at the dead man. "Look

what the fuck you did! Ruined my damn coat, and now you're bleeding all over my carpet." He stormed over to the body and kicked it hard in the head. "Goddamn dago motherfuckers," Wrisberg said. "Can't trust none of you to act like a man's supposed to."

No wonder the guy was so fat, Tommy thought. He lived maybe eight blocks from work and had to take the car back and forth every day? Judging from what was in the magazine article, though, it seemed to be McCauley's style. He could shoot off his mouth all night on the radio, talk tough when he was in a locked room speaking into a microphone with armed guards downstairs watching over the locked front door, but he didn't have the courage to handle walking down the street after dark. Not even from the Gold Coast, maybe the safest neighborhood in all of the city.

Tommy almost panicked when McCauley pulled into the descending drive of one of the lower-rise apartment buildings on North Lake Shore Drive. He relaxed when he saw that the steel door took some time to raise and lower. He reached up, as if he were pressing a garage door button, then followed the Lincoln in and down. McCauley pulled into what was obviously his designated parking spot, and Tommy passed him, driving slowly, and pulled into a spot marked VISITOR. He turned off the Buick and waited until he spotted McCauley lumbering toward the elevator. Then he reached under the seat, grabbed his pistol, shoved it into his waistband, and pulled his shirttail out to cover it.

As McCauley pressed the elevator button, Tommy got out of the car.

*   *   *

The fat man was breathing hard, as if he'd just run a couple of miles rather than simply walked—and walked very slowly— from his car to the underground garage's elevator. He raised his eyebrows at Tommy as he saw him walking toward him, too dumb to be scared, then he half frowned and turned to look away, at the steel of the elevator door. Tommy began to whistle a tuneless little melody.

They stood side by side, Tommy's hands over his groin, clasped together, further hiding the pistol. At last the elevator door opened. Tommy stepped in first, moved far back into the cab, allowed the huge man to stand facing the front of the elevator. Tommy did it as if deferring to the man. McCauley pressed the button for the fifth floor and said, with just a touch of impatience, "What floor you heading for, there, partner?" He was talking to an obvious incompetent, a lower form of human evolution from himself.

"I'm going to five, too," Tommy said, with a touch of surprise in his voice.

"Small world, i'n it?" Listen to the bastard. "I'n it," like an Englishman. Tommy smiled, being patient and slick for maybe the fourth time in his life. In a few minutes, he'd have this tub of guts calling him 'sir.' McCauley startled him by asking, "You visiting the D'Amatos?" Then he laughed patronizingly. Tommy had heard con men laughing in much the same manner. McCauley added, "I guess you'd have to be; they're the only Italians on the floor."

Tommy bit his tongue before he said, "I'm his brother, uh, Timmy."

"Brother?" McCauley turned to face him, suspicious now. "I've known Allison and Jim for a year now. He's never mentioned a brother."

Was this elevator wired for sound? It wouldn't surprise Tommy. He had to play out the string.

He said, "Jim's always been a closemouthed son of a bitch, i'n he?" The fat man looked at Tommy, seemed to get it, and smirked, then turned to face the front again as the elevator stopped and its door opened wide. He stepped out and, ignorant son of a bitch that he was, just stood there. Tommy stepped out past him, turned to his right, and heard a sharp intake of breath come from McCauley, and he realized that he'd turned the wrong way.

All right, to hell with it. He reached under his shirt and into his waistband, pulled the pistol out of his pants just as the elevator doors whooshed closed.

"One word, one fucking sound out of you, and I'll deflate you like a balloon, you hear me, fat boy?"

McCauley raised his hands over his head and nodded hard enough to make all ten of his chins jiggle.

"You owe me *money!*" They were words Tommy had been waiting to speak since he was ten years old and had seen Paul Newman in *The Hustler* on late-night television. Some older guy, an outfit guy, not a pool player—George C. Scott, that's who it was—had shouted the words at Fast Eddie Felson after Eddie had at last beaten Minnesota Fats. The only problem was, from then until now, nobody had ever owed Tommy any money. It had always been the other way around. Well, tonight was his night.

There was no doubt about that. The talk radio guy, McCauley, had pissed his pants already, let it go before Tommy had ever touched him. He was quivering now, sitting on his couch while Tommy stood over him, the guy terrified, his hands held down, fingers together out straight, covering his groin and looking as if he were praying to the devil. He wouldn't look at Tommy.

The apartment wasn't too bad, though it was a lot less than Tommy had expected in this neighborhood. Small, little rooms. A tiny kitchen with no place to sit down. The tub of guts had furnished it okay, with pretend leather furniture and a large-screen TV. The TV had been running when they'd walked into the apartment, the sound muted. The flickering light it cast had scared the shit out of Tommy when they'd first come into the place; he'd had a moment of panic and had shot the television set, thinking somebody was in the apartment. McCauley hurriedly told him that the place was totally soundproof; the gunshot wouldn't be a problem. As soon as he'd said it, he'd realized his mistake. Tommy had grinned, and McCauley had had his accident.

Now Tommy walked over to McCauley and touched the still-warm gun barrel to the top of the man's head. McCauley made a little whimpering sound and shook some more. Tommy could see his tits jiggling under the Grateful Dead T-shirt he was wearing. In the joint, he would—Tommy stopped himself. They weren't in the joint. And he wasn't here to get laid.

He said, "Twenty-two grand, asshole. That's *my* money now that we're talking about. I bought out your contract." He removed the barrel from the top of McCauley's head. The man looked up at him, gratitude in his eyes.

"What?"

"You heard me. I bought out your contract. You don't owe your bookie anymore, Ray, you owe *me*. Bookies, they get involved with their clients sometimes, form re*lat*ionships and shit like that. Sometimes they get so tight with you guys they ain't got the heart to collect. That's when they come to me, 'cause I got that heart. So I bought out your contract. You owe me twenty-two grand. And you're gonna pay me, right now, or I swear to God, I'm gonna put you on a weight-loss program better than Jenny Craig." Tommy leaned forward, stared directly into McCauley's eyes, and looked crazy at him. Looking crazy was one of the few things Tommy was exceptionally good at.

"I'll tape your mouth, get one of your kitchen knives, and cut about fifty pounds of ugly fat off your ass, right here, right now."

"But I don't—"

"Shut *up!*"

Tommy slapped McCauley lightly on the side of his head with the pistol. It was enough to shut him up, to send him over onto his side, holding his head and bawling as if Tommy had smacked him a good one. Big fucking baby. Tough guy, eh? A fighter? And he liked to talk, ask questions.

Tommy said, "There's nothing any of you can do to me that hasn't been done before," trying to quote McCauley. The man got his point, looked up at him, his fingers over his face, looking through the soft, pudgy webs at his worst nightmare. He didn't open his mouth to speak this time, though. Good. Tommy must have had his attention.

"Anyone ever flatten your nose for you, Ray?" Tommy barely moved, just shifted his weight. He hit McCauley in the middle of his face with the pistol. The man screamed as blood spurted out through his fingers. "One more word, *one more word out of you,* and I start to slice and dice, you understand me?" McCauley nodded rapidly again, horrified, sniveling. Tommy owned him. He chuckled, patted McCauley's hip, and suddenly dropped down next to him on the fake leather sofa.

"Now, we're going to have a little talk, you and me. I want my money, and you're gonna pay me. You don't open your mouth unless it's to tell me how you're gonna pay me my money, all right, Ray babe?"

Jake walked out of the room, feeling beaten down, wanting a drink to kill the dull, throbbing aches that seemed to have settled in his head and stomach. The tape recorder was in his hand, but the microcassette it had held was in his pocket. He looked at the cop who was still standing guard outside the door.

"He's dead."

The cop smirked. "Doctor come in when I wasn't looking, declare him that way, or what?"

Jake felt the repressed anger bubble to the surface.

The cop said, "He got pretty talkative there at the end, huh? He tell you which alderman's kid with a Homicide shield killed him?"

Jake tried, he really tried, to stay in control of his emotions. He said, "He was calling out to God, that's all."

"*Sure* he was," the cop said.

Before he could stop himself, Jake said, "Look, it's nobody's fault but your own that you're fifty years old and still a patrolman." He started to walk away. The cop shouted at his back.

"Go fuck yourself, all right, Mr. Big Shot? Don't think we all ain't heard the rumors about *you*." Jake stopped. He turned to look back at the patrolman. "That's right." The officer's voice had lost a little of its anger, now that Jake was looking at the man. Still, he continued in the same vein. "The apple don't fall very far from the tree, does it?"

Jake lifted the recorder. He began to walk back toward the officer, pressing a button, as if turning the machine on.

"You want to make accusations? You got a big mouth?"

"It's free speech." The cop was staring at the recorder now.

"I heard that same excuse an hour ago from one of our friends in the media. Come on, give some of that free speech away, then." Jake was almost at the man now, advancing quickly. The officer took a quick step backward. Jake said, "You don't think I have enough shit in my life without bitter slobs like you spreading lies?"

The cop grunted. "Yeah, I heard. Your job's to take shit. And to wait for the Rat Patrol to take away your pension, then lock your ass up. I know all about you Homicide guys." The cop gave Jake what he probably thought to be a withering, morally superior look. He said, "And my job's to stand out here until I get relieved."

Jake understood then. The guy was just another slacker, putting in his eight hours. To hell with it. He lowered the recorder, turned, and walked away, down the corridor leading to the Emergency Room. The officer didn't say anything this time.

Jake needed to use the bathroom but hadn't wanted to use the one back in the room, not with a dead body lying five feet away. He didn't know why, but within seconds of Duette's death, Jake began to feel afraid. He didn't know what was wrong with him these days.

Or maybe he did. He thought about it as he walked, thinking of Mondo, and as he did, things he'd been wondering about for some time now fell into place.

Mondo didn't suspect him of anything; that was the best news Jake had had in a while. He had in fact been worried that Jake knew something he himself didn't, was concerned that IAD, OPS, the captain, or God knew who else was investigating *him,* for God's sake. Mondo, as had almost every cop Jake had ever known, had had his share of problems, in his life as well as his career. But there wasn't even the faintest scent of corruption about him, let alone having its ugly stain stamped upon his forehead.

Which wasn't the case concerning a number of other officers in the department. Particularly these days, when stains were being invented by the headhunters, the Rat Patrol, the media, and gossips like the fat bastard who'd been guarding Duette's door. Jake walked back the way he'd come, ignoring several exit signs. At this hour of the early morning, the doors would more than likely be alarmed, and he didn't want to draw attention to himself. He had a meeting to attend.

Jake heard the shouting before he entered the ER proper, and it dragged him out of his reverie. A vaguely familiar voice was shouting curses, screaming in anger. Jake ran the last few steps down the hall, turned into the ER, and saw who it was that was causing all the trouble.

A badly beaten obese man was charging around the Emergency Room with two uniformed police officers worriedly following him. An empty wheelchair was sitting off to the side. Several paramedics were watching the scene, half amused. Jake looked at the man, frowning. He knew him from somewhere. Where had he seen him before? And why was his voice familiar?

Jake looked around. The other cubicles were all still filled, the curtains still pulled tightly shut. The orderlies and doctors and nurses behind the island weren't paying the man much attention; this sort of thing happened frequently these days in hospital emergency rooms. Jake looked at the man, puzzled. Then he remembered where he'd seen him before, why he recognized his voice.

He'd seen the man's image on various billboards around the city. It was the late-night talk radio host, Ray McCauley.

Who was now shouting, "That fucking bitch, it's all her *fault*! You go out there and arrest her; she made this happen; it's her fault I got beaten half to death!"

The cops were looking at each other, wondering what they should do. You couldn't just slap a celebrity around, not in public, at least. Particularly one who had daily access to a fifty-thousand-watt radio transmitter. A hospital security guard came running through the doorway, stopped short, looked at the two cops, then shook his head at their timidity, pulled his club, and began to walk toward McCauley.

"You touch me and I'll own this fucking hospital!" McCauley screamed, pointing a finger at the man. "Don't you know who I *am*?!"

The two police officers stepped in to apprehend the guard before he could hurt the man. McCauley suddenly bent over at the waist, his hands going up to grip his chest, his face betraying his fear and confusion. He shouted in pain; his voice rose, and the pained tone was now blended with anger and terror.

McCauley collapsed face forward to the floor and fell silent, the fat of his back jiggling for just a moment before his body stilled.

The doctor who had earlier acted as Jake's escort jumped over the barrier and put her head to McCauley's chest. "Get over here, *now*!" she shouted, and several others raced over to her, joined by the paramedics. "Get a gurney. Get his ass into Surgery. Goddamnit, move!"

Jake stepped around them all, his face blank, trying to show professional disinterest. His curiosity was piqued, though; he felt the old urge to jump in with both feet, try to discover what had happened to the man, how he'd wound up like this, what had brought him into an ER in the middle of the night, horribly beaten. And what "bitch" was he referring to? Jake wanted to know. But he couldn't take the time to find out.

Just a year ago, Jake would have jumped right into the center of the thing, would have demanded to have been made a part of the investigation.

But he wasn't the man he had been a year ago. Things were rapidly changing for Jake.

Jake pushed the man out of his thoughts and walked through the door and on into the waiting room, which had somewhat thinned out since he'd passed through an hour before. He felt empty inside, lonely and afraid. He saw the Delaney-Hinckle woman staring at him, and he felt his jaw tighten. But her earlier insolence seemed to have abandoned her; the cocky attitude was gone. She was staring at the door, her mouth open as wide as her eyes.

Well, hey now, what was *this* all about? This sudden change of demeanor. Jake almost smiled when he flashed on it; he'd seen McCauley before, sure, and remembered him from more than billboards. He'd seen that fat body below a cocky smile, staring out from the cover of this month's issue of *Chicago Alive!* magazine.

Jake walked past the woman without giving her a second thought. It was another act that would have been unthinkable for him to perform a year ago. But Jake didn't dwell on his shortcomings; he had other things on his mind.

Things he started to think about in the late, stark comfort of a nearly empty Rush Street bar, as he sat alone in a booth that was as far away from the door as possible, drinking beer and waiting. The place had a 5 A.M. license; Jake had plenty of time. He listened to strange, soft music coming from the jukebox. Jake didn't recognize it; he hadn't paid any attention to music since he'd graduated from college. He didn't have to wait very long.

Patrol Officer Billy Wozak, out of uniform and wearing an expensive suit, entered the lounge first. He stood there looking around, spotted Jake, then turned to the door, made a small jerk with his head, and Homicide Detective Sergeant Michael Anson followed his nephew inside. Anson stared hard at Jake as the two men walked toward the booth. Wozak swaggered as if he were more than a patrolman, as if he were the superintendent of police. The kid had a superior air about him that always made Jake want to slap him. Anson pointed for Jake to slide around in the booth; he wanted to be able to watch the door himself. Jake did so, and Anson took his seat. Wozak had made a detour to the bar. When he came over to the booth, he was carrying two drinks. He didn't bring another beer for Jake. Wozak sat down next to his uncle, across from Jake, and both men sat there staring at him.

Anson took a sip of his drink. He put the glass down on the table, closed his eyes, and sighed. Jake fiddled with his Rolex and watched as some of the tension drained from the man. "Jesus," Anson said. Wozak took a sip of his drink, his cold eyes never leaving Jake's face. Jake put his left arm on the table, at an angle, and lounged toward the man. He stayed that way, steady, a casual gesture of relaxed camaraderie that Anson ignored.

"You didn't call Genco?"

Billy Wozak answered. He said, "Does it look like we called Genco? No, *he's* at home, while we're here, listening to this shit. What the fuck. Even if you hadn't said not to tell him, he's supposed to drop everything to come out for a late-night meet with you?"

Jake said, "Let me tell you something, Billy. I don't like you. I have never liked you. If your uncle wasn't doing business with me, I wouldn't waste my time even talking to you." Wozak sat up straight. The two men glared at each other. Anson waved an angry hand in the air.

"We got nothing better to discuss than this schoolyard shit?

This is what you dragged me out of my house for? Billy, do me a favor, will you? Take your drink, go over to the bar, and hit on one of the broads, bullshit with the bartender, do whatever you got to do, but let me talk with Jake, all right?" Wozak turned his glare to his uncle. Anson made a *move it* gesture with his hands, and Wozak angrily snatched up his drink, got out of the booth, and stomped over to the bar. Jake did not enjoy having his back turned toward the man, but there didn't seem to be anything he could do about it at this point.

"Why you got to aggravate the kid all the time, Jake? What's the matter with you?"

"He's a tough guy when he thinks he's in control, Mike. I think he'll fold under pressure. I don't trust him."

"Yeah? Well, that makes you even."

"You sure he won't go to Genco, tell him we had a meet? If he sees a chance to make some money?"

"He's my *nephew,* Jake, come on."

"He's out of line. What is he, twenty-three? And he thinks he's too important to show up for a meeting like this one?"

"A meeting like *what* one? I told you on the phone, I still don't know what the hell you were talking about."

"Then why'd you bother showing up?"

Anson changed the subject. "Where'd you call from?"

"First, from my apartment, then the hospital."

"Good thing you called me instead of Genco. Al don't ever talk business on the phone, you know that."

"He leaves that to you."

"And *I* try to leave it to Billy." Anson paused, took another sip of his drink. "Christ, that tastes good tonight." He pretended disinterest in the reason Jake had called him, said, "You recover from Saturday night all right? You was pretty *bombalied,* kid."

"I slept all day Sunday. Didn't get out of bed except to go to the bathroom."

"Is that right? I thought you said you had to get up early, that you had to pick up your kid."

Jake immediately lied. "I had to pass it up. Don't think my ex didn't let me know about it."

"Ah, they're all bitches, you know it? These days, if you ain't kissing their asses, they don't think their *needs* are being met." Anson cooly finished his drink, then fixed Jake with an appraising eye. "You gotta start eating more, Jake; you're getting too skinny."

Jake sat looking at him. Anson didn't even blink. Jake said, "I've got court in the morning, Mike."

"I was wondering why you were playing around with beer. Yeah, all right. Just trying to make conversation." He reached into his suit jacket and pulled out an envelope. "I guess you been waiting for this, right?"

"You keep it. I'm through running errands."

"You're *what*?" Surprised, Anson angrily tossed the envelope onto the table. It skimmed across and fell into Jake's lap. Anson chortled, shaking his head. Jake had to admire his coolness under pressure. Genco was all muscle and mouth; from the very beginning, Jake had pegged Anson as the smarter of the two, the one more apt to use intelligence rather than toughness.

"After all these months, you still don't get it, do you, Jake? What do you think this is, some part-time security job you can walk away from whenever you feel like it? You think *you* get to call the shots, who meets you at what time? Where and fucking when? You got to get all that shit out of your head."

"Do I?"

"I didn't call Genco *only* because I don't want to waste his time with this kind of crap. Don't think you're ever gonna be important enough to drive a wedge between us."

"I was supposed to run a few names for you on the computer, Mike, let you know what we were investigating once a week. I was supposed to use the resources of the Special Victims Bureau to help you guys out from time to time."

"And we pay you for it; it ain't like you're doing us any favors."

"The money comes in handy," Jake conceded. "My wife left

me, and I can't pay my bills on what I make. I explained all that to you the first time you approached me." Jake paused and lowered his voice to say, "But I refuse to be a part of any murders. I told you that up front, too, Mike."

"Murder? What murder? Where the hell you get this murder shit?"

Jake's voice was tight. He sat forward in the booth. "I called you from Duette's *death*bed, Mike, goddamnit!"

"Yeah, you told me that on the phone. I know who Duette is. I was as surprised as you to find out he was in the hospital." Anson paused, then compounded his lie. "I been looking for him myself, you know that."

"Know it? *Know* it! I looked up his *name* for you! *My* goddamn number's on the computer log! If anyone checks . . . " Jake could hardly control his anger.

"If anyone checks, you tell them whatever you want. Tell them you were checking him out in conjunction with another case. I don't care what the hell you tell them, as long as it don't ever come back to haunt me."

"I'm Homicide, Mike, the same as you. What business do I have looking up thieves on the computer?"

"A guy like Duette, he's killed a few people, believe me. Whoever killed him, he did society a favor." Anson looked over at the bar, and Jake wanted to look around, to see what Wozak was doing. Did some signal pass between them? Was he in danger here? Jake picked up his beer and took a drink, left his hand on the bottle when he put it back on the table. He'd smash Wozak's head with it if he had to, buy time to pull his weapon.

Anson looked back over at Jake and said, "Look, kid, I worked with your old man for ten years. I been a copper since you were in kindergarten, for Christ's sake. I know what I'm doing. I offer you a chance to make a few bucks, you ought to be grateful." Jake started as Wozak brought his uncle another drink. He picked up Anson's empty glass and turned away from Jake without comment. "You were grateful enough when I come to you." Anson's tone was accusatory.

"I told you and Genco both up front, information was all you were getting, that's all you were buying from me. And none of it was stuff you couldn't get somewhere else if you wanted it bad enough."

"We can't get what's inside that Special Victims Bureau computer, pally. We need *you* for that." Anson shook his head. Jake concentrated on the shininess of the man's suit. He did not want to see Anson's face. "Take a look in the envelope. Go on, take a look." Jake plucked the envelope off his lap and didn't lift it above the table as he opened it and looked inside. He had to squint in the dimness. He closed his eyes, then closed the envelope. He dropped it back into his lap.

"What the hell is this?"

"A bonus. What I figured was, if you were calling me at home, you were getting antsy, losing your nerve. What I did was, I decided I'd give you a vote of confidence. So I doubled your weekly take."

"Doubled my take."

"There's a grand there, kid. And I need another name, right away, tonight, if you can get it."

"This is supposed to make me accept murder as part of my job description? A lousy thousand fucking dollars?"

"It ain't like you worked for it. You lucked into the Duette thing."

"Lucked into the . . . " Jake was astonished. He said, "IAD's crawling all around Homicide, looking to pinch guys who pay their *alimony* late, and you sit here talking about luck? Do you know what your partner pulled last night, in *spite* of the heat?"

Anson seemed relieved by what Jake had said. "Genco's not a stupid man." Anson shrugged. "He gets stupid, he's on his own. Like everybody else."

Jake sat silently, trying to figure out what was going on. Anson took his time. He looked around the bar, then casually back at Jake.

"So, Jake," he said, laying one arm across the back of the

booth, settling in as if he were just making conversation, "What's his name, Duette, did he say anything before he died? Give up any names?"

"I talked to him." Jake's statement caused Anson to lose some of his studied composure.

"Were you alone?"

"As alone as we are right now. That's one of the reasons why I didn't want Genco here."

"And why's that, Jake?"

" 'Cause Duette named him."

"No shit?" Even in the dim light, Jake could see Anson's face go pale. "He mention . . . any other names?"

"Just one."

Anson nodded, lips pursed, eyebrows slightly raised. He said, "Good thing it was just you in that room, ain't it, Jake?" When Jake didn't answer, Anson said, "So what's this, a holdup? You want more money?"

"You aren't hearing me, are you, Mike?" Jake leaned forward and spoke in a harsh whisper. "Your partner killed Duette, goddamnit, and I know you were there, too!"

Anson's coolness scared Jake more than if the man had exploded. It confirmed Jake's suspicion that Anson had killed in cold blood before.

Anson said, "Jake, Jake, Jake." He shook his head, as if frustrated at having to explain the complexity of life to an adult. "We did what we had to do with that punk, Jake. He spat in Genco's face! You know Al Genco; what do you think would happen to somebody who pulled that?"

"So you killed him."

"Genco and me, we had a talk with the guy."

"A discussion he didn't survive."

"Okay, let's quit playing around. You did the right thing in coming to me."

"I'm in charge of the investigation, Mike. You hear me? I caught the case."

"How much?"

Jake shook his head. He picked up the envelope and tossed it back across the table. Anson tried to grab it, but it hit his chest. He slapped at it, held it there, then looked at Jake angrily.

"You want to watch yourself, Phillips. You want to watch the games you play with me."

"You want me to risk my pension and my freedom for a lousy five hundred a week."

"You weren't bitching about it when I came to you, when I made you the offer."

"That was before you guys killed Duette."

"That'll be awful hard to prove in a court of law, Phillips." Anson dropped the envelope on the table, left it lying there between them. "You got a couple of thirty-year coppers, supervisory rank, pensions locked in, long-term marriages, kids all went to college. What jury's gonna take the word of a burned-out drunk over those two guys?"

Jake paused, as if thinking it over. Then he said, "How about a jury that hears the tape?" and Anson widened his eyes.

"You got this all on tape."

Jake reached out and patted Anson's arm. He said, "Don't worry, Mike. Your name isn't even on the tape."

"You said he mentioned two guys."

"Genco."

"Goddamnit, Jake!" Anson shouted, then caught himself, and with an obvious force of will spoke softly again. "Who was the other guy?"

"Lemelli."

"Lemelli. Oh, Jesus." Anson sat back and looked up at the ceiling. He looked back down at Jake, wired now, on the edge of violence. "You got Duette saying Genco and Lemelli killed him?"

"I got Duette saying Genco killed him on Lemelli's orders."

Anson sat back and processed the information. At last, he said, "What do you want, Jake?"

"I'm tired of working these streets day in and day out for nothing—" Anson waved a hand at him, made a rolling motion with it.

"Come on, goddamnit, save the speech for later. What do you *want*?"

"I want a meet with Lemelli."

"That ain't possible. Lemelli don't even hardly ever meet with *me*."

Jake started to rise. "Then I'll turn the tape over to my supervisor, Lieutenant Mondello."

Anson grabbed Jake's arm. Jake looked down at him. "Sit down, Jake, let's talk this over." Jake felt Anson's finger shaking. Slowly, he sat down.

Anson said, "Listen, you got to meet with the guy in his basement *swimming* pool, for God's sake, or in his sauna, always naked. He has his house swept every *day;* you know what that gotta cost him? He don't meet with you, Jake; he only meets with me and Genco."

"I'm tired of working for nothing. You put me in a position where I'm risking jail time for your five hundred a week. I hand this tape over to you and who gets it, Genco? *He* gets to convert it into cash? Maybe not, because his name is on it. But yours isn't. You can hold them both up, can't you, Mike?"

"Genco and me go way back."

"Like you went with my father."

"Your father would have burned the tape and kept his mouth shut. He never took the outfit's money."

"Bull*shit,* he didn't."

"All right, let's not argue. And let's not use names it ain't healthy to use. What you're saying is, you want a meet with the Man. Say I can set that up, say I luck into that. Then what?"

"*Then what*'ll be between him and me."

Anson shook his head. "Jake, you don't know this guy, he's nuts; he's a psycho."

"The type to beat a guy to death?" Anson glared at Jake.

"You ain't got no evidence that I had anything to do with that."

"And a thirty-year, long-time married guy like yourself, someone's survived as long as you have, Mike, by now, I'd think he'd be asking himself, What's in it for me if I set up the meet?"

"The thought had crossed my mind."

Jake said, "Smart guy like you should have already figured that out," then rose and walked away from the booth. Anson didn't try to stop him this time.

But someone else did, and without laying a finger on him.

Dabney Delaney-Hinckle was sitting in a booth with a big bearded guy, watching him like a hawk. Jake stopped, shocked at the sight of her. He caught himself and walked over to the bar, ordered another beer. He watched in the mirror as Anson passed behind him. Anson didn't even signal to his nephew; the kid just got off his stool and hurried after his uncle. Jake turned and watched them leave the tavern. Then he took his beer and walked over to where Delaney-Hinckle and the man were sitting.

"Jake, say hello to Tony." Jake nodded at the man, ignoring Tony's offered hand. "Tony's the night manager here." She gave him a bright smile. "You want to talk to me now, Jake?" the reporter asked, her smile turning absolutely radiant.

It was the sort of thing that had made Kevin Wrisberg a legend years ago, in his prime as a rising street player—calling men on his car phone to come meet him in the middle of the night, then having them help him dispose of a dead white man's body. The two men, Ingram Pleasant, and his younger half brother, Rasheed Moore, were too intimidated and awestricken to complain or to ask any questions. They had both been working for Wrisberg long enough to understand that they would wind up right alongside the white man if they were dumb enough to do either.

Wrisberg had carried the body down to the car and had thrown it roughly onto the floor in back—having to sweat in the heat while he twisted and shoved to make the big body fit into the small space back there while he kept one eye out for the law—then covered it with a blanket so no casual observer could see what it was. His already large resentment over his circumstances had increased in direct proportion to the work he was forced to perform, and he had lashed out at the body several times as he worked. There had been a time when such labor would have been beneath him. Rick's corpse took the blame and the battering for Wrisberg's entire life.

There was a time not too long ago when he could have left Rick's body on the floor in the back, he knew. In this neighborhood he was known, and he paid the local precinct coppers enough each month that they would have never bothered him. Enough so that when a vice raid did have to come down, he'd have enough advance warning to get his boys and his bitches off the streets. Even now, with his recent reverses, the police were way behind him when it came to what was happening on the street. Most of them would still be thinking that Wrisberg was on top of the action. He knew better, but he wasn't about to tell them, not the cops or anyone else who accepted his generous gratuities.

It was an arrangement that worked well for everyone, or had until just lately.

Yet even though the Man still probably wouldn't stop him without good cause, he knew better than to think that he could get away with flaunting a murder right in their faces. Sworn members of the police department were likely to take that as an insult. Well, some of them would, at least. And they would demand a fortune in cash to keep them from running Wrisberg in and charging him with murder. What they wouldn't know, and what Wrisberg wouldn't tell them, was that he no longer had that sort of money to throw around.

He would, though, and soon. Right after he got his hands on the hundred thousand dollars, which he now had to cut up into exactly one single share. Then it would be time for Kevin Wrisberg to pull on Outtie Five Hundred and get his ass into the wind.

But all that was ahead of him. If he was going to get out of this alive, he had to take it one step at a time.

So now he drove slowly down Emerald Avenue, going the posted speed limit. The street was, for the most part, empty. The few men and women who were wandering around weren't the type to notice anything other than their need for whatever owned what was left of their souls. Ingram was sitting in the seat beside Wrisberg, and Rasheed was in the back, sitting sideways so his feet would never have to touch the corpse. He was bitching back there, too, loudmouth motherfucker, all the time crying.

"Come on, man." Rasheed's voice was a child's whine, without a trace of disrespect, though, fear driving him to tread where he would never dare step without it. "Can't we just dump him in any alley? Shit."

Wrisberg ignored him. He wished he'd had the foresight to bring a broom handle, or maybe a baseball bat would have been long enough. One end under his seat, the other under Rick the dago. Jiggle his foot and watch Rasheed soil his pants. He smiled at the thought.

Ingram was the older brother but was by far the smaller of the two men. Ingram stood around five feet three and at the outside weighed maybe a hundred and twenty-five pounds. Tight muscled with a baby face, he wore the same brimless black leather hat year round. He had an attitude about his size. And about his name. Wrisberg had known him since the time that it had been *Pleh*-sent. Since coming into a little money, though, he'd insisted that it was Plah-*zant*. When Wrisberg wanted to get

Ingram's goat, he referred to him as Frenchy. Tonight Ingram was wearing a black T-shirt with a pocket, and black pants. Oversized jeans which he'd thrown on quickly when he'd gotten the call from Wrisberg. The pants were hanging low, way down on Ingram's hips. He had a pack of Kools stuck into the pocket of the T-shirt.

His brother, Rasheed, was something else, closer to a monster than a man. Wrisberg had never wanted to meet Rasheed's daddy; he suspected that the boy's mama had been involved with an actual ape. Rasheed was very wide and heavy, with thick lips and a thicker skull. A ridged forehead that looked like a black mountain above his eyes. He was missing several teeth and had scars from street fights and long-ago brawls from the juvie jail all over his face. He had five different holes in him where he'd been shot by a single policeman and lived. He was Ingram's right hand; he idolized his brother. The truth was that Rasheed was more than a little slow in his head, but the boy had his uses. Oh yes, he did have those.

"There's one over there, Kev." Ingram's voice was low and professional. This was the first time Wrisberg had ever used him for anything like this, and he was going out of his way to prove himself worthy of the honor. "That alley there got a manhole in it."

"You sure, Frenchy?"

Ingram paused, then said, "Dropped shit down it once before."

"Rasheed." When he didn't get an answer quickly enough, Wrisberg shouted the name. "Rasheed!"

"Yeah, what's up?"

"Stop shivering in fear back there long enough for you to tell me you remember what it is I told you to do."

"Get out, dump the body. What so hard 'bout that?"

"You sure you can touch it?" Ingram asked him sarcastically. He seemed to be taking his anger at Wrisberg out on Rasheed. Wrisberg had to get them both under control, and right away.

He said, "Shut the fuck up, what's wrong with the two of you tonight? Now I asked you a question, Rasheed, you give me half an answer. What I tell you to do?"

"Get the body into the sewer, cover it up, come out and wait on the street." Sometimes this boy was funny. He talked like he was reciting a memorized poem for the teacher, one he was a little embarrassed to have to speak in public. "What you think I be, stupid?"

Instead of responding, Wrisberg shook his head, then cut his lights and slowed nearly to a stop as he entered the mouth of the alley. He was driving very carefully, so that his fenders wouldn't so much as touch a badly placed garbage can. He wasn't as worried about scratching the car as he was about leaving any trace of his having been there. You never knew about the Homicide squad these days, what they could discover with only a tiny bit of evidence to work with, what with all that *Silence of the Lambs* shit they kept coming up with to catch you. Enough men whom Wrisberg had thought to be too smart to ever take a fall had gone down for the long count after the Homicide boys had started in on their asses.

He stopped when Ingram gave the word, and hit the button that unlocked the doors.

"Move it!"

Ingram leaped out and pulled up his seat, and Rasheed was out in an instant, pulling on Rick's arm before he even turned around. They had the body out of the car in seconds. As soon as they did, Wrisberg leaned over and pulled the door shut, then smoothly drove down the alley, getting out of there as quickly as his cautious nature allowed. He turned right out of the alley, then went slowly around the block. By the time he hit the mouth of the alley on Emerald, Rasheed and Ingram were out there waiting for him, out of breath and scared, worriedly looking around.

This was Disciple territory, and they had no gang affiliations—a deadly mix for young black men in the wrong neighborhood, dawn breaking over another brutally hot summer night.

Wrisberg pulled to the curb, and the two men leaped quickly into the car. "Shit, *shit!*" Wrisberg shouted. "Get the fuck—goddamnit, don't either one of you touch *shit* in this car with them filthy hands, you hear me?"

Ingram and Rasheed looked at each other, but neither man spoke a word in response.

As he dropped them both off in front of Ingram's mother's apartment, he handed them each two hundred dollars for the night's work, then asked Ingram to hold back a second. Rasheed got out, closed the door, and stood waiting for his brother outside, on the corner. Wrisberg didn't like that. You could never trust a crazy man.

He said, "Ingram, you know that fat guy, that radio talk dude?"

"Yeah, sure, man. Ray, my goodest client." Despite his casual response, Ingram's voice betrayed his fear. Twenty-two grand of Wrisberg's money was in McCauley's pocket.

"You forget about him, don't take nothing from him no more, no bets, no collections, nothing."

"You collectin' it yourself?" Ingram spoke without thought. Wrisberg pinned him with a glare, and Ingram looked away, breathing heavily. He waited, building his courage. When Wrisberg didn't bother to answer, Ingram continued, carefully, but with heat.

"Man, that ain't right, and you know it. I'da got it, sooner or later. There's twenny-two cees involved, Kev; you know that better than I do. I get my ten points off whatever I collect from the losers." There was still no answer from Wrisberg. Ingram took in a deep breath, then let it out, then turned to face his boss. His voice sounded as frightened as Rasheed's had sounded when he'd been seated in the back and a dead white man had been right there under his hundred-and-eighty-dollar Nikes.

Rasheed said, "Come on . . ."

"That white boy give you ten points of what he win? You're lucky I don't charge you ten points off the vig! He was your motherfucking collection, you took the bets, you supposed to collect. You didn't. That means *I* got to come into it, micromanage every motherfucking thing, like I got time for that. What you think I owe you for doing your damn work?" Ingram shrugged, then tossed his head around back and forth resentfully, snorting through his nose but not saying anything right out loud.

Without warning Wrisberg angrily slapped him in the head with the back of his hand, and Ingram ducked down, frightened. He held his hands up to cover his head, and slowly let them down when he realized Wrisberg wasn't going to hit him twice. Ingram was next to tears. Wrisberg waited patiently. He didn't speak until Ingram cast a frightened look his way.

"You come begging me for a job, and what do I do? I pull you out of the fast food restaurant, I give your ass a job. And you make more money with me in a night than you would in a month of flipping chickens at the Colonel's." Wrisberg was speaking slowly and carefully, nearly whispering every word, but whispering them with venom.

"Forty-one goddamn different gangs in this city, and I'm the only man alive can slide through maybe twenty of them undamaged, do business with them, hand them all over a piece of the action and get their protection and respect in return. That respect extends to my men, too, to the nongangbanging neutrons, boys like *you,* Ingram, who can damn near walk any street in this city in safety, just because you *work* for me. I got out of prison last time, six years ago, in Ohio? You ever hear about that? You was still in grade school back then, probably. There was a black stretch Cadillac limo waiting on my ass, right outside the gate, so all the hacks and my own homeboys could see it from inside; six different gangs called a one-day truce to come celebrate with me, to welcome my ass home."

Wrisberg reached out and Ingram ducked, but not quickly enough. Wrisberg caught the collar of his shirt, pulled him up straight, and held him so that the younger man would have to look him in the face. When Wrisberg spoke now his voice held a tone of incredulity.

"And you're going to come on to me like I owe you something?" Wrisberg shook his head in disbelief. "Like *I* owe *you*?"

"I'm sorry, Kev, I was out of line, I know that, I was wrong, man, I didn't—"

"Shut the fuck up." Wrisberg cut him off, then pushed Ingram away from him, shoved him against the car door. He shook his head, his lips pursed in distaste. He reached into the pocket of his fine blue pants, and Ingram wailed aloud. Wrisberg snorted, as if expecting such behavior from a man like Ingram. He pulled out a wad of bills, quickly riffled through them. Held a sheaf of them in his left hand while he returned most of the roll to his pocket.

Ingram's eyes never left Wrisberg's right hand. He believed he was about to die, which was exactly what Wrisberg wanted. Wrisberg pushed the wad of bills in his left hand toward Ingram, held them out in front of the man's face.

"Go on, take it."

"Wha—what's that?"

"What you think? Twenty-two hundred dollars. Your commission for the fat man's money."

"No!" The terror in Ingram's voice couldn't possibly have been anything less than genuine. He shrunk back from the money as if it were afire. Wrisberg raised his voice, his scream booming inside the car.

"What'd I tell you!"

"I don't want it, man, I was wrong, Kev!"

"Kev, my ass. I ought to make you call me massah."

"I will you tell me to, Jesus, just don't make me take that."

As if against his better judgment, Wrisberg slowly shoved the bills back into his own pocket. He shook his head again, this time being the forgiving, benevolent father figure.

"You gonna ever question my shit again?"

"No sir, I ain't."

"You gonna ever second-guess me anymore?"

"No sir." Ingram spoke immediately, a marine responding to a drill instructor.

"You gonna do whatever I tell you to do and do it without challenging me?"

"Yes sir, I give you my word, this won't never happen again, I was out of line, I know it."

"Good. Now get the fuck out of my short, and don't you ever bite the hand that feeds you again, you understand me, Frenchy?"

"Yes sir, I do." Ingram was looking through the windshield, straight ahead, afraid to look Wrisberg in the eye. Rasheed was staring in at them, his mouth open, his eyes wide. Wrisberg smiled gently.

"Hey, Ingram?"

"Yes sir?"

"Call me Kev, man; knock that 'sir' shit off."

"Thanks, Kev."

"You can go now."

Relieved at the prospect of being able to live another day, Ingram nearly leaped out of the vehicle. He stood on the curb, watching, shaking inside, as Wrisberg put the car into gear and tore away from the scene with a squeal of tires.

Rasheed and Ingram stood there and watched him until the purple neon underneath the car disappeared from their sight. Rasheed, glaring up the street, shook his head in repressed anger.

Rasheed said, "Man wear his ass on his shoulder all the time, don't he? Bad act, 'specially for a man who ain't shit no more. One of these days I might just have to cap that motherfucker."

Ingram waited a second, until he was sure that his voice wouldn't break. Then he said, "There's better ways than that to take a man like him down, my brother. Now come on, we got to hurry. Get the short while I keep an eye on where he goes." Ingram was in a hurry, but not too concerned. He knew it wouldn't be hard to follow the man with all that neon blaring out from the underside of the car.

———————

There wasn't much that Dabney Delaney-Hinckle hated more than dealing with the senior management of *Chicago Alive!* magazine. As a contributing editor, though, there were times when she had no choice but to do so. Yet she did whatever she could to avoid what she considered to be pseudointellectual confrontations, rather than "barnstorming sessions," as they were referred to by the bosses.

Dabney never attended the frequent social gatherings, the parties thrown by various editors, writers, and networkers at the magazine, nor did she show up at the quarterly dinners the magazine publishers threw, dinners that were intended to boost morale but that she saw as a mere excuse to get drunk at the company's expense. She never posed for group pictures. She had vehemently refused an invitation to join the magazine's editorial board. And when through business circumstance she was forced into the infrequent face-to-face conference, Dabney would try to arrange to deal with them in the afternoon, managing to get through meetings with them from the perspective that a meal and some time on the street would give her. She tried desperately to always arrange for such meetings to occur directly after lunch, at a time when she knew that the two men who were the true power at the magazine would be bloated from their meals, relaxed from the expense-account drinks they'd consumed.

But today was their idea of an emergency, and she had to meet with them at seven. It had been a demand made by Morris Mosslin, executive editor and HMFIC—head motherfucker in charge—who had dragged Dabney out of a disturbing dream at a little after five with his phone call.

Now, still half asleep, hair still damp from her shower, carrying a paper cup of coffee in her left hand, her right hanging onto the strap of her suitcase purse, Dabney was ushered into the inner sanctum by the secretary everybody referred to as the Dragon Lady, a white-haired, pompous widow, the type who related proximity to power to actual personal authority without ever understanding that she could easily be replaced by a semitrained retardate. Dabney didn't hold it against the woman; she'd seen worse when she'd been breaking into the business, working as a reporter for a radio station, where teenage interns to popular DJs had labored under the delusion that they themselves were somehow talented. The Dragon Lady didn't seem upset at being called out at this ungodly hour. Maybe she didn't ever sleep, just sat awake in her tiny apartment at night, thinking of ways to better serve her masters.

"Miss Delaney-Hinckle, sir," the Dragon Lady announced, then closed the door behind Dabney. The two men in the room didn't seem to notice her loudly declared arrival. Dabney stood silently in front of the closed dark-wood double doors, checking out the atmosphere, absorbing the vibes. She didn't like what she was picking up; though silent, the room seemed charged with hostility.

Morris was sitting in his massive leather judge's chair in front of his equally massive wooden desk. His tie was partially pulled down, his sleeves were rolled up, and he was staring down with distraught thoughtfulness at a sheaf of fax papers he was holding in one hand, peering at them through the bifocal half glasses that were usually pushed up into his hair when he wasn't using them for reading.

The chair had been custom-made for him, as had been the desk. Both had been built as a scheme to try and disguise his tiny physical stature. Dabney thought the furniture was a mistake; it made him look like a child playing grown-up. Common gossip had it that Morris's feet didn't touch the carpet when he was seated on his throne.

He looked up suddenly, pinned Dabney with a glare, then tossed the fax sheets casually onto his desktop with an over-wrought sigh. Morris lifted one arm up, put it behind his head, then casually laid his hand on his opposite shoulder. He bowed his head slightly, stretching, and his elbow pointed at her like the barrel of a gun. Morris straightened up, pursed his lips, and looked at her in what he probably thought of as unsavory contemplation when he practiced the move, as he undoubtedly did, in front of his bathroom mirror.

Ron Halls, on the other hand, didn't seem to be contemplat-ing anything. He appeared to be as happy to be here at this time of day as Dabney was herself. He was a heavy man, much taller than his tiny, slender boss, with a thick beard that did little to compensate for the lack of hair on his head. Halls had just turned forty, but his beard was entirely gray. Dabney believed he colored it—along with the fringe of hair on the sides and at the back of his head—to give himself the appearance of mature and pensive wisdom.

Appearances could be deceiving; Halls was now making a disgusting, throat-clearing noise. He wiped at his nose with the back of his hand. He swallowed whatever it was he had coughed up, and looked guiltily away from Dabney.

Dabney, straight faced, watched him, hiding her contempt. She'd once complained about his attitude to the EEOC rep, and Halls had never forgiven her. It had been the accumulation of escalating and disgusting remarks that had finally driven Dabney to form a public protest. It had all begun the first time they'd met, when he'd said to her (in what she was later to learn to be his regular self-introductory statement with females), "The name's Halls; rhymes with balls." When her complaint had led to mandatory sensitivity training for all full-time maga-zine staffers, he'd taken it upon himself to send an internal memo to all of the magazine's employees, telling them they owed their thanks to Dabney's politically correct attitude for this intrusion upon their lives. Dabney now wondered if he'd begun his morning with a drink.

Patiently waiting, she looked back at Morris. When he at last figured out that she wasn't going to be the first to break the silence, he began to speak himself, with studied deliberation.

"It seems that we have something of a problem this morning, Dabney."

He didn't ask or indicate in any way that Dabney should sit down, so she felt compelled to do so, taking the leather chair that had been strategically positioned so that Morris could even look down at a basketball player should one happen to be sitting in it. She put her coffee on Morris's desk. She set her heavy purse down on the floor at her feet. She removed the Pearlcorder from a pocket of the bag, smiled sweetly at Morris and turned it on, then placed it on the edge of the desk, next to her cup of coffee. Morris's pompous, smug, disapproving look immediately vanished, replaced by one that Dabney believed betrayed his average state of mind: frightened insecurity.

"Could we possibly hold this meeting without electronic memorialization?"

"No, we can't," Dabney said. Halls looked quizzically up from the couch, rubbing at his runny nose again with the back of his hand. Dabney was glad that he hadn't gotten up to shake hands when she'd entered the room; God alone only knew what might be crawling around on his pudgy little fingers. She *did* know that he would soon seek an excuse to leave the room. The two men shared a bathroom, which connected their respective well-appointed offices. Halls would excuse himself, saying that he had to use the john, then would go through the connecting door, on into his own office, and run to where he kept the bottle hidden in the bottom left-hand drawer of his desk.

"You don't need to be a trained investigator—which I am, by the way, Morris—to understand the purpose of your phone call and this meeting. You called my apartment before dawn for the same reason that the police execute no-knock warrants at that time, to throw me off base at the time of day when people are the most psychologically vulnerable. You demanded that I meet you here in two hours, wouldn't tell me what it was about—as if I couldn't figure *that* one out—and hung up before I could think to ask if I needed to bring a lawyer." Dabney smiled and shook her head at the look of shock that Morris was affecting. Halls was staring at her strangely. Halls always stared at her strangely.

"Well, I've got one, Morris. A lawyer, I mean. And a very good one, in fact. I wouldn't think of calling her at this ungodly hour, but I'm sharp enough to know that she'd want me to tape-record what is said at this meeting." There was a soft grunt from the couch, and Morris shot his second in command a hateful glance. Dabney knew that the grunt had been loud enough to be picked up by the blessedly sensitive little recording device.

Morris, looking at the recorder, his mind obviously racing as he sought a way to shift this turn of events to his advantage, said, "Oh, come on now, Dabs. You can't believe I would actually do that, do you? Called at *that* time for *that* reason?" He chuckled softly, then said, "Young lady, you give me too much credit; it's not as if I'm The Prince." His tone was patronizing, surprised. He waited a few seconds, then casually said, "We really don't need our private conversations bugged, now, do we?"

"Bugging implies duplicity, and that's not the case here, Morris. You're aware that I turned on the recorder. But if it bothers you so much, I guess I can turn it off, as soon as you answer one question: is *Chicago Alive!* magazine completely indemnifying me against any charges, brought by anyone at any time, now or in the future, concerning the article I wrote about Ray McCauley, or about any other article I've written since I've been here?"

"Is *that* what this is about?" Morris said in disbelief, as he shook his head. When he spoke, it was loudly, and he leaned toward the recorder.

"Abso*lutely* we at the magazine indemnify you; not only that, but we stand behind you one hundred percent, and behind the integrity of your story." He paused, smirking at Dabney. He turned to Halls, as if showing off, a teacher giving a student an on-the-job lesson in how subordinates should be handled.

"Satisfied, Dabney? Or would you like those assurances in writing?"

"I'd think the tape will be good enough." Dabney leaned over and turned off the recorder. She returned the machine to her purse. She picked up her coffee, took an exploratory sip, then closed her eyes and drank deeply. She sighed and returned the cup to the desk, ignoring the pointed stare that Morris was giving the coffee. She smiled at him and said, in her most condescending voice, "Thank you, Morris; now would you please explain why in the *fuck* you dragged me out of bed at five in the morning for this meeting?"

A phone call awakened Lieutenant Alex Mondello also that Tuesday morning, but unlike Dabney Delaney-Hinckle, Mondo had grown quite used to late-night and early-morning calls. It came along with the badge, the gun, the rank, and the authority. He had left instructions for the sergeant who was his second in command, explaining to her via written memo as well as by voice mail that he had worked eighteen hours the previous day and would be in to the bureau around noon. Still, he wasn't the least bit surprised when the call came in at 7:08.

He knew the exact time because he'd trained himself to look at the clock first when the phone rang or his beeper went off; he could often tell by the time of day who might be calling, and of course he knew what the phone call would concern; men such as Mondo dealt only in death. He had also trained himself over the course of the years to come fully awake at the first ring of the telephone. So now Mondo sat up in bed in the small bedroom of his rented three-room apartment. He shook his head to clear it, reached over and picked up the phone before it completed the second ring.

"Mondello." His voice was thick with sleep, and he quietly cleared his throat. Beside him, Elaine Hoffman rolled over onto her back. His back was to her, but he felt her sit up, felt her arm slide around his waist, felt her fingers tickling his abdomen. Mondo listened for a moment, then gently touched his fingers to Elaine's and lightly squeezed. She withdrew her hand and lay back. Mondo spoke softly, a rare compassion in his tone. He mostly listened, then after a time said, "Is there anything I can *do*?" He listened for a time, then said, "Jesus, sir, I'm sorry." He replaced the receiver softly, then rubbed his face harshly, digging his fingers into his eyes. He automatically reached for the cigarettes on the bed stand, picked them up and began shaking one out, then looked at the pack and threw it harshly back onto the stand.

"Shit!"

"What's wrong?" Elaine asked, and Mondo didn't turn around to speak to her face-to-face; he hadn't yet brushed his teeth. From somewhere outside came the sound of car horns blaring. Mondo felt the air conditioning blowing down onto his back, though he didn't think it was the cool air that caused him to suddenly shiver.

He said, "That was Merlin Royal."

"Captain Royal? What did he want?"

"Remember a couple of weeks ago, when they said he was preemphysemic? That's what all those big-shot doctors thought; at least that's what they told him. He cut back on the Pall Malls; that was his way of looking out for his health." The irony in Mondo's tone was as heavy in this statement as the anger was in the next when he said, "The MRI was the first indicator that they were mistaken, but the scope found masses in both lungs and spreading."

"*Cancer?*"

"He'd have six months to a year, if he got lucky and responded to treatment. He's decided not to let them experiment with him, though. He's going to tough it out on his own. He probably won't see Labor Day."

"The IAD Homicide probe didn't help matters much, either, I'd bet. My God." Elaine reached over and grabbed angrily for Mondo's pack of cigarettes, muttering, "These fucking things . . . ," but he grabbed her wrist and stopped her.

"Don't do that. Crushing them won't solve anything; I'll just buy another pack." Elaine sat back, accepting it; petulance wasn't in her.

She said, "Have you ever met his wife?"

"Agnes? I've seen her at weddings and retirement parties; I never spent any time really talking with her."

"Should I call her, do you think? Offer support?"

"Oh, no, don't do that, Elaine. He asked me not to tell anyone. I'm sure he knows about us, but still, he'd see it as my having broken a confidence." Mondo paused, and Elaine touched his shoulder, a sign of gratitude for his willingness to tell her about Royal, in spite of the captain's desire for secrecy.

"I won't tell anyone."

"Come on, I know that. He's putting in his papers today, effective immediately. That way he won't have to even bother with the probe, let alone worry about it. If he's off the department, he can concentrate on what's important, rather than worrying about whether they're going to come around with their trumped-up charges, threaten to take his medical benefits away if he refuses to tell them whatever lies they feel like hearing. He says he's not even going to wait around to train his replacement." Mondo paused, wondering.

He said, "They won't promote from within Homicide; not with everything that's going on right now, the cloud that's hanging over us, the probe. Whoever takes over is going to have to walk into the Homicide captaincy blind."

"What will this mean for Special Victims?"

"The replacement will be briefed; hopefully he'll be told that even though we're technically still a part of Homicide, we're autonomous, that I report to him, but he has no power over the bureau."

"Yeah, and I'll believe that when I see it in writing. Royal accepted that, even promoted it with the bosses so it would cut back on interdepartmental political interference. And it's not like there isn't enough back stabbing and gossip going around about the bureau as it is, especially now. A fractious captain could make waves; an asshole could tip the boat."

"Probably not far enough over to drown us, though, Elaine."

"Unless one of us screws up." For the first time, Mondo turned to face her.

"We're all good, Elaine. I've checked over and over on that, called everyone I'd ever done anything for. IAD's investigation doesn't involve us."

"You're forgetting about *Sergeant* Jake Phillips, Mondo, a probable drunk who has administrative responsibilities within the Special Victims Bureau." They'd had this argument before. "And that reporter—what's her name?—she's been snooping around, Mondo. We don't need bad exposure in the press right now, with all that's going on."

"Elaine, come on. Jake's my friend, and he's one of the best detectives we have. I don't know what you have against him."

"He's been slipping, Mondo, and we both know it. And I'll tell you what I have against him. I was never close to him; I was never his friend. I can *see* how he's been screwing up. You can't, because you're too close to him."

"I'd notice if he was on the edge. He's in some trouble, but he's dealing with it."

Elaine paused, her eyes narrowing. "Dealing with it how?"

"I can't tell you that, Elaine."

"You told me about the captain. Just give me a yes or no: is Jake getting counseling?"

"As his superior officer, I have to decline to answer that, Elaine."

"I think you just did."

"All right, say you figured it out. Say he's getting counseling. Let's even stretch it a little bit, say he's seeing a psychologist. About his marital problems, some other things. Would that appease you?"

"Depends on how long he's been going."

"Elaine, I trust him as much as anyone in the bureau." That stopped her. She knew precisely what he was telling her. Elaine thought for a moment.

"If you trust him so much, would you mind if I did a little checking around?"

"What kind of checking around?"

"Get me his private log-in number. I want to look in the computer, see what he's called up. I want to check with the hospital, see if any calls went out of Duette's room last night. I want to check his home number, see who he's been calling."

"The hospital, that's one thing; it'd be part of his bill. His home number, forget about it, unless you've got a court order, and I won't consider allowing one to be written up to review."

"No, no, that's all right; I understand. Just let me look around, Mondo, when I get a chance."

"You get a lot of free time, do you?" Mondo smiled. "Your boss isn't working you hard enough?"

Elaine reached up and absently rubbed Mondo's shoulder, thinking.

He said, "If it'll make you feel better, look into it. I'll have the log-in number for you by the time you get to your desk." Mondo got off the bed. "Breakfast'll be ready by eight, steak and eggs sound good?"

T hough she tried mightily, Dabney couldn't manage to keep her contempt off her face or out of her voice as the two men questioned her; they'd become suddenly emboldened after she'd turned off the tape recorder. They told her how representatives from the print, radio, and television press had bothered them throughout the night, calling them at home with the money question: had Dabney Delaney-Hinckle's article caused Ray McCauley to be killed? Both men had been blissfully asleep when the calls started to come in; neither man had been aware that anything had happened to the talk radio host.

There was still enough of the journalist left deep down inside Morris that he was able to disengage himself from the first call and make a few calls himself in pursuit of the few known facts: McCauley had apparently been accosted—the police at that point had not known where or by whom—sometime after the end of his radio show and had been beaten within an inch of his life. Decades of smoking, drinking, and abusing illogal drugs had pushed his obese body beyond that last inch; his cause of death, pending autopsy, was now tentatively being referred to as a heart attack.

Dabney knew the questions to ask: Had he been in a bar brawl following the show? Had any bizarre calls come into the studio, or to his home? Had any credible witnesses seen him leave the radio station? Had he left with another person? Was there any empirical evidence linking the magazine article to the beating—such as a copy found somewhere, in a place that might end up being the murder scene? The editors had no answers for her; she didn't know if that was due to the dearth of provable facts, or to their personal lack of journalistic talent, but she was certain she would find out the truth just as soon as she got out of this office.

For now, however, having heard their fears and being acutely aware that those fears went deeper than could be accounted for by their ethical concerns, or their journalistic integrity—they were probably living in terror of a lawsuit—Dabney decided that it was time to once again go on the offensive.

"Gentlemen. I have every word McCauley's quoted as saying in the article not only in my notes, but on tape. I transcribed those tapes word for word in my piece; all I left out were a bunch of inarticulate grunts, 'umm's,' and 'you know's,' and I only left them out so as not to torture the reader with

McCauley's inarticulateness. Those tapes are now locked safely inside a safe deposit box at a bank other than the one that keeps my personal accounts; the box is in a lawyer's name, and *not* the lawyer I referred to earlier. As always in my work, I refused to use any unnamed sources; unless their jobs or personal safety would be jeopardized by attribution, I consider people who won't speak out and put their names on the record to be cowardly snipers.

"I didn't invent any statements or quotes, nor did I pull a Janet Malcolm and condense any quotes, using my own interpretation of their intent. I did everything by the book, and if either of you bothered to read the piece, you'd see that I was not only balanced but objective, leaving my own feelings about the man out of the piece until the final paragraph, when I just couldn't resist." Both Mosslin and Halls were hanging on her every word. Halls's mouth was open as wide as his wet eyes; Dabney could hear his labored breathing. He hadn't even excused himself to use the toilet yet. Good. She had a couple of other things to run by them before she was through.

Dabney reached down into her purse, removed a stack of computer sheets, placed them on her lap, and referred to them as she spoke, flipping back and forth as if she hadn't memorized and prepared in advance almost every word she was about to speak. The only thing she hadn't planned was how soon she'd have to speak the well-rehearsed lines.

"Now, that's settled, as far as I'm concerned. But as long as we're together, let's make good and damn sure we all know where the others stand." Dabney flipped through the pages for effect, then said, "Last month's cover story was on Schwinn bicycles." She raised her eyebrows and looked at Morris just long enough for him to catch her ironic, bemused expression. "The month before that, the lead was Elvis impersonators—the title was, just a second, "Chicago's Elvi," it says here. In April, you ran a cover story I wrote about the Hollywood Pictures film being shot in Chicago, *The Savage*. My *Savage* piece outsold

your next two issues com*bined* by a margin of three to one."
Dabney looked quickly up at Morris.

"All this information came out of your computers. These are
your spreadsheets, taken from your databases, gentlemen, not
from mine.

"Now, we don't need to run down all the cover stories of the
previous twelve months, or the years before that since I've been
working here, but it really should be noted that even before my
Savage piece ran, your largest circulation periods by far were in
months where I wrote the cover story, second only to the issues
when I didn't have the cover, but where I wrote the inside lead
story." Dabney folded the papers, then replaced them in her
purse.

"Not being a publicity whore myself, the competition—and
in particular the electronic media—doesn't have my private,
unlisted home phone number, so they couldn't call me in the
middle of the night to ask me about the tragic life and times of
that great First Amendment advocate Ray McCauley. But I'll
just bet my listed voice mail is all filled up with messages.
Some of which I'll return just as soon as I walk out of this office.
Not to mention that I'm sure the police will want to speak with
me, sooner or later. This entire McCauley situation could wind
up being a gold mine. A career maker, in fact." Dabney held up
a hand to cut Halls off; he had opened his mouth as if to say
something, but Dabney was on a roll and didn't want to lose her
momentum.

She said, "Let me put my cards faceup on the table, gentlemen. Whatever might have happened last night aside, and
regardless of whether my piece had anything to do with it, I'm
still the best goddamn reporter you've ever had working here,
and we all know it. You've paid well for my talents; I'm not
complaining about that. The facts remain that Chris Newman
has been recruiting me to come over to *Chicago* magazine; your
counterparts at the *Chicago Tribune,* Metro *and* Tempo sec-
tions, and at the *Tribune* magazine, have been courting me for

two years; the *Sun-Times* has been pressing me to write an exclusive Sunday-through-Thursday column, page three, with my picture above the byline.

"The problem, from my personal point of view, is that every one of those markets wants me to come on board as a full-time reporter. Now, I've exploited each of those markets from time to time in a freelance capacity, within the boundaries of my contract with this magazine, and I'll more than likely do so again. That's something for me to decide at another time. The question before us now, however, is this: do I give up my freelance status and all the personal freedom it allows me, with the upside being that I get to dump you two frightened, insecure, lawyer-intimidated, ball-less wonders, to go over to one of those other markets?"

"*What* did she just say?" Halls demanded. Morris cut him off with an angry chop of his hand.

"You heard her." He spat the words at Halls with contempt, without looking at him. He turned his iciest stare Dabney's way. "Ball-less *wonder*?" he repeated. There was a note of near awe in his tone.

"You heard me as well as Halls did, Morris. Remember what you said to me when I approached you with the McCauley piece?" Dabney cranked her voice down into a basso imitation of a male whine. " 'I just don't *know*, Dabs, I somehow just can't get my *arms* around this piece . . .' And I've got a memo right here from *Mr.* Halls"—she dug around in her purse and pulled it out—"concerning my outline for the 'Cops' Wives' piece." Dabney read aloud. " 'Seeing as this is Everywoman's story, maybe we should think about all of you sharing a by-line.' "

"I thought that was a damned good idea, and I still do; it's *their* story, after all," Halls said. Dabney let her silence eloquently speak her opinion for her, but only momentarily.

When she was sure she'd made her point, she said, "And what about your *opinion* that in a free society, some people just have to die, we can't protect them? Do you remember that?"

"I certainly *do!*" Halls said. He sat up as tall as he could to say, "And I *still* believe that!"

"Do you want to volunteer to go first?"

Before Halls could answer, Morris cleared his throat.

He said, "You're getting dangerously close to the edge, Ms. Delaney-Hinckle."

"Fuck the edge; I'm way past your edge. I'm insubordinate, I'm impertinent, I'm disobedient, and I'm rude. But I deliver, don't I? And I've changed my mind on this story; it's only gonna be about one family. I'm calling it "The Socialite and the Sergeant," or maybe "The Special Victim." In case you don't recall our in-depth conver*sation*, it's about one of the bureau hotshots, a Chicago copper who's stalking and threatening his soon-to-be-ex North Shore, social register wife. I caught him last night in a rendezvous with what could only be an outfit guy or a cop bagman. He promised to give me full disclosure about his marital problems if I forgot what I saw. I agreed, but that doesn't mean I have to *keep* the gloves off." Dabney paused for effect. "Gentlemen, the story I'm proposing might bring you your first Pulitzer."

Morris immediately said, "A brutal cop? Dabs, that's too damned close to home for you—"

"Let *me* worry about how close to home it is."

Halls said, "You can't go around trying to save the entire fucking world because of your own personal tragedy—you lose your objec*tivity* . . ."

"Spoken by a master of objectivity."

"Dabs, if I may—"

"No, you may not." Dabney cut Halls off.

"I think we need to know what your personal relationship is with your subject, Dabney!"

"My *rela*—"

"You heard me!" Halls had worked himself into a fit of self-righteousness. He was so excited that he almost stood up. "What's your re*la*tionship, *Ms.* Delaney-Hinckle! Don't you think for a moment that we haven't heard the rumors!"

Dabney finally understood what he was saying, and could only stare at him for a second, her mouth open in shock. Finally, she shook her head. "Let me tell you something; I'm writing it, and you boys are going to run it—whether you can get your arms around it or not—on the cover of October's issue, on sale the first of September. And you're giving me expenses, the check to be cut today. I'll be needing some equipment: a night-shooting camera, a long-distance mike, and a trained somebody—I don't care who it is, as long as he's good—to use them both."

"Or?"

"Or I resign right here this morning, take the story *and* my sudden celebrity down the street to Christine Newman, *and* I'll write a front-page *Tribune* "Tempo" article about how you two fuckups run this magazine, 'Halls, it rhymes with balls,' and all."

"Fuck her, *and* fuck her goddamn personal crusade . . . Get her *out* of here, Morris." Morris didn't respond at first, just continued to glare at Dabney. She held his stare with a steady gaze.

"You're a cunt with teeth, aren't you?"

Dabney grunted her disgust. "A regular bitch on wheels. It's the way I am when some asshole wakes me up at dawn, shouting demands." Dabney lifted her purse to her shoulder and rose.

"One would think that assholes wake you up at dawn with regularity—to throw you out of their apartment before they have to get up for work."

Dabney turned without response and headed for the door. She knew what she'd be giving up, what she'd be leaving behind, but she didn't care. She'd had enough of this place, and more than enough of these men.

She heard Morris call her name just as the door was closing behind her. She ignored him. The Dragon Lady looked up in surprise, then Mosslin called Dabney's name again, much more loudly, with a hint of outrage in his voice, and the Dragon

Lady's expression slowly changed to one that betrayed her mounting terror. She rose quickly from her desk and hurried to Dabney's side, tried to stop her from opening the outer door, tried to bar Dabney's exit with her tiny, ancient frame.

"You can't go! He's not done with you yet!" Dabney stepped past her easily, then stopped and spoke to her as she pulled the door to the hallway toward her.

"It's the nineties, honey," Dabney Delaney-Hinckle said. "*Men* don't decide when they're through with *us; we* decide when we're through with *men*." She left the old woman standing there trembling, terrified at the prospect of having to face the wrath of her bosses.

As she rode down in the elevator, Dabney had second thoughts about a couple of things, but not about leaving the magazine. The truth was, the sight of the frightened old woman dulled the edge of Dabney's triumph. And she suspected that there might have been a kernel of truth in what Halls had said about her objectivity, about her personal crusade . . .

There was, nevertheless, a surprisingly light spring in her step as she pushed through the main entrance doors and walked out onto Michigan Avenue.

———

Jake was the first witness called to testify that morning. He sat in the witness chair, a duly sworn officer of the court who proceeded to give three straight hours of testimony in a soft but firm voice, doing his best to project a calm, professional demeanor.

The ability to pull that off hadn't come easily.

Jake had a slight hangover, but nothing to worry about. He was thinking straight, although he was very tired. He had dragged himself out of bed in time to take a long cold shower, shave carefully, brush his teeth, dress, and go out to eat a big breakfast before coming to the Criminal Courts Building. He'd also taken a Xanax to control his nerves.

The sixty-year-old patent-attorney defendant had killed his socialite wife. He'd denied it publicly for months, had even posted a substantial reward for the conviction of his wife's killer.

He had gone on denying the crime, personally and through his lawyer, granting constant interviews to the media, and he had more than his share of supporters. Jake had known from the beginning what the man and his lawyer were doing. They didn't care about supporters; they didn't care about justice.

They'd been trying to influence the potential jury pool.

Because of disclosure, both sides knew how damning the actual evidence was against the defendant.

Jake had put together enough evidence to convince a jury of retardates that the man had murdered his wife. He had everything except a videotape of the crime and a signed confession.

Still, as everyone in law enforcement knew, what it all really came down to was lawyer against lawyer. Whom the jury liked and whom they didn't. Which juror thought it was impossible for such a small, timid, shy man to commit a brutal murder; which juror was worried about the money he was losing from his job while having to perform his public duty. Which juror was worried about her husband, about the quality of her child care.

Evidence wasn't the most important factor in trials anymore, if it ever had been. Far more important was the way the jury related to the defendant, the way the jury felt about the lawyers.

Jake didn't have to worry too much about what they thought of him. His testimony, he knew, was unimpeachable. He was in fact surprised that he'd been on the stand as long as he had. But the two prosecutors had wanted to take him through every step, slowly and carefully.

The patent attorney, Pommerantz, had never spoken a word

directly to Jake. Because of his strong ties to the community (not to mention his political clout), he'd been set free on a million-dollar bond the day he'd been indicted, which had been more than a year ago. The buzz was that he'd taken the Fifth inside the grand jury room and that he wouldn't be taking the stand in his own defense at the trial.

The prosecutor had taken Jake through the case slowly, bit by bit. He'd spoken just as slowly, precisely, looking at the jurors as he answered, rather than at the lawyer. Jake had been waiting for this day since he'd first seen the dead woman's body. Her head had been nearly cut off.

She'd been stabbed a total of seventy-two times.

Yet with all the damning evidence Jake had procured, Pommerantz had been set free on bond. It didn't do much for Jake's already distorted view of the criminal justice system. Still, he was a part of it, and he'd had the chance to tell his story.

Now it was the defense attorney's turn.

Jake steeled himself and opened his coat so the jurors could see his belt badge. He wanted to give them the impression that he was the last line of defense between them and people like this. He had seen the polls; he knew what the public's opinion was of lawyers. He also knew what their opinions were of cops.

The lawyer was tall, with a helmet of silver hair combed straight back, held in place with some sort of shiny gel. The man had to be in his seventies. He had no fat on him that Jake could see. His suit was expensive; his ring was made of gold and diamonds. Pommerantz, who'd seemed nearly bored by Jake's recitation of events for the prosecution, now sat forward, as if looking forward to his lawyer's cross-examination. Jake heard the courtroom door open and dared a brief glance over as the lawyer approached him.

Dabney Delaney-Hinckle had just taken a seat in the press row.

"Officer Phillips . . ." The lawyer paused and smiled paternally. "Do you prefer Officer Phillips or Sergeant Phillips?"

"Either one's fine with me, Counselor."

"Officer Phillips, is it true that at the exact time you were investigating my client, you were yourself involved in a rather messy marital separation?"

"Objection!" The chief assistant state's attorney was on her feet, fuming. Her assistant was shaking his head.

"Germane to statements about to be entered into the record, Your Honor."

"Proceed very carefully, Counselor," the judge admonished. No cameras were allowed in Illinois courtrooms. There wasn't a lot of posing here at Twenty-sixth and California.

"While interviewing my client on the night of the murder, did you state"—the lawyer referred to a sheaf of papers in his hands, transcripts of Jake's recorded, one-sided interviews with Pommerantz—"that you know how it is, how women can sometimes"—the lawyer put a touch of anger in his tone, obviously lowering it so as to distance himself from the statement in the eyes of the jury—"be 'bitches, pains in the ass'?"

The assistant state's attorney was on her feet again. "Your Honor . . ."

"Sustained."

The lawyer appeared shocked.

"Your Honor!"

"Sustained, Counsel."

"May we approach the bench?"

"No, sir, you may not."

Jake looked over at Delaney-Hinckle as the lawyer reshaped his line of questioning. Her head was lowered. She was scribbling furiously on a legal pad.

"Officer Phillips, did you ever state to anyone that 'only a husband could kill a woman that way,' referring to the many knife wounds?"

"No sir, I did not."

"Oh, you *didn't*." Delaney-Hinckle looked up. Their eyes met. Jake looked back at the lawyer impassively, as if he hadn't recognized her.

"And did you ever tell my client"—the lawyer turned to the

jury box now—" 'Listen, I've thought about killing my wife myself'?"

"No, sir, that was never stated." Jake looked at the jury with outrage. "And such statements are *not* in the transcripts of any of my interviews with the murder suspect."

The prosecutor was on her feet again. The judge waved her down. He turned to the defense lawyer. "Proceed, Counsel, and I suggest you immediately change your line of questioning." The tone of his voice left no doubt that it was in the defense's best interest to do so.

So far, Jake wasn't worried; he was, in fact, elated. Impeachment of the investigative police officer's testimony had become the primary way for defense attorneys to win acquittals for their clients, and it was the only way this particular lawyer would ever win one in this case. Jake had the guy nailed cold. He'd found the bloody clothes, the murder weapon, and he had receipts and eyewitness statements that Pommerantz had bought the weapon and had been observed wearing the clothing before the murder. The DNA evidence would bear him out on this. As far as he could see, the lawyer hadn't laid a glove on him with his speculation and outright lies. If the jury bothered to read the transcripts of the very brief interviews, of the few questions Jake had been allowed to ask Pommerantz by this very same silver-haired legal eagle, they would know that he'd never said anything like that, that all three statements had been manufactured by the defense team.

Although he might have said those exact things if he'd ever had a chance to question Pommerantz alone. It was the way to get a suspect to confess; he had to think you were sympathetic to him. The lawyer knew that. Which was why he was lying now. Still, defense lawyers all believed that every juror they faced was dumber, less educated, and in lower-status jobs than they themselves were; they in fact hired jury consultants to make certain that this was the case.

With a jury, you never knew.

"Let me see here . . ." The lawyer riffled through more papers, impatiently, as if doing it only to appease a harsh, disapproving judge who was prejudiced against him. "Ah, here it is." The lawyer looked up. "Detective Phillips, does the name Marcus Monroe mean anything to you?"

Jake looked over at the prosecutor's table. "I know who Marcus Monroe is, yes sir."

"Is it true that Marcus Monroe is in fact *suing* you, Officer?"

Jake gave a shy smile.

"A police officer hasn't really earned his shield until he or she has a lawsuit filed against him, Counselor." The packed courtroom snickered. Jake peeked over at the jury. Several of the jurors were smiling at him, but one of the black jurors was glaring. Shit. He knew better than to improvise. The assistant state's attorney was glaring at him, too.

"What you're saying is, in the parlance of the Chicago Police Department, you haven't earned your badge until you've brutalized an African-American citizen?"

"No sir, that's not what I'm saying. There was a brutality charge against me filed with the OPS—"

"Would you explain to the court what the OPS is?"

"It's the Office of Professional Standards. They investigate civilian complaints of brutality against the police. I was cleared after a complete, very thorough investigation."

"Do you know how many complaints each year are cleared by the OPS?"

"I have no idea, sir."

"Eighty percent sound about right to you?"

"I have no idea what their clearance rate is, sir."

"Still, does it surprise you that so many claims are considered to be unfounded?"

"No sir, that does not surprise me. It only proves that the police are doing their job, and the citizens we arrest almost *always* claim brutality."

"But you didn't arrest Marcus Monroe, did you?"

"No sir, I did not. I street-adjusted it."

"Which means you were judge and jury, is that correct?" Jake opened his mouth to reply, but the lawyer hurried on. "You in fact warned Mr. Monroe to stay off the street you yourself live on, didn't you? You threatened to kill Mr. Monroe if you ever saw him on Dearborn Street again, didn't you?"

"No sir, I did not," Jake lied.

The lawyer turned to the jury with a look that told them that they all knew the detective was lying, before he turned back to Jake.

"Marcus Monroe *is* suing you, though?"

The prosecutor was on her feet again. "Your Honor, this Monroe character is *not* on the witness list. I object to this line of questioning."

"Sustained."

The lawyer opened his mouth to complain, but the judge repeated himself, loudly. "Sus*tained,* Counselor."

The defense lawyer shook his head and threw up his hands, as if he were being handcuffed by the judge. The judge said, "Would counsel approach the bench please?" and the stenographer and all four lawyers walked over for a sidebar.

Jake put as innocent an expression on his face as he could muster, then looked over at the jury as if he were one of them, outside of and above the legislative wrangling of the lawyers. He could hear the judge's heated voice berating the defense attorney. Good. This case was as open-and-shut as any Jake had ever investigated. This trial should be nothing more than a formality. Jake told himself that the defense was simply trying to force the judge to walk into reversible error that could save Pommerantz on appeal. The public never heard about such things. To cops, lawyers, and judges, it was common knowledge. Jake wasn't even worried about the black members of the jury. Pommerantz was a rich, spoiled white man who'd been allowed bond. Not exactly the type to engender sympathy from their community.

Jake looked out at the gallery. Several of the dead woman's relatives, including her three daughters, nodded at him in support. They had all agreed to testify for the prosecution against their father. Jake was growing bored, his mind on other things. He nodded back at them, a sign of solidarity that he hoped would win some points for them with the jury. He looked to the press section, where Delaney-Hinckle had been sitting. An old, bald reporter with a red face and veins all over his nose had taken her place. He wondered where she'd gone. He looked back at the seats reserved for family members.

Marsha was sitting directly behind the dead woman's daughters. He'd heard the door open and close several times, which always happened during sidebars. People went to the bathroom; reporters went into the hall to make cellular calls. Jake had paid no attention. He sat straighter in his chair and smiled nervously at her. The attorneys were heading back to their respective tables.

The defense lawyer's voice was filled with disgust as he nearly shouted, "I have no further questions of this witness." Jake was shocked. The prosecutor rose and approached Jake confidently, carrying several pieces of paper in her hands.

"Sergeant Phillips, have you ever been arrested for any crimes against citizens?"

"No, ma'am."

"So you were *not* arrested for allegedly *brutalizing* someone named Marcus Monroe."

"No, I wasn't."

"*Did* you brutalize Mr. Monroe, Sergeant?"

"No, ma'am, I did not."

"And how many police officers do you know who have had such charges leveled against them in their careers?"

"Detectives, you mean? Veterans?"

"If you will."

"Every single one of them, ma'am."

"So it's a game."

"Objection!"

"Sustained."

"In your opinion, Sergeant—"

"Objection! She's calling for speculation."

"Overruled."

"In your *opinion,* Sergeant, are these charges generally justified?"

"In only a tiny fraction of cases, ma'am."

"Thank you." She turned to the judge. "I only have a few more questions and the detective's testimony will be complete, Your Honor. Before lunch, if it's all right."

"Proceed."

"Sergeant Phillips, I'd like you to look over the typed transcripts of the brief conversations you had with the defendant, which was taped by my office, with the defendant's counsel present." Jake took the papers she'd been holding, looked at them briefly.

"Is there *any* remark in there where you referred to women as 'bitches' or 'pains in the ass'?"

"No ma'am."

"Is there *any* remark in there where you state 'only a husband could kill a woman that way'?"

"No ma'am."

"Is there *any* remark in there where you said you 'thought about killing your wife yourself'?"

"None at all, ma'am."

"Thank you, Sergeant."

Jake began to rise, and the prosecutor said, "Oh, just one more thing, Sergeant," and Jake sat back down. Defense attorneys didn't hold the patent on the manipulation of witnesses.

"Sir, in questioning any murder suspect, have you *ever* made derogatory statements about your own wife?" She was pouring it on for the jury. Jake wanted to kiss her.

Jake looked over at Marsha, who had entered the courtroom after the defense lawyer's initial charge. She looked puzzled. Jake felt the entire jury, the entire courtroom watching him. He shook his head and spoke very softly.

"I love my wife more than any other human being I've ever known in my life."

"Even though you're still separated."

He looked directly at Marsha when he said, "It's only made my love stronger."

"Thank you, Sergeant. You may step down."

━━━━━━━━━━━━━━━

Marsha sat across from Jake in a booth in a greasy spoon just a couple of blocks from the courthouse. Jake was sipping coffee. Marsha had a Coke. He had locked his weapon in the trunk of his department vehicle. They were awkward with each other, shy, as if on a first date. In a way, they were.

"Did you mean what you said, Jake? In the courtroom? Or was that just nonsense to impress the jury?"

"I could have told them I hated your guts, that I beat you once a week and I wanted a divorce, and it wouldn't have changed things much for them. The evidence speaks for itself."

"It's not the lawyers, huh? It's all the assholes who plead not guilty." Jake smiled at the recitation of the police officer's inside joke.

"I've never not been in love with you, Marsha."

Marsha lowered her head. Jake was afraid that if he reached out to touch her, she'd feel she was being manipulated, so he didn't, but it was difficult. Marsha looked back up at him.

"I spoke to the reporter this morning. She came out to the house. That's how I found out that you were in court this morning on the Pommerantz case. I remember how hard you worked on that one."

"I still can't believe the guy gets to go home every day, to the same house where we found his wife's body."

"Well, it doesn't look as if he'll be going back there very long."

"I wish you'd heard the prosecutor's examination. They took

me through everything, inch by inch. By the time they finished, there wasn't anything Pommerantz's guy *could* do but to fold his hand with me and hope to confuse the jury with their DNA experts."

"She taped everything; the reporter, I mean."

"All I ask is for the truth. And Florence said something I agreed with: you're the most honest person I've ever known."

Jake was surprised at the bitterness in Marsha's voice when she said, "I was totally honest with her; I told her I changed my mind; I didn't want to do her story." Jake looked at her. Marsha smiled at his confusion, paused, dropped the smile, then said, "Can I be honest with you now, Jake? Totally?"

"Of course." Jake's heart was pounding. He was certain she was going to ask for a divorce.

"I've—I've been seeing someone."

Jake couldn't answer for a minute. At last, fighting his jealousy and a mixture of other emotions, he said, "I don't blame you." Jake swallowed and looked directly at her. "You're young, you're beautiful, you're in premed." He forced a sad smile.

But he had to look away from Marsha when he said, "I hope he's smarter than I was." The words were harder to say than Jake could have ever imagined. They'd been so happy together, so much in love for what seemed like so long. He'd known her ten years, a third of his life, and for him, there had never been any other woman. Jake felt tears welling up in the back of his eyes, and he blinked rapidly, still not looking at Marsha. He couldn't let her see him weak; he couldn't let anyone see him weak.

"That's not what I'm saying. He's not the first man I've dated." Jake looked back at her. Was she rubbing it in? Marsha shook her head and looked directly into Jake's eyes. "None of them stack up, kiddo." Jake's heart leaped into his mouth. He didn't dare try to speak.

Marsha said, "I remember when we were first dating, and when you were a rookie, Jake. Oh, do I remember those days. I'd watch you from the window when you walked out of the apartment, in your uniform, and I'd be so proud. You had your degree; you could have done anything you'd wanted with your life. But you wanted to be a cop; you wanted to help people. At least that's what I thought at first."

"That's all it ever was, Marsha. What it still is. There aren't five cops in this city would have done what I did to try and acquire evidence against Pommerantz. He's successful, he's rich, he's connected. And his friends won't forget who did this to him, either."

"Jake, you're still just chasing a dream."

"And that's so bad, Marsha?"

"It is when you're trying to destroy the memory of your father. All you're trying to do anymore is to prove that the Phillips name is golden, that it's above reproach. Maybe that's all it's ever been, I don't know. You're trying to wipe out what he did, and you're wasting your life doing it."

"Marsha, that's not—"

Marsha cut him off by reaching over and taking his hand.

"Yes it is, Jake. You're not cut out to be a cop. You never were."

"I'm a good cop!"

"Yes, that's true. You'd have been good at whatever you went into; it's the way you are."

Jake didn't answer her. He swallowed again. He held her hand as if it were a life raft in high waves.

He surprised himself by blurting out, "I don't care about the job anymore, Marsha. I don't care about the Special Victims Bureau. All I care about is you and the baby." Jake lowered his head; his shoulders shook. Marsha tightened her grip in his hand. He felt her reach out with her free hand and rub his head. "I'll quit, I don't give a damn about any of it, just come home." Jake looked up, tears spilling down his cheeks.

"Let's start fresh, Marsha, you and me and Lynne. Come home. Please."

Marsha's voice was very soft as she said, "And what about the drinking, Jake?"

"I'll never touch another drop again for as long as I live. I promise."

"It'll take time, Jake. I love you, but I have to know you aren't an alcoholic, and that if you are, that you'll seek help. If that's the case, I'll be there for you, I promise, as long as you're trying. But I need to know that you won't put me or Lynne in jeopardy. And I have to tell you, Jake, I'm concerned that somewhere down the road, if we're back together, you'll resent me, blame me for making you give up your career."

"I've never blamed anyone for my problems."

"And that's *part* of your problem, Jake, can't you see that? Your father was a crooked policeman! You wanted to prove to yourself that you could be better than him. But you've done that and now you're thirty years old and I don't want to be a policeman's widow; I don't want to have to worry about you every time you walk out the door; I'm tired of your fucking *crusade*!"

"Then I'll quit, Marsha. I don't give a *damn* about the department anymore. All I care about is you. And Lynne. That's all I care about." Jake took a minute to get himself under control.

"I'm involved in something right now, Marsha, something heavy. I should have a meeting to wrap it all up in the next few days. After that, I'll resign. I promise."

"Don't do it yet, Jake. See if you can quit drinking first. Take your time; think about this; see if it's what you really want."

"What I want? It's what I've been praying for! It's all I've thought about for ten *months*!"

"Me, too. My doctor told me I should have had this confrontation with you months ago. He was the only one I told about how I felt, about how much I still loved you. I went out with other men, Jake—don't take this the wrong way—but I *wanted* to get over you. I wanted to put you out of my life, but I couldn't. And it always came down to confronting you, and whenever I confronted you, you withdrew into silence; you rejected me. And when I got up the nerve to do it, well, by that time, you were drinking. And I started to get scared of you, of the man you'd become."

"He's dead, he's gone. I won't ever let anyone scare you again."

"No, don't say that. *I* won't let anyone scare me again, Jake."

Jake nodded.

He said, "Can we at least start—seeing each other again?"

"I'd like that. The three of us, too—you, me, and Lynne, as a family."

Jake's beeper went off. He shut it off without looking at it. "Florence said we were making more progress than I knew."

"I have a lot of problems to work through, Jake."

"Don't say that, Marsha; that's not true! The only problems you had were the ones I caused you."

Marsha squeezed his hand. Jake felt resurrected. He thought about the events he'd set into motion six months ago and had to close his eyes in regret, had to fight not to wince.

"Answer your beeper, Jake."

"Later."

"You should know . . . Dabney . . . she told me she was going ahead with the story anyway."

Jake pretended a nonchalance he did not feel. "She can do what she wants; it's a free country."

"She got angry when I told her I'd decided not to participate in the story. She said a lot of bad things about you, Jake."

"I could go to a hundred sources in the press, and a number of them would tell me all kinds of vicious rumors about her, too. That doesn't make them true."

"Jake?" Jake raised his eyebrows, not wanting to speak. He didn't want anything to spoil this moment, to change the way he was feeling. "Tell me, Jake, reassure me—"

"I love you, Marsha—"

"No. That's not what I wanted. What I want you to tell me is that you're still the man I married. That somewhere, deep inside that gruff exterior, the Jake Phillips I fell in love with is still"—Marsha smiled—"I don't know, lurking, I guess."

Jake covered their hands with his free hand, gently squeezed, and looked at her with every ounce of sincerity he still had within him.

"He's not only lurking; he's chomping at the bit. I won't ask you not to see other men. I won't make any demands. All I ask is that you give me time, Marsha. And I have to tell you something else." Marsha waited expectantly. Jake gathered his thoughts.

"Is there another woman, Jake?"

"There hasn't been any other woman for me since the first time I laid eyes on you."

Marsha rubbed at her eyes. "My God, I feel like a teenager."

"Marsha, listen to me. This is important."

She sobered at the tone of his voice, looked at him expectantly.

"I know a lot of our problems had to do with trust. I'm asking you to trust me now, just once, this last time. I've gotten myself into something, something that's not good. It's . . . ugly. I've got a way out, I think. I mean, I know. Resigning from the department won't be good enough to fix this; I've got to do something else."

Marsha didn't seem to understand; she was looking at him oddly, then with growing horror.

"Jake, you didn't . . . You've got that new Rolex; that wasn't cheap. The bills, the rent." Marsha paused. "Don't tell me you—"

"Don't ask me, and I won't have to tell you."

Marsha shook her head and pulled her hand free. Jake could see that she was closing in within herself. He wondered if she was sorry that she'd come to him, that she'd said the things she had.

She said, "You have no idea how hard it was for me to do what I just did, to say the things I said. Please, Jake, don't do this to me, not again. Don't close me out."

"The only way to bring you in is to close you out on this one, Marsha."

"You're telling me I don't really *want* to know, right? Like I've never heard that one before." Marsha grabbed her purse from the seat beside her, put the strap on her shoulder.

Jake hurriedly said, "I'm telling you that I'm leaving the department, that our marriage is more important to me than any job. I'm telling you that I love you, that I'd rather die than live without you."

Marsha's voice was icy as she said, "And you're also telling me that there are still things the little woman just can't be trusted to know."

"We've been separated a long time, Marsha. I got into some things . . ."

Marsha leaned forward, as if giving him one more chance. "Yes? You were saying? You got into some things?" Jake looked away. "*What* things, Jake?"

"I can't tell you that, not now."

"When, Jake? When you finally decide you can trust me?"

"That's not it."

"That's *exactly* it, Jake." Marsha rose, and Jake looked up at her. He didn't think he had the strength to get to his feet and try to stop her. "Give me a call when you've straightened your priorities out, Jake. We'll see what happens then, all right?"

"Marsha, please . . ." Jake spoke the words to Marsha's back. He watched her with a heavy heart as she walked determinedly away from him and through the door of the restaurant.

Elaine sat at her desk in the squad room, looking over Ray McCauley's effects, what he'd had on his person at the time of his death. Everything had been tagged and inventoried, then placed inside a large plastic Baggie, which Elaine had emptied out onto her desk. All the official reports and memoranda were also on her desk, police and medical reports, both written and visual, Polaroid pictures as well as a single, well-typed summary.

Elaine and Kenny Lynch were now working on the case together; they'd just gotten back from McCauley's apartment building. Kenny was a good detective, and Elaine enjoyed working with him. Happily married for a couple of decades now, Kenny was one of the few detectives in the bureau—maybe even in the department—who never seemed to be condescending to Elaine. Not to mention that he was one of the few who had never hit on her, either, didn't sexualize every man-woman relationship, didn't make snide remarks that couldn't specifically be referred to as sexual come-ons but that nevertheless were. Lynch's reticence could be partially explained by the fact that he had been partnered with Mondo for something like seven years. Elaine liked to think otherwise; she thought that Lynch respected her as a detective.

The division of labor that Kenny had established was as smart as it was equitable, the work distributed so that neither detective would cross over the other one's path. With frequent discussion between them whenever something new and important was uncovered, the procedure was a time-saver as well as an exhibition of trust. Neither detective would be looking over the other's shoulder, double-checking the other's work.

Elaine's job was to establish motive; Kenny's was to locate the suspect. Elaine looked through the tiny little phone book which she'd removed from McCauley's wallet, checked the phone numbers in the book against a typed list she'd made of his friends and immediate family, numbers that had been taken from McCauley's personal home book. Her job at the moment was to establish a definite, ongoing link between Ray McCauley and the man who they suspected—suspected, hell; the man they were absolutely *certain*—had killed him. They couldn't depend on a guy like this ever breaking down and confessing.

Elaine looked up from the phone book, sighed at the stack of paperwork that a celebrity's death generated, and glanced furtively into Mondo's office. He was on the phone, gazing up at the ceiling, his expression somewhat grave. He looked a lot older than he had just a few months back, as if time, for Mondo, had doubled its already rapid pace. His hair had more gray in it; the bald spot on the crown was expanding. The lines in his face were deeper, and he frowned more often than he smiled.

She noticed Mondo's head begin to move, and she lowered her own head before he could catch her studying him. She looked back down at the phone book, began to check off the numbers again, worrying about Mondo, and herself, as she did so.

She had found out—as had everyone in the unit, through the police department grapevine that seemed as all-knowing as it was accurate—that the Duette homicide had been taken away from the Special Victims Bureau. IAD was investigating it, in conjunction with a handpicked squad of Homicide detectives. This did not sit well with Mondo.

And it did not bode well for the future of the Special Victims Bureau.

It showed a decided lack of confidence. And once the brass lost confidence in your group, it didn't take long before the media got hold of it through careful, well-orchestrated leaks; and from there the negative stories began to appear; and then, well then, Elaine knew—she had seen it happen over and over again in her career—it was only a matter of time before your unit got disbanded.

If Special Victims was disbanded for the second time, it would never get a third chance, and Mondo would blame himself.

Elaine, on the other hand, would blame Jake Phillips. He wasn't the only member of the bureau who had been singled out for OPS scrutiny, but he was the first who hadn't been relieved from duty as soon as the investigation began. As far as Elaine was concerned, he hadn't lived up to the standards of the unit; he had engaged in behavior detrimental not only to the unit but to the entire department as well.

What irked her the most was that Mondo had always defended him.

What was this? Elaine stopped thinking about Jake for the moment.

A number she didn't have on her list, with a 504 prefix and initials instead of a name. "I.P.—B." was written next to the number. The 504 prefix meant a beeper or cell phone, neither instrument being uncommon. So why the secrecy? No other number that Elaine had encountered in the book was so encoded.

She looked over at Kenny Lynch, who was talking into his telephone. She should wait for him; he was the senior man; she should see what he wanted her to do.

Then again, she didn't have to; she knew what he'd want her to do. Kenny was a by-the-book copper, a guy who'd studied every night for six months before taking the sergeant's exam. A guy who'd gone to *study* groups for it, for God's sake. He'd know the case law involved, the precedents that had been set, as well as where, when, and in what jurisdiction those precedents had been made. He'd lecture her about how some killer in Mississippi had gotten off the hook because the local police had gone through a contact at the phone company informally, rather than doing the proper thing, waiting for a court order that would authorize the release of a suspect's telephone number.

He would, in effect, waste time. In light of what was occurring within the Homicide department in general and Special Victims specifically, time was the one thing they might not have a whole lot of.

If Kenny told her to wait on such a court order, they could be stuck here all day before they found out whose number this was. It might be important; then again, it might not. She suspected for a number of precise reasons that it was, indeed, important.

The phone on her desk rang. Elaine snatched it up.

"Special Victims Bureau, Hoffman." It was the billing department at the hospital, finally returning her call. Elaine wrote down the information she was given, thanked the woman, and hung up. Then sat looking down at a telephone number that had been called from the hospital room where Jimmy Duette had died.

Elaine reached into her purse, found the personal phone book whose numbers would never be transferred to the Rolodex on her desk, looked through it until she found the number she now needed, then picked up the phone, dialed that number, asked for the proper extension, and within five minutes had two identifications: the first was Ingram Pleasant's name, phone number, and billing address; the second number, the one she'd gotten from the billing office at the hospital, baffled her somewhat. The number was listed to a Michael Anson. Michael Anson, Elaine knew, was a Homicide detective sergeant with more than a hint of suspicion surrounding him.

Elaine took her purse with her when she left the squad room. She also had Ray McCauley's wallet with her, the phone book stuffed back in its place. She'd put the rest of his effects back inside the Baggie, and leaving it unsealed, she'd locked it inside her desk. Elaine walked down the hall, into the small cubicle that held the bureau's computer. The room was, blessedly, empty. Good.

Elaine sat down at the computer desk, punched in the information she wanted, took McCauley's wallet out of her purse, and removed the phone book while she waited. She removed one of McCauley's personal cards from its little holder, placed it facedown on the table. She took a pen out of her purse, then opened the telephone book, looked at the number, then copied the beeper number down on the back of McCauley's card. In block letters, she wrote the name INGRAM PLEASANT above the number. She returned the phone book to the wallet, put the wallet back into her purse. She covered the card with her hand.

Ingram's name popped up on the screen, along with his list of arrests. He'd had only two of them as an adult, both of them for syndicated gambling. The *B* behind his initials, then, more than likely stood for "bookie." Pleasant had been sentenced to probation the first time, had received a two-year extension of that probation for the second conviction. This did not surprise Elaine; bookies never went to jail. What *did* surprise her was the lack of mob or gang members' names at the bottom of the page, under the heading of Known Criminal Associates. Could you operate as a bookie today without backing from one or the other? Ray McCauley's name wasn't listed down there, either, but that didn't surprise Elaine. He wasn't a known criminal. The name "Kevin Wrisberg" was listed. Elaine did not immediately recognize the name, though it had a vaguely familiar ring.

Elaine punched in Jake's security code, which Mondo had given her earlier, and checked the listings he'd most recently looked up. It didn't surprise her when the name Jimmy Duette turned up on the screen. He was one of the officers investigating the man's death; she'd be surprised if he hadn't looked him up.

What did surprise her was the date of the computer search: Jake had dialed up information on Duette on Sunday night. When he should have been off duty.

Elaine deleted the information, shut off the monitor, then, at the bottom of Ray McCauley's business card, on the back, under Ingram Pleasant's name and beeper number, she wrote, once again in block letters, BOOKIE.

If anyone looked into it, she'd say she found the card with the name, number, and job description when she'd gone through McCauley's wallet. Which would justify her coming into the computer room and accessing it with her coded password number. Elaine was solid, and she knew it.

She knew, too, that in her profession, if you were ever going to get anything done, you had to take shortcuts from time to time.

Elaine once again removed the wallet from her purse, stuck the card she'd doctored inside, put the wallet back, then went to tell Kenny Lynch about the good fortune that she'd had. When she did, he looked up at her with a lottery winner's grin on his face, then put the word out to two junior squad members to go out and pick the kid up, bring his ass in for questioning.

The two Homicide detectives sat in the second-to-the-last booth of a coffee shop on Division Street, the sergeant and the lieutenant, both of them dressed in light casual summer clothing rather than their usual suits. It never dawned on either man that the way they sat, the manner in which they ordered their coffee, the way they looked at people, their sheer attitudes alone—who and what they *were*—identified them as police officers as readily as if they'd had their badges hanging from their necks, and nothing they were capable of doing would make anyone conclude otherwise.

They talked as they waited, the only customers left in the place after the lunchtime rush, the two of them smoking cigarettes and drinking coffee. The waitress was off somewhere in the back. When she did appear, she made it apparent that she wanted them out of there.

There was nobody around to hear them; nevertheless the two of them spoke in low, worried tones about matters that seemed to be quickly escalating out of their control.

"You shouldn't have dumped the body in the golf course, Al. Even if the fence *was* already torn down. That was your first mistake," Sergeant Michael Anson said in a scolding tone of voice. His partner was taken aback.

"My first mistake?" Lieutenant Alfonse Genco was incredulous. *My* first mistake?! What are you, fucking nuts? Was I out there alone last night?"

"You're the senior man, Al; it's always been you who calls the shots."

"Hey, *I* didn't call any shots. I only did what the Man told me to do." At this point, Genco didn't appear to be too worried, but the first faint inklings that something was radically wrong were beginning to pierce through into his thought processes.

Anson was being too cute, as well as cocky, and he'd never had the courage to pull off either one without strong support from a higher source. Until now, Genco had always been that source of strength. Now Genco narrowed his eyes and stared across at the man, wondering what was going on.

Anson was definitely being cute now when he said, "Now, Al, that ain't quite the truth, either, and you know it."

"First it's all my fault, and now I'm a liar." Genco was glaring hard across the table at Anson. Anson was clearly frightened, but he didn't look away, nor did he back down. He asserted himself, speaking in a level tone of voice. Enjoying the shift in the relationship. Genco thought that he was an ass-kissing little prick.

As if reciting from memory, Anson said, "The Man told you to grab the hillbilly and to find out what he knew. He didn't say shit about killing him in the basement of a police station, for Christ's sake."

"He didn't know nothing."

"We're not sure of that, either."

Genco had had enough. "*We*? What 'we' are you talking about now? I thought it was *me* who did all the fucking up." Genco was leaning across the table now, his belly cleaved by green Formica. Anson leaned back, held up both hands in a placating gesture. His expression changed as he understood what it was that Genco was really saying. Genco felt hatred for the man.

"Al, now calm down." Genco did the opposite, leaning closer still, his face growing red. Anson's back was flattened against fake blue leather. With a surprisingly fast gesture, Genco grabbed one of Anson's hands in one of his own and began slowly to squeeze.

"You sell me out to that swamp-guinea outfit punk? You talking to the Man behind my back?"

"Come on, Al, it ain't like that." Anson was trying to pull his hand free. It was like an ant trying to uproot an oak tree through brute force. "Let go of me." Genco squeezed harder. "Come on, Al, I *mean* it!"

"What are you gonna do, tell Lemelli on me?" Genco let go of Anson's hand, pushed it away from him in disgust, and sat back on his side of the booth.

Anson rubbed his hand. Genco looked at it. He was pleased to see that it was discolored and rapidly swelling. "You're a bullying son of a bitch, you know it? Who you think I am, Duette?"

"No, I wouldn't compare you to Duette. Duette at least had some balls. Spit into my face himself, knowing damn well I'd kill him for it. He didn't run around behind my back and go crying to his girlfriend, Lemelli."

Anson threw his good hand up in despair. "Okay, all right, you want to know what happened? Yeah, he called me," Anson lied, then lowered his voice and whispered, "Lemelli him*self*." The badge of honor was in his tone, on his face.

He continued in a normal, angry tone. "He wanted to know how you could have fucked everything up so bad. How the guy wound up dead without telling you nothing, then wound up *not* dead an hour later in the hospital, long enough for the bulls from Special Victims to get to him."

"We don't know that for a fact yet."

"*I* know it for a fact; I checked it out while your lazy ass was still asleep. Why do you think we're meeting here? You figure I just couldn't wait until three o'clock to see your ass at work? We're waiting for confir*mat*ion, Al.

"And he wants to know why he ain't got all of his money back, after you told him he'd have it just as soon as you snatched up Duette."

"Yeah? He wanted to know that, did he?" Genco paused and nodded, as if considering a reasonable request. He said, "Did you tell him that *you* were the one that proclaimed yourself the new medical examiner and pronounced Duette dead?" Anson's mouth opened as he remembered that to be true. Genco smiled and nodded.

"I figured that might have slipped your mind, what with all the bad-mouthing of me you were probably doing at the time." Genco leaned back and sipped his coffee, sighed, and lit a cigarette. "You little ass wipe. You fucking traitor." Anson flinched with every word. Genco held his eye, looking dangerously close to violence. "Shitheel.

"Did you happen to tell him—between giving him little informational tidbits about how badly I fucked up—that it was *you* who dragged Duette into the car and that there might have been witnesses on the street who saw you do it?" Genco was smiling now; his fingers were no longer shaking.

"Did you mention to him that *I* did all the heavy work at the station? That you sat around on your skinny little ass all night and watched me? That, or you went outside to bullshit with your half-a-retard nephew?" Genco nodded toward the window. He could see Wozak standing outside next to Anson's car, waiting for his uncle.

"You're in as much trouble as me, if not more. I can put the kibosh on this. I can handle Lemelli, and he knows it. Why you think he called you? He knew he wouldn't be able to shake *me*, to get me crapping in my panties. It never dawned on you, never penetrated your thick skull, that we ain't got to worry about outfit punks like Lemelli? I been dealing with him for over twenty years; I know how to handle him. You stupid bastard, *he* don't own *me; I* own *him*!" Genco felt an inward gladness at Anson's loss of composure. Mr. Cool now looked as if he were about to suffer a heart attack. Genco leaned even closer toward him and smiled.

"It's the Rat Patrol; it's Special Victims. *That's* what you got to worry about. But if you want me to save your ass now, after what you did? Then you're going to have to understand something." Genco paused and waited as Anson seemed to think through what he'd been told. After a long time, Anson slowly nodded.

"What's that?"

"You're saying you want my help? Is that what you're saying?"

Anson nodded again, which was good enough for Genco; he'd made his point.

He said, "I'm the boss here, Michael. Not Lemelli, not any of the guineas; me. I've always been the boss between the two of us, and I always *will* be the boss." He pointed the cigarette at Anson, to further emphasize his statement. "You want to change them dynamics? You want to be the Man? Let me tell you something, Michael, you ain't got what it takes. And I'll tell you something else. You get away with this only once. If you *ever* try and go around me, or behind my back again, to Lemelli, to the Rat Patrol, to the punk we got in Special Victims, or to anyone or anything else, I swear to God I will personally kill you, and I'll get away with killing you. Do you understand what I'm saying?"

Anson was sitting back in the booth aghast, his face ashen with fear. He opened and closed his damaged hand slowly, wincing unconsciously every time he opened it. He stared wide eyed at Genco for a time before he was able to speak.

"He—listen, Al, no offense, but what did you want me to do? Tell him to go to hell?"

"That's exactly what you should have told him. Who the hell is he? He *pays* us not to pinch him; what does that make him, our boss? You should have stood up for once in your miserable life; that's what you should have done. You should have told him to go to hell, then you should have told him to call me, that it was my call and I made it, and that you stood behind me on it."

"Al, don't take this the wrong way, but you don't understand; he's really pissed."

Genco waved his hand in the air, as if dismissing Anson's concerns. "He's really *pissed*? Did he *frighten* you? I'm concerned for you, I really am, Michael. All these years I known you, I never took you for a pussy."

"This ain't some two-bit dope dealer we're talking about here, Al! It's the Man, for God's sake!"

"Yeah, Lemelli, that's exactly who he is. The *Man*." Genco grunted in disgust, then leaned back in the booth and lifted his cigarette dramatically, holding it over his water cup with the tips of two of his fingers. When he spoke his voice was filled with his disdain for both Anson and Lemelli.

"He's the *Man*," Genco repeated. "He's got the money, which we've been know to take, and he's got the power. He terrorizes all the niggers, spics, and dagos who work for him. But you know something? I'm still the cops, Michael. I still carry the shield. And if he bothers me, if he threatens me, if he so much as makes a phone call to me in a tone of voice that I don't like . . ." Genco let the cigarette fall into his water glass. He listened to it hiss, then he looked up at his partner.

"I snuff his criminoid ass out just as easy as that."

Anson was looking at him strangely, as if wondering if he were a genius, insane, or both. His mouth was open, and it moved up and down as if he were trying to speak but couldn't. Genco winked at him.

"You let me handle Lemelli. What we got to do is stick to-gether if our own people come calling, 'cause that's all we got to worry about, and if we stand up, and if your *nephew* stands up, we're solid. Now you tell me something, Michael. What were you talking about, what did you mean before, when you said that we're waiting for confirmation? Confirmation of what?"

A voice behind him said, "Confirmation of *this*." Genco turned and immediately understood that Anson's terror hadn't been caused by what he'd said, that Anson hadn't been shaking in fear over his horror of Alfonse Genco. He understood this as his own face grew pale, as his hands began to tremble and there was a rumbling in his stomach.

One of Lemelli's bodyguards had spoken.

Pete Lemelli himself was sitting across from that bodyguard, with another guard, staring at Genco with wide, hate-filled eyes and lips so thin Genco could barely see them.

Without a word, Lemelli rose with the second bodyguard, nodded once, horribly, at Genco, then turned his back on them all and disappeared into the rear of the restaurant. The second bodyguard watched Genco closely, waiting until he sensed that Lemelli was out of the man's sight, then shook his head, sighed, and gave Genco a sad look. He stood up, came over, and slid into the booth beside Anson. There wasn't enough room for him on Genco's side.

"How you doing, Frankie?" Anson said in a shaky voice, and Genco looked at him. Frankie? Genco could never remember any of these guys' names, and Anson was asshole buddies with this character?

Frankie ignored Anson. In a conversational tone, he said, "You fucked up, Al."

"Fuck me." It was all Genco could think of to say. He was amazed at the quiver in his voice. He sat back, appalled and fascinated, looking at Anson as he might look at a dancing snake. He took a deep breath, then said to Frankie, "Look, it was just talk." It was obvious even to him that he was begging.

Frankie shook his head. "You're out, Al. That's it. You're out. Not another dime from us. And we want you to retire."

"Retire?" Genco said it as if the idea had never crossed his mind before.

"That's right, retire. The Man don't want you in a position where you can compromise us. Mike's taking over your spot with us. Anything happens to him, Al, well, we know where to find you, don't we?" Genco knew what the man was truly saying. He was saying that they knew where to find Genco's wife, find his kids. Unable to speak now, Genco nodded his head.

"There's a kid got a tape from Duette last night, got some circumstantial evidence on it, Duette talking some shit while he was out of his mind, delirious, making up paranoid fantasies. Still, the Man wants it."

"What kid? What tape?" He turned to Anson. "What the fuck is he talking about!"

"Jake Phillips. He taped Duette's deathbed confession." Anson's voice was calm and relaxed. Genco began to see him in an entirely different light. Anson turned to Frankie. "I beeped the kid, he's meeting us here; he'll be here any minute now."

"He's meeting *you* here." Frankie leaned away from Anson. "Christ, you ever hear of Listerine?" Then he said to Genco, "You get that tape, Al." He rose from the booth, spoke down to Anson. "He don't get it, you know what time the meet is tomorrow, right?"

Genco said, "*What* meet?"

Anson said, "We'll be there."

Genco said, "Who'll be there?" as Frankie turned and walked away in the same direction Lemelli had gone.

Anson, who now seemed as calm and in control as he'd been when he'd first come into the restaurant, as if he'd never betrayed his best friend, hadn't sold him out to the outfit, said to him, "Phillips, Al. If you don't get the tape, the Man'll have to meet with Phillips himself. He'd rather not do that. If it happens, though, Jake'll be taking *my* place."

"And you'll be taking mine."

"Watch your tone of voice with me, Al, you heard what Frankie said."

"You cock*sucker*!" Genco growled, but Anson acted as if Genco hadn't said a word, was in fact smiling as he got to his feet, his hand out in greeting, saying to Jake Phillips, "Hey! How you doing, son?"

They awakened Ingram, pounding on his door, shouting his name, and even half asleep he instinctively knew two things: it was the polices; and if they had a warrant, they wouldn't be knocking. His door would have been kicked off the hinges right away, and he'd have been dragged out of his apartment, handcuffed and naked, with a blanket thrown over him in case a television camera crew had been sent out to cover the arrest.

Ingram threw himself out of bed, leaped over to his brother's, and covered Rasheed's mouth with his hand. Thank God Rasheed was a heavy sleeper. He was the type of boy who would have gone over and opened the door just to see what the polices wanted, the type who prided himself on being smarter than the polices, who believed he was smart enough to be able to talk himself out of all his legal problems. Which was the main reason that Rasheed had spent more than half his life in some sort of state confinement.

Rasheed's eyes popped open, and Ingram saw terror within them. He shook his head, removed his hand, and put a finger to his lips.

"Shhh."

"Wuzup?" Rasheed whispered. The terror was gone now, and Rasheed's eyes just looked sleepy.

"The polices's at the door. Stay there; we ain't home."

"Sure we is."

"Not for them, Rasheed."

Ingram sat on the side of Rasheed's bed until he heard the sound of the police's footsteps pounding down his stairway as they left. It sounded like there were only two of them. That didn't mean they didn't leave a third man standing in front of the door or someone out in the street in a car.

Shit, what was he supposed to do now? Ingram got off Rasheed's bed, walked around the bedroom, unaware that he was naked, lost in thought, and grateful that his mama still had her job. She, too, would have let the polices in, but for reasons that were entirely different from those of her son Rasheed.

What could they want from him? Did they know about the body? That he and Rasheed had helped dispose of it? That didn't make sense; if they had, they'd have come in droves, and his ass—along with his brother's—would be in the back of a car right now, heading for the county.

So, they didn't know about the dead white man; at least they couldn't connect it to Ingram, if they did. What else could they want? Wrisberg, that's what else they could want. And they might even somehow know that Ingram could actually deliver him.

Ingram began to throw on his clothes, his standard summer street uniform, oversized shorts, an extra-large Bulls Jersey tank top with *23* stamped on the front and back, his Nikes, and his brimless leather hat. Ingram never went anywhere without his hat.

"Where you going?" Rasheed asked.

"I want you to listen to me, Rasheed, all right? I'm going out front, brother, and I'm going to have me a look around. I want to know what's going on. If there someone out there, the polices, and they grab me? You go to where we followed Kevin to last night, all right? You tell him what going on, and tell him I under arrest for something."

"What if he tell me to go fuck myself?"

"He won't. Not as long as I'm with the polices."

"Man, I'll never remember all that." Sometimes Rasheed had insights that his brother couldn't figure him having. Ingram stood still, looking at him, saw what was happening, and knew Rasheed wasn't having one of them now. The boy wasn't concerned about what he might or might not be able to remember. Rasheed was only worried that Ingram would go outside and get himself arrested. Ingram smiled, lowered then shook his head, knowing what Rasheed was going to say next before the boy even opened his mouth. Blood sure is thicker than water, same last name or not.

Rasheed said, "Let *me* go out there. The polices grab me, you do better with Wrisberg than I can. I never been any good at talking to people, you know that."

"I'm going to go out, Rasheed," Ingram said, his voice surprisingly soft, filled with emotion. He went over to the door of the tiny bedroom, stepped through it, then turned back to his brother. "You watch from the window in the front room, all right?"

It popped into Jake's mind unbidden, when the man called him son: pop him. Hit him once, and very, very hard. Drop him and then draw down on Genco before he or Wozak could react. Jake was acutely aware of the fact that if he did, everything he'd worked so hard to put together would come tumbling down around his ears. Jake was so surprised to see Genco that he had literally begun to tremble at the sight of the man. And he was so angry at the sergeant's greeting that a flash of red crossed his vision, Anson fading into and then out of focus as Jake forced himself to calm down, took the offered hand, and slid into the booth beside Anson.

"I'm good, Mike." Jake cursed himself, then waited until he was sure of his voice before he turned to the other man. "Lieutenant Genco, how you doing?" There wasn't a lot of enthusiasm in his voice. Wozak stood at the head of the table, as if ready to defend either man if Jake should make a move he didn't care for.

Genco looked up at him and half nodded. Jake rested his left arm on the table and sat still, trying to watch all three men at the same time.

"You got the tape?" Anson's voice was filled with suspicion.

Jake said. "I was in court all morning; then there were some things I had to take care of." He glared at Anson, signaling his betrayal.

Anson said nervously, "I asked you if you had the tape."

Jake said, "I'm running late for . . . an appointment. I think I'll have a cup of coffee." Jake waved a hand. Anson glared at him. Genco didn't seem to care either way. The waitress reluctantly brought over a cup and Wozak stepped aside as she poured for Jake first, then refilled Anson's cup. When she went to give

Genco a refill, he held his hand over his cup. She shrugged and walked away. Jake watched her put the pot back, then go through a door that led into the kitchen.

Jake couldn't tell if he was being snubbed or if Genco had just had enough coffee for one morning. Jake's already jittery nerves grew worse under the man's intense and ugly glare. The woman didn't ask Wozak if he wanted anything.

Genco spoke his first words to Jake after the waitress had left them alone. "What's that in your pocket?"

Jake said, "That's a tape recorder," then turned to Anson. "How much you tell him?" He heard Genco mutter a curse under his breath.

The tension in the booth was incredible, and more than a little frightening. Jake didn't know if he was its cause or if there'd been serious trouble between the two men before he'd arrived. He didn't know if Anson had told Genco everything or if the sergeant was playing it cool. Anson seemed friendly enough. Jake decided that Anson had somehow been coerced into bringing Genco to the meeting. His decision didn't calm him; he'd been wrong enough times in his life before. This time, if he was wrong, there'd be a price to pay.

Slowly, so as not to further agitate either one of them, Jake slipped his right hand into his pocket and came out with Elaine's microcassette recorder. He put it on the table so that both men could see that it hadn't yet been turned on.

"I want that fucking tape, kid," Genco said, menacingly.

Jake said, "First, you want to hear what's on it. And then the tape is staying with me."

Genco wouldn't speak now, was merely staring at the machine, curiously but intently. Jake had only met the man a handful of times before, so he couldn't tell if his hateful, enraged look was simply his everyday expression. Jake had known plenty of other cops like that before, who woke up pissed off and walked around throughout the day looking for somebody or something to vent it on. They never had far to look before finding it, either. Wozak was such an officer. Jake felt

Wozak staring at him, kept him in his peripheral vision. Genco gestured at Jake, turned to Anson, and made a rolling motion with his finger, and Anson touched his hands lightly to Jake's chest, then around his back, then down his backside, around and into his groin.

"What the hell is *this*?"

"Can't be too careful, can we, Jake? With all that's going on." Jake glared at Anson as the older man spoke to him.

"After six months, you're going to shake me down?"

Anson's voice was patient. "That'd be the time to wear a wire, wouldn't it?"

Jake impatiently waited until Anson was finished before he spoke, and when he did he worked hard to keep his voice level and his tone even.

Neither man would ever understand the courage it took for Jake to say, "You watch too much television, Lieutenant." Jake averted his gaze, then looked up and stared hard at Genco. "They got things now about the size and look of a button, could fit right there on my shirt—camera, in color, with sound. Rat Patrol doesn't wire cops anymore, at least not with all that old-time crap *we* have to use with our regular informants. What they do is, they dress you up. Put the camera in your tie, even; the sound wire in your collar . . ."

Genco said, "So, did somebody dress you today, Jake, or is that snappy suit all yours?"

Jake forced a smile. "Lieutenant Genco, Sergeant Anson?" Jake didn't acknowledge Wozak as he reached out carefully and touched the recorder with his hand. He didn't care anymore what Anson had told Genco. He would now have to prove his point. He raised his eyebrows and waited for Genco to nod before he continued. "I want you to listen carefully to this, I made this tape early this morning; it's Jimmy Duette's deathbed confession."

Jake hit the play button, and the two men leaned forward, listening intently. First they heard Jake's urgent voice, speaking to Duette, imploring him to tell Jake who'd beaten him. Now

Jake was telling Duette that he was going to die, there was no way around that and the both of them knew it, and wouldn't Duette feel better knowing that the men who'd killed him went to prison for it?

Softly, almost too softly for even the sensitive microphone to pick up, Duette's voice came through the speaker. Jake adjusted the volume dial upward until it would go no further. Duette's words were as slurred as Jake's, but the names he spoke— Genco's and Lemelli's—were easily recognizable. Wozak was leaning on the table with his palms, listening intently to the tape. The other two men looked at each other, then Genco stared at Jake, but Jake raised his right hand to silence him before he could open his mouth.

The tape continued to roll.

Jake's voice came crashing out of the speaker. "Do you swear"—Jake hurriedly turned the volume down—"Jimmy Duette, that a sworn police officer, Lieutenant Al Genco, picked you up tonight, did this to you, beat you to death on the orders of Pete Lemelli?" Jake hurriedly turned the volume up again.

Through smashed lips and shattered teeth, a swollen, chewed tongue, a smashed cheek, came Duette's voice. "Ah— do—so—sway-uh . . . Genco—did—it—for—the—dago—for Lemelli." Every word was labored, tortured Duette to speak it. Jake turned the recorder off.

"I didn't know then that Mike was in on it, too."

"Until he kindly informed you," Genco said.

"Hear that last bit, after he says 'Lemelli'?" Jake asked now. "That soft, gentle little sigh? That's Duette dying, gentlemen. Now, do you still believe that the Rat Patrol dressed me this morning, Lieutenant? If I was with them, on their side? Guess what. I wouldn't even have to be here; your ass would be in custody."

"Maybe, maybe not. Or maybe they thought that this tape wasn't good enough. Maybe they figured out that a half-bright second-year law school student would have that taped confession tossed out as inadmissable before any jury could even get close to hearing it. Maybe they even thought you were slick enough to talk us into a so-called real confession." Wozak was still leaning on the table. Jake wanted to push his arms away, wanted to smash his face into the Formica.

Instead, Jake said, "Or maybe they would be fully aware, as the three of us are, that it would still be good enough to get you bounced out of the department, admissable in court or not. Maybe they knew that it would be good enough for the U.S. attorney to open an investigation on Pete Lemelli. Maybe they knew that just the threat of such an investigation would"—Jake looked at Genco and lowered his voice—"change your life radically for the worst." That stopped him. He was staring at Jake warily, but listening. Anson for some reason didn't seem at all concerned by what Jake had just said, but Genco was staring at him with an intensity that was palpable.

"Your name ain't even on it," he hissed at Anson. Anson shrugged. Beneath the table, Jake moved his hand a little closer to his weapon.

"I don't know what you're talking about."

Genco said, "You miserable little—"

"Al, remember Frankie . . ."

Jake interrupted them. "As I told Mike last night, I was alone when I recorded this. No one else still alive has heard it."

Genco, glaring at Anson, said, "Last night," then turned to Jake. "How many copies you got of that tape."

"This is it, Lieutenant."

Genco shot another hateful look at Anson, then turned to Jake and said, "And what do you want for it? Say you wanted to do a fellow copper a solid, wanted to let him take it off your hands, so that he wouldn't have to worry about some psychopathic liar's deathbed statement maybe destroying his family, taking his pension away from him and his loved ones. If you did that, what would you want in return?"

"I don't care about your pension, Genco, and I don't care about your family." Genco looked as if he were about to leap across the table. He was actually shaking with rage. Jake moved one leg out of the booth. His right hand was inches from his pistol. He would have to move fast if a man this size came at him. He said, "I told Sergeant Anson what I wanted last night."

"He didn't share that information with me."

"And I'm not giving it to you."

"Why's that?"

Jake was surprised at how level his voice sounded as he said, "Because you're a murdering piece of shit, that's why. I would never do business with anyone who could do what you did to Duette." Wozak stood up at this and grunted. Anson, beside Jake, held his breath.

Genco said, "But you'd do business with Anson. He was there last night, too; he's as guilty as I am."

"It's not the same thing."

Genco paused. Jake could see him fighting to get his emotions under control. Still, he didn't relax. He stared directly across the table at Genco. The fear was making his hamstrings sing.

At last, Genco said, "You got a wife and kid, Phillips. I know where they are. Give me that tape, now, or—I give you my fucking word—something real bad's gonna happen to them."

Jake's hamstrings stopped singing; his fear was replaced with rage. He moved his hands a few inches and drew his weapon smoothly and laid it flat across the table, leveled it at Genco's belly. Genco sat back in shock. His eyes narrowed, and he kept his wrists on the table but raised his fingers up, as if in surrender. Wozak was breathing heavily, but he didn't move. Anson, next to Jake, sighed.

Jake's voice was a hiss as he said, "If there's even one strange phone call, one unknown fucking car on my wife's street, you're dead, Genco, you and everyone you love. Let me put it this way; if my kid falls down and skins her *knee*, I'll cap one of *your* knees, just on the off chance that you wished my daughter harm. You believe me, *Lieutenant*?"

Anson said, "You lay down with dogs, you get up with fleas."

"Shut up," Jake snapped, without bothering to look at him.

He pulled the hammer back with his thumb. "I asked you a question, Genco."

"I believe you, Jake."

Jake nodded. He slowly let the hammer down and put the gun on his lap under the table. It was still pointing at Genco. If a gunfight broke out, Genco would go first.

"So we don't get the tape? That's what you're saying?" Anson was speaking conversationally. Jake didn't respond. He and Genco stared at each other. Anson said, "I told Frankie it wouldn't work."

"Tell you what, Jake," Anson said. "Meet me at my house tomorrow morning at, say, seven."

"What for."

"We're gonna take an early morning swim. With the Man."

Jake looked over at Anson now as he put things together. "What was this, some kind of fucking *test*?"

Anson smiled at him. "If it was, you sure passed, didn't you, kid?"

Jake held his weapon beside his leg and rose from the booth. Wozak stepped back, giving him room. Jake stowed his weapon and turned away, with Anson and Wozak following, Anson giving Jake further instructions even as Jake stalked out of the place, leaving Genco sitting alone, pondering his now suddenly dim future.

Tommy Malardi awakened to the sound of the ringing telephone, a sound he at some level realized he'd been hearing off and on now for hours. When he fully understood that he hadn't been dreaming, that the phone *had* been disturbing him at regular intervals since early that morning, he angrily struck out at it with one beefy arm, got lucky and hit it, swiped the instrument right off the nightstand. It fell to the floor with a startled, short ring, an outraged electronic *ouch*.

"Leave-me-the-fuck-a*lone!*" Tommy shouted, in case anyone was still on the line. He thought about who might be calling, what might be so urgent. Was it Rick trying to reach him? He probably wanted his car back. Or was it Wrisberg? They could be checking up on him, would have thought that Tommy wasn't up to performing a simple job. If that's what they were doing, screw the both of them.

The answering machine was hooked up in the living room and would have clicked on after four rings the first time somebody called. Tommy might have vaguely heard that, or else he'd slept right through it. After the first time somebody called, the toll saver device on the machine would make it pick up after the second ring, until after Tommy listened to the messages or rewound the machine.

Now he lay there resentfully wondering how often he'd heard the noise, how many double second-long rings had shattered his peaceful sleep. He should have turned the ringer off. Usually, nobody ever called him.

He remembered what Wrisberg had said something about needing proof that the job was done. Shit. He didn't *have* any proof. At least none that he'd show Wrisberg.

Tommy heard a nearly mechanical noise coming from the direction of the receiver, a high-pitched, angry voice, shouting his name. He thought that the voice was a woman's. A woman? Tommy sat up in bed.

He shouted, "What!"

The voice coming from the floor responded, but he couldn't tell what it was saying.

Tommy got out of bed, cursing under his breath, and staggered over to where the phone had landed. He picked up the receiver and fell back onto the bed. The springs squeaked until his muscular form stopped bouncing.

"What?" he said before he even stopped moving.

"Tommy? It's your Auntie Gracia."

Tommy was stunned. "Auntie *Gracia*?" Rick's mother. Shit! Had she heard him shout fuck at her? Tommy was certain she had. Damn it! Just when things were starting to go good with Rick again.

"I'm on the line, too, Tommy." Tommy recognized this voice—this disdainful, know-it-all snap—as his mother's. Tommy hated to talk to his mother. She always spoke to him in a tone that conveyed the unshakable, automatic belief that Tommy was nothing more than a dunce. She was doing it again now, whether she knew it or not, the stupid woman identifying herself, as if Tommy didn't have the required smarts to recognize his own mother's voice. Tommy fought his resentment, assuming that somebody in the family had died.

"Ma . . . Auntie Gracia . . . What's the matter?"

"You know where my Ricky is at?" Auntie Gracia asked, before Tommy's mom could respond. Auntie Gracia's voice was quivering with her lifelong theatric false courage. She was such a pro at it that Tommy couldn't tell if she was really worried about Rick, or if Auntie Gracia was just putting on an act to impress Tommy and his mom.

He tried to act surprised when he said, "Rick? Ain't he at home with Marie?"

Tommy's aunt said, "Marie been calling me up all morning, she's frantic. She ain't seen Ricky since he left the house last night."

Tommy's mom said, "He said he was going to meet *you*, Tommy. When he left the house last night, he said that." Accusation was dripping from Tommy's mom's tone. "We been trying to call you up on the telephone all goddamn morning. Marie and us, both—all three of us, I mean. Auntie Gracia and me, we're on three-way calling." No shit, Tommy thought. Why did she *always* have to act like he was a retard?

"Ma—"

"I know that tone; I heard it before." Tommy's mom jumped all over this now, her mind reacting quickly, the woman thinking she knew him and not about to let him get away with anything. "You say 'Ma' like that every time you're getting ready to tell a lie. You been doing it ex*act*ly like that since you were just a little boy."

"Ma, would you please stop? I ain't nobody's little boy no more."

"Were you with Ricky last night or not, Tommy?" Auntie Gracia wanted to know.

Tommy had to think fast. He didn't want to get Rick in trouble, but still, he didn't know what Rick would tell Marie— or his mother—once he hopped out of whoever's bed he was in and came rolling into his house. He rubbed his brow, cursing himself for answering the phone in the first place, then said, "We was at some bar together. I left him there around two o'clock."

His aunt grabbed at this the way a detective grabs at the first inkling of remorse during a suspect interview. Only, Auntie Gracia was far less subtle. Tommy revised his thinking. She was probably acting more the way one of those asshole private investigators would act.

She gasped, then said in a breathless voice, "Was he alone when you left him?"

"Auntie Gracia, come on, I can't tell you that." Tommy had to fight the urge to tell her that her precious little Ricky had been with five known serial killers.

"This is life-and-death!" Auntie Gracia, like her sister, Tommy's mother, also had a tendency to grossly overreact. Tommy had planned on that, and had to stop a chuckle before it escaped.

His smile didn't reach his voice when he said, "Well . . . not really."

"Tommy, damnit to hell, was he alone or not!" his mother shouted.

"All right, you want to know? No, he wasn't alone. But it's not what you think; he was with . . . some guy." Auntie Gracia gasped again, and Tommy's smile broadened. He put wicked recrimination into his tone. "Auntie Gracia, shame on you for what you're thinking!"

"What guy! What are you talking about! One of Ricky's friends was with him?"

"Exactly. I didn't catch the guy's name; the place was noisy, and I was talking to a girl." Tommy pretended that somebody had punched him in the ribs. He said, "Oof!" paused, then let a little bit of a chuckle into his voice as he added, "I was with the love of my life, Katrine."

His mother shouted, "Who's this Ka*trine*? That ain't nobody's real name; that's one of them stage names, I know it. Tommy, are you with some whore again?" She pronounced the word as Tommy's father used to: *hoo-ah.* "Ain't you never heard of the AIDS?" She wasn't about to let Aunt Gracia's missing son upstage her, so she would give her *own* kid a fatal disease in order to keep the two of them on a level playing field.

Tommy ignored the remark. He said, "Anyway, Rick was talking to one of his friends. We left around two, and I came home, that's all I know."

"What did he look like, this friend of Ricky's? Marie knows all of Ricky's friends. She can call him up and find out if Ricky's there." Auntie Gracia wasn't being mollified; she had too great a need to play the martyr to be comforted by what Tommy was saying. Tommy, for his part, was getting bored with the entire thing. His cousin Rick and Wrisberg aside, his patience was wearing pretty thin.

He said, "For Christ's sake, I don't remember what the guy looked like! He was just a guy, some guy. A white guy, tall, that's all I remember."

"Tommy, you listen to me, you think hard and you re*mem*ber, you understand me?"

"Ma, relax, would you? It's too early for this bullshit—"

"It's after two-thirty in the goddamn afternoon!"

"I had a long night!"

"With some whore, you had a long night!" She probably thought that she'd zinged him pretty good with that one. "Now you tell me right this minute, where were you, and who was you with last night! You can do that, or you can forget you got a mother!''

Tommy, finally having enough of all this, said, "I forgot about that a long time ago," then dropped the phone back to the floor.

He lay back in bed, the cold air pouring down on him from the vent above his headboard, and listened as the two women screamed at him from the receiver on the floor. Tommy smiled. Thought about touching himself, getting himself stiff as he listened to their screaming, then decided not to do it. That was too sick even for him.

When he was certain that he wouldn't be falling back to sleep, he tossed back the sheets and got out of bed. Tommy left the phone off the hook, stepped around the phone, walked over to his dresser. He opened the top drawer as if to confirm to himself that what had happened last night had really, truly occurred.

It had.

Inside the top drawer, under Tommy's colored bikini under-wear, was the money. Two thousand dollars even in cash, and a check for twenty thousand dollars, made out to Thomas G. Malardi. Tommy was proud of himself for looking at the check-book register, making sure that McCauley had that kind of money in his checking account. He had assured the guy that if he didn't, or if he stopped payment on the check, that he would come back and kill his head. He'd told the fat boy that after he did that, he would find his daughter and kill her, too.

Now Tommy took it all back with him to the bed, dropped onto his back, and held the money up, along with the check, looking at more cash than he'd ever seen at one time before in his life. Well, it would be, at least, as soon as he got motivated, got himself cleaned up, and got his ass over to the First Chicago bank.

Twenty-two thousand dollars, Tommy thought. For one night's work. Couple of hours, really. Talk about the big time. He could live for months on that kind of money. Well, it would pay for a month, at least, of living pretty high on the hog. Tommy was a real sport when he had the cash to be one. A tipper who wore nice clothes, spent the greenbacks on the babes.

The best news was that there was even more where that came from, now that Wrisberg and Rick would know that he was a force to be reckoned with, that Tommy could be counted on to do the job and do it right.

He had a moment's hesitation about hanging up on Rick's mother, then decided that Rick wouldn't let his feelings for the woman interfere with his business. Rick, Tommy knew, was a pretty heavy hitter. He didn't get that way by being a sentimental slob.

Tommy left the money on the bed as he showered, left it there still as he threw on a robe and opened his apartment door. It was another hot one out there, Christ. No one had stolen his paper. It sat there on the wooden landing, rolled around inside a thin blue plastic bag, the paper almost leaning against Tommy's door. Tommy brought the paper in, dropped it on the kitchen table. He made a pot of strong coffee, grinding the espresso-mixed-with-French-roast beans himself. House blend, Malardi style. Tommy got dressed while the coffee brewed. He let his hair dry while he blew on and sipped his mug of hot coffee, dipping a cinnamon roll into it, then sucking the coffee off the roll. Tommy began to leaf through the paper, starting with the gossip columns. When he was done with them, he turned to the front page, saw that the headline was a question:

POLICE KILLERS ON THE LOOSE?

Tommy didn't put together that the dead man in the story was the same man Wrisberg had been talking about to Rick just a little over twelve hours ago. He scanned the story, then turned the page, not even bothering to finish it; he knew cops would kill you if they got even half a chance, and thought they could get away with it. He would be surprised to discover that anyone doubted such a simple truth.

The issue of the paper he was reading had been put to bed at one that morning, before he'd even gone off on his rendezvous with Ray McCauley. Therefore there was no mention of Mc-Cauley's death in the paper. Tommy didn't think to turn on the TV; nothing was on at this hour except for soaps and the ignorant talk shows, which weren't much different than the soaps. It would never dawn on Tommy to turn the television to *Chicagoland Television News* or to flip the radio to one of the all-news stations. As he dressed, all Tommy could think about was getting to the bank before it closed—what were their hours? They were independent bastards.

Deep in such selfish thoughts, Tommy was ignorantly, blissfully unaware of McCauley's death as he left the apartment, closed and locked the door behind him, then looked, as he always did, up and down the stairway as if the FBI might be out there, lying in wait for him to come out. When he was sure that nobody was there, not even someone who would be impressed by his vigilance and who would then talk about it to somebody else in the neighborhood—"That guy down the hall, Jesus, you ever see him? I'll bet he's connected!"—a disappointed Tommy Malardi sauntered, swaggered, really, down the stairs and down the street a little ways, to where he'd parked Rick's car.

And son of a bitch if some small time, two-bit asshole of a junkie hadn't busted out the driver's window, gone into the car, and torn out Rick's radio. Tommy saw the broken window from ten feet away, stopped, then raced over to the vehicle, as if he had a chance to catch the thieves in the act. "God*damnit!*" leaped out of his throat before he thought about how shouting words like that on the street would look, and caught himself.

Tommy slammed the flat of his hand on top of the car, shook his head, opened the door, and pushed the small pieces of broken safety glass off the seat and out into the street, using the side of his palm. He looked around the car. The stereo was gone; the glove compartment had been opened and torn apart. The copy of *Chicago Alive!* magazine was even missing from

the front seat. Tommy started in shock, then looked around
suspiciously, saw no one watching him through either the
windshield or the back window. He leaned down, felt around
under the front seat, waving his hand around down there,
growing more and more frantic when his fingers didn't touch
cold steel.

"God*damnit!*" Tommy screamed aloud, no longer caring
what anyone saw, heard, or thought. He somehow managed to
kneel down on the floor of the passenger side, looked down,
and sighed with relief when he saw that they'd missed it, that
his pistol was still there, safe.

Mondo was in his corner office when Jake entered the squad-
room at a quarter to three that afternoon. Mondo looked up,
spotted him, and gave him a short, choppy, *come here* wave.
Jake did not at all care for the look on the lieutenant's face.
Mondo seemed to notice it; a veil draped across his face, seal-
ing off all emotion. That frightened Jake more than the vicious
look had.

Jake, buying time, held up a finger, asking for a minute, as he
went over and waited for Elaine to get off the phone so he could
return her microcassette recorder.

What did Mondo want from him? What was this all about?
Jake tried to fight his rising suspicions, tried to subsume them
before they totally overwhelmed him.

Elaine said into the phone, "What I'm asking is, do you have
a single computer that is accessed by every branch?" She listened, and Jake watched her, grateful for the time to think even
as he resented the fact that she was ignoring him. Her hair was
down around her shoulders, her brow knitted in concentration.
She interrupted whomever she was speaking to.

"So if the checks are drawn downtown, and Malar—" Elaine looked up at Jake suspiciously, then cautiously continued. "And the guy we're looking for tried to cash the check in, say, Lonbard, the flag would still fly?" She listened for only a brief time now before cutting the speaker off again.

"Listen, I don't care about your lawyer, about liability, or about any other of your arguments. We got a suspected killer's name right out of the checkbook register, sir, and we got a court order directing you to work with us. Now if you'd rather face contempt charges—"

Jake heard a man's excited voice coming over the line, even through Elaine's hair. The man seemed to be speaking words of conciliation. Elaine spoke over him.

"We need a call as soon as that flag flies, sir," she said, then added, "This is a celebrity death we're talking about here. If for some . . . unforeseen *reason* . . . say, the president of the bank puts a delay on the call because he's worried about liability? Guess what? The media that's been hounding our asses for twelve hours will get directed toward you. Ever have them biting on it before? It's a lot of fun." Elaine paused. Jake heard outrage coming through the phone.

"No, that's not a threat, sir. Every line in the department is taped, did you know that? I was gonna threaten you, I'd do it from a pay phone. All I'm saying to you is, if we don't get the call, if that check clears, and the man leaves without our getting the chance to peacefully arrest him, a contempt charge will be the least of your worries." Elaine sighed loudly into the phone as the man spoke to her again. This time he seemed to be pleading.

"Sir? Listen to me. I give you my word, we'll do our best to make the arrest outside of the bank. But we have to know he's there; we have to know he's inside. There're four exits to cover, and God knows which route he'll take; it'll take us some time to set up. Sir . . . sir . . ." Elaine couldn't seem to get a word in edgewise. Frustrated, she began to shout. "Just do it, pal, you hear me? Keep your rent-a-cops away from him, and do what the court ordered!" She slammed down the phone, looked up at Jake, still angry.

"You couldn't put that on the desk?"

"I was curious. Who wrote a check out to his killer? That's dumber than we usually get . . ."

Elaine ignored Jake and took the machine from him solemnly, coldly, as she asked him if Duette had said anything before he'd died. Jake didn't like her tone, or the superior look she gave him. He didn't like the way she'd ignored him; she hadn't even had the respect to try and evade his question. He told her if she wanted to know, she should have stayed in the room with him; they could have had a good time after Duette went on to his reward. Elaine shook her head, then picked up the phone, dismissing him from her mind. She was absently checking the recorder as Jake walked away from her, as if she feared that Jake had stolen some of the inner components.

Jake did a quick look around the room; he did *not* want to go in and face Mondo just yet. He could feel Mondo staring at him through his office window.

Jake spotted one of the Internal Affairs rats standing way over in the corner, with his back to Jake, standing there slouched in his shirtsleeves, casually talking to Rickover. What was his name? Thompson? Jake thought that was right.

They were always in the squad room these days, talking, making it an ordeal for any of the Homicide cops to even come into their own office. They played up particularly to the Special Victims members, pretending as if every bureau detective was completely above suspicion and reproach, attempting to make friends while their minds worked overtime trying to solicit enough information out of you to destroy your life; but now Jake had a quick and sudden insight, and the reality of what was happening, what was really going on, hit him with chilling clarity.

Jesus Christ, it was obvious. The guy, Thompson, was hiding from him, trying to hide from Jake. He was trying too hard to act normal, as if he belonged. This wasn't your typical, everyday attempt to get information for their probe from a real, working street cop.

Thompson was acting as if Jake wasn't supposed to see him.

Jake shot a quick look over at Mondo's office.

Mondo hadn't moved, was still sitting behind his desk, leaning back in his chair, arms folded, watching Jake with an unreadable look. Inscrutable, he was. Jake felt as if a large predator were closing in on him.

Jake walked over to his desk, picked up the phone, and punched in the four interoffice digits. He sorted through his drawers as the phone rang on the other end, using it as an excuse to not have to look at Mondo or to feel the man's eyes on the back of his own neck. It didn't take away the sensation of being watched, though. Jake felt not only Mondo's eyes but those of Kenny Lynch—who had the desk right next to Jake's—and Elaine Hoffman's, too. Lynch was on the phone himself, obviously talking to another sergeant in another part of the city.

The phone rang in Jake's ear for the third time. Where the hell was this guy? Where was his secretary?

Lynch said, "It's that idiot, Tommy Malardi; he's a half a retard, at least. Cousin to Richard Malardi, the thief? We got him on a security video camera following McCauley through the garage, and into the elevator at McCauley's apartment building. Another camera picked them both up inside the elevator—"

A woman finally picked up at the other end.

"This is Sergeant Phillips, is he in?"

Lynch said, "He got a P.O. box for his home address; it's on his driver's license, we can't find him from that. Could you have one of your TAC teams run over to Richard's house from time to time? He's in your district."

The woman sounded distracted as she said, "Uh, no, Sergeant, I'll . . . uh . . . I'll have to tell him you called."

"Tell him it's important. Tell him"—Jake couldn't go too far with her— "I've got trouble with Mondo." Jake slammed the phone down without saying another word to the woman. He stood there breathing heavily, trying to catch his breath.

Lynch was looking at him oddly. Jake looked away. Lynch said into the phone, "If they catch hold of Richard, see if they can pry Tommy's address out of him, all right? It's a murder case now, and a guy like Richard, he'd trade his *mother* away on a murder case, for the chance for us to owe him that big. Naw, he wouldn't be involved in this stupidity." Lynch listened for a second, then chuckled. Jake heard Mondo's office door open. He didn't look over there.

He listened in as Lynch said, "Listen to this, Sarge, you want to talk about *dumb*? Tommy obviously braces the guy, extorts him, beats the shit out of him, then takes a *personal check* from McCauley for twenty thousand dollars."

Jake tried to look around casually as Lynch laughed out loud into the phone. Mondo was leaning against the door frame, arms crossed, looking right at him. He crooked a finger at Jake.

Lynch said, "It's just a matter of finding this goof now. I appreciate it, Sarge. Yeah. Me, or Elaine Hoffman. I owe you one, thank you."

There were perhaps eight other squad members in the room, but Jake wasn't reading them, didn't feel any animosity coming from them, at least. The slob from the Rat Patrol wasn't around anymore; he'd probably slipped out when Jake was going through his desk.

Jake walked toward Mondo's office. Mondo stepped inside, leaving the door open for him.

———————

"**J**ake, what's going on?" Mondo didn't equivocate. He sat straight in his chair, looking Jake directly in the eye, his expression neither warm nor cold, his expression blank, giving Jake nothing to work with.

"What do you mean, court? I killed them—Ackerman, that defense attorney, barely cross-examinod."

"That's not what I mean."

Jake openod his hands. "What?"

"We lost the Duette case, Jake; IAD took it over."

"*What?*"

"You heard me."

Mondo reminded Jake of a jungle cat watching a zebra, scrutinizing his every move, waiting for a chance to pounce. Jake didn't know what to say, didn't know how to act.

"IAD's convinced it's cops involved, Jake."

"I was at home, Mondo; you called me, remember?"

"I wasn't checking your alibi. I was simply stating a fact."

"Mondo—"

Mondo was looking up at the window, past Juke's shoulder. He held up a hand. "Wait—don't say another word."

Hoffman walked in, followed by Lynch. Jake watched as Elaine glared at him as if he were a suspect. He felt himself starting to sweat.

"You read him his rights yet?"

"Elaine, come on," Mondo said, but he didn't seem startled by the question.

"Come on, what?" She stood on Jake's right side, her hand close to her hip, as if she suspected she might need her weapon in a hurry. Jake looked from her to Lynch, who was on his other side. The accusatory air that was so strong in the room—against him—was one Jake had worked hard to evoke in other people, at other times, in other rooms, as he'd grilled suspects, working them into corners. Being aware that this was SOP didn't do much for him; Jake felt panic rising along with his ever-present paranoia.

"Hold on a minute here—"

Hoffman ignored him. "How long are you going to let this go on? What are you waiting for? IAD to shut us down? Jesus Christ, Mondo, we're already catching hell in the press as being another Red Squad; there's a reporter calling everyone in the bureau at *home*—God knows how she got the numbers—trying to pry information out of us about him."

"Elaine, calm down. Sit down, both of you." Lynch did as he was told, taking a chair that was situated a little behind Jake, on the left. Hoffman remained standing. Mondo said, "The press doesn't dictate bureau policy."

"Evidence of criminal activity should."

"What criminal activity!" Jake nearly shouted.

Mondo looked directly at Jake and asked, "Why did you look up Duette's name on the computer on Sunday, Jake?"

Jake blurted out the first thing that came to mind. "His name came up in the course of another investigation!"

Elaine landed on that one hard. "On your day off? You wander in here on Sunday, Phillips, what, you had a sudden, shrewd insight into a case you were working? Just wondered if Jimmy Duette somehow managed to fit into the scheme of things?"

"I—"

"Why'd you call Mike Anson from Duette's hospital room last night, Jake?"

"What?"

Mondo didn't bother to repeat himself. Jake felt Elaine's glare as a physical thing. He didn't look at her, kept his gaze directed at Mondo, as his mouth worked, opening and closing, as his mind raced for an answer. He rejected each lie as it came to mind, knew how easy it would be for the three people in this room to tear his lies apart.

He understood that he'd been set up and that there was nothing he could do about it.

"He's a friend of mine." Jake knew how lame the answer sounded. He fought the urge to close his eyes, so he wouldn't have to look at Mondo anymore.

"A friend of yours." Mondo's reply left no doubt as to how he felt about Jake's statement.

Jake said, "If you feel you have to, Mondo, read me my rights. Outside of that, I have nothing more to say without an FOP rep right here at my side."

"So, the suspect's crying for his lawyer." Hoffman's voice was as icy as her glare. Jake and Mondo looked at each other for what seemed to Jake to be a very long time. "Got a right to protect his constitutional freedoms."

Mondo said softly, "I could suspend you for five days right here on the spot, for cause, you understand that? Without pay. You get a hearing before the board at the end of that time."

"Is that what you want to do?"

"It wasn't when you came in here, Jake; honest to God, it wasn't." Jake fought to keep any expression off his face. He was breathing heavily; he couldn't change that. "I wanted to know what was going on. That was all I wanted."

"And these two just happened to wander in on their own."

Lynch spoke for the first time since entering the room. "You're damn right we did. We've got a vested interest in the bureau, Jake. We've worked with you long enough. We have a right to know what you're up to, what you're doing." His voice was less harsh than Elaine's, less judgmental than Mondo's. He seemed to still be reluctantly giving Jake the benefit of the doubt.

Hoffman said, "I want to place him under arrest, Mondo. Let him clam up."

Mondo shook his head at Elaine. "We won't pinch one of our own." He turned to Jake. "You're out of Special Victims, Jake."

"You don't understand what's going on, Mondo." Jake shot a hateful glare toward Hoffman. "And neither does she."

"I understand that you refused to answer reasonable questions asked of you by your superior and your coworkers. And you understand that working Special Victims isn't a right, it's a privilege."

"And you're revoking it."

"On the spot. I put a call in to the patrol captain; he can reassign you wherever he wants."

"Just like that."

"Don't think you're off the hook, ace," Hoffman said at Jake's shoulder. "*I'm* going to have a talk with IAD and tell them all I know. They'll investigate you from top to bottom. None of us will be surprised if you wind up being charged with accessory murder before and after the fact."

"Would you be surprised, Mondo?" Jake asked, and Mondo nodded, slowly, as if thinking back over the past year.

"Yes, Jake, I would be."

"So that's it. I can go?"

"Clear your desk; give Lynch your files. When you're done with that, you're free to go," Mondo said.

"For the moment," Hoffman added.

Jake rose shakily to his feet, not looking at Hoffman. Lynch had a weary look about him—the old-time copper who'd seen it all but still had enough heart left in him to feel bad when he saw it again. Lynch got to his feet, too, nodded to Jake, as if in farewell.

As Jake reached for the door handle, he heard Mondo say, "Detective Hoffman? Stay here a minute, would you?"

"What the hell was *that* all about?"

"If there's one thing I can't stand, it's a dirty cop."

"You have nothing but suspicion that Jake's dirty."

"Pretty strong suspicions, Mondo. No matter how much you like him, you have to admit that."

"You don't want to be countermanding my orders in front of my subordinate officers again, Elaine. It undermines my authority. And you know better than to drop all your cards on the table, too."

"I didn't, Mondo."

"What?"

Mondo's phone rang before Elaine could answer. He picked it up and was surprised to hear Captain Merlin Royal's husky voice on the other end. He listened for a minute, then hung up, a puzzled expression on his face.

"We'll finish this discussion later. I've got to go see the captain."

Elaine said, "Mondo?" Mondo heard the warning in her voice and raised his eyebrows.

Elaine reached into her pocket and held up the tape from her recorder, put it on the desk, and pushed it toward Mondo. "I told you I didn't play all my cards. This tape is an unused microcassette from Radio Shack, Mondo."

"And?"

"I had a brand-new cassette in there last night. A Sony tape, Mondo, fresh out of a pack of five."

Mondo looked at Elaine for a moment, eyes narrowing, having to think for a moment.

"Jake had that recorder in Duette's room with a fresh Sony tape inside, and the tape's been switched? Is that what you're telling me? You're absolutely certain, Elaine?"

"It's not the same cassette, Mondo; Phillips switched the tapes." She paused and seemed to soften. She said, "He's dirty, Mondo. Phillips went bad. Even you have to believe it now."

One of the Internal Affairs officers, Thompson, was just leaving the captain's office when Mondo came walking into the regular Homicide squad room. He stopped when he saw the man, stood staring at him. Thompson looked at Mondo, then offered him the condescending, wintry smile that the Rat Patrol must teach during internal training, the sort that said a silent "fuck you" while presenting an appearance of civility. Mondo turned and watched him pass, turned back, and there was the boss.

"You want to come on in here, Mondello, or you want to stand out there all day with your mouth hanging open?" Captain Royal said from his doorway. It was obvious from his tone and his stance that if Mondo did go in, he wasn't going to like what the captain had to say. It was as if the captain had never gotten sick, as if nothing had changed, as if no phone call had been made to Mondo early that morning. Royal walked back into his office, and Mondo sneaked a quick look around, trying to spot Thompson. He didn't see him anywhere in the squad room. He followed Royal into the office and closed the door behind himself.

"You all right, Captain?" Mondo said. He was sitting in the uncomfortable wooden chair set directly across from the captain's desk. Royal sat observing him, in his leather judge's chair. The electronic air cleaner that usually whirred away on the desk was missing; the windows, usually stained with small brown spots of nicotine, were clean. The stench of stale smoke, which for years had invaded a visitor's clothing and hair, was gone. The office had an empty feel to it, as if the captain had abandoned it, and the office didn't care one damn bit, was merely awaiting his replacement.

"If I get lucky, I've got ninety days to live. I guess you could say that I'm not 'all right.' "

Mondo cleared his throat.

"Was Thompson in here about Phillips?"

The captain's expression never wavered. He said, "Now why would IAD be concerned about Jake Phillips?"

"Sir?"

"Phillips is a good man, Mondo. We need him in Special Victims."

Mondo took a deep breath, let it out, then told the captain everything he knew or suspected.

When he was done, the captain looked at him for a time before saying, "I want Phillips back in Special Victims, Mondello."

Mondo fought his anger. This was Captain Royal. He would eat Mondo's anger alive. "Sir, why are you protecting him?"

The statement stopped Royal. His face tightened, and Mondo knew that at best he'd phrased the question wrongly. He tried again, took another tack.

"Sir, pardon me, but can I say something here?"

Captain Royal pursed his lips and thought about Mondo's question. Mondo watched as the captain automatically, unconsciously reached into his shirt pocket and seemed momentarily surprised to find that the pocket was empty. For just a half second, a flash of horror crossed the captain's face as he probably thought about how the missing cigarettes—his longtime, beloved friends—had wound up betraying him. Mondo suspected that in spite of it all, the captain sorely missed the cigarettes.

Royal nodded; he'd allow Mondo to speak.

"You were right there for me last year, when Special Victims was reactivated. You gave me an autonomy that hasn't been seen in—well—in a while." Mondo didn't want to discuss what had happened to the previous special, autonomous unit within the Chicago Police Department. It had become corrupt, filled with officers who'd become brutal dope millionaires, virtual bodyguards for the dealers, until the feds had brought them down, giving the department a black eye in one of the department's most horrid public relations blunders. The newspapers and TV news had been filled with the lurid details, and the public had claimed, through their voice on the radio talk shows, to have lost their confidence in their sworn police officials.

Mondo shared their outrage, but knew something that few of the voting public had bothered to discover after they moved on to other issues: most of the officers who'd been arrested and later convicted were now already out on parole from various federal penitentiaries.

Now Mondo said, "You helped the unit get its life back, even after the . . . problem . . . we had with Tulio, Captain. It doesn't look good that we had the Duette case taken away from us, Captain. It makes us look as if we're under suspicion. And now I have to ask you, don't let my bureau die." Mondo regretted using the word the second he heard himself say it. He quickly added, "Don't let us go down like this, without a fight." He paused. The captain's expression still hadn't changed.

"And I need to ask you again, Captain, man-to-man; was Internal Affairs in here about Phillips?"

"None of your goddamn business," Royal said. He nodded for emphasis, or perhaps to convince Mondo that in spite of his illness, he was still in charge. He let the silence fester between them, until Mondo looked away.

"I've been a cop since you were in high school; you don't think I know how to play the game by now?" Royal swiveled his chair around and looked out his window. Now that it had been cleaned, he could see people swimming in a rooftop pool, directly across the street. It was mostly young women and little children, with just a sprinkling of men.

Mondo watched the captain's head bob, and kept silent. He knew that the captain did this only when enraged. He hoped that the man's rage wasn't directed at him or, more important, at the Special Victims Bureau. Another thought struck him, a thought that filled him with terror.

Was Internal Affairs focusing their investigation on the captain? Mondo was grateful that the captain's back was to him as he sat, stunned, thinking about that.

Had Mondo ever heard a word, even a hint of scandal concerning the man? Of course, there was the usual nonsense that top administrators had to live with, some disgruntled detective making up lies to justify getting bounced out of Homicide.

Mondo's thoughts were cut off as the captain swiveled back, his decision made. There was a far-off, almost dreamy expression on Royal's face.

"I seen a lot of things happen in Special Victims, you know, Mondo. Man, you mentioned what happened with Tony Tulio; does *that* bring back some memories. That deal almost brought down the house. It got the unit disbanded, as you mentioned, for a time."

Mondo listened to the man's rumination, marveling at how a dying man could allow such a small but nevertheless joyful smile to swim at the corners of his mouth.

"I was one of the few who fought to have the original unit put together in the first place; did you know that, Mondo? What a concept it was. An elite squadron of top cops, handpicked, tough, and incorruptible. The new untouchables. Take on only the worst, the unsolvable cases." The captain chuckled.

"We had our problems right from the beginning, too, and not only from the outsiders; there were plenty inside the department who didn't like the idea. It was too ... too non-multi*cult*ural for those simpleminded morons." Mondo couldn't decide what was going on. Was the captain rationalizing something here. Was there something Mondo was supposed to be picking up between the man's words? Or was Mondo looking only for that, while the captain was simply reminiscing?

The captain said, "Got our asses straightened up with the

press right quick, too. You remember the picketers outside? The press reported, and the public believed, that we only took on cases involving rich white people." The captain shook his head. "I wondered what they thought *I* was? A public relations ploy? The token Ne-gro?" Royal grunted. "Once they get that shit in their heads, it's impossible to get it out." Royal dropped his bemused expression and looked at Mondo straight on.

"You think I'm here today because I want to be here? You think my wife isn't at home, hurt and more than just a little pissed off? She was shouting at me, before I left, thinks the department brought on the stress that made me smoke the way I did. She knows I was smoking before I got into high school, but she got to get mad at *something,* and she doesn't want to get mad at me. I suppose that'll come later." The captain shook his head.

"Maybe she's right. Maybe I should have stayed at home and let everything pass me by. I spent my entire life looking out for a department that at first didn't want me, then later wanted to use me, and now trots me out as a *symbol,* 'Look how high the ghetto-born can rise in our department!' " Royal waited, but Mondo didn't allow even a fraction of his feelings to be exposed on his face.

Royal said, "None of them ever understood it. None of them—including my own wife—ever figured it out. Me? I personally never gave a shit about public perceptions. I never gave a shit about power or personal prestige. And I never gave even *half* a shit about the money. I know my career isn't going to amount to even a footnote in the department's history. But see, that's not why I got in this in the first place."

The captain was speaking forcefully, not recalling now, but explaining. His arms were folded on his desk, his fingers wrapped around massive biceps that would soon be toneless and bony.

He said, "I'm in this—and stayed in it to the end—because I believe that *every single citizen in the city of Chicago* deserves to live in safety. Because I believe that everything I did, from the day I was sworn in at the academy, until the day they pull the plug on the life-support machine, gave them a little more of an opportunity to have that safety."

The captain never lost eye contact with Mondo; he now widened his eyes just a little. There was something swimming around in there that Mondo couldn't figure out. Was it anger? Disdain? It could even be fear. Another thought struck him and gave Mondo pause.

Did the captain think that *Mondo* was guilty of something, as well as Jake?

"I wouldn't have thought a kid like Phillips would have been calculating enough or sophisticated enough to stand on his rights. I'm surprised he even asked for the union rep; he has the support of the FOP for nothing. Their army of lawyers would have taken the case all the way to the Supreme Court, and it wouldn't cost Phillips a dime." The captain nodded, as if making certain connections.

"He's got that right, you know, without you suspending him for it, or kicking him out of the unit."

Royal leaned forward now, putting his weight onto his elbows, his eyes opening wide. He nodded his head twice, as if to emphasize something to himself and himself alone.

"I wasn't sure I was going to tell you this, but you hit the nail on the head. You were right earlier, I *am* protecting Phillips. The truth is, I'm only here today because, as your immediate supervisor—and as your friend—I am asking you to call off the dogs on Phillips, Mondo."

What was the captain saying? What was going on? Mondo knew that some of his suspicions—his paranoia—were caused by all the investigating that had been going on. There was a sudden climate of suspicion and fear within the entire Homicide department these days; guarded, skeptical men had been pushed beyond their usual cynicism. Perhaps he was here because he was respected, and was about to learn what the captain probably thought of as a Truth.

Or perhaps he was supposed to figure it all out on his own.

"Gimme a smoke," Royal said, then dug around in a drawer until he found an old, heavy glass ashtray.

He placed it on the desk between them. Mondo didn't try to argue. He dug out his pack and tossed it on the desk. The captain gave the pack a strange look, then shook out a single cigarette, bit off the filter, spit it onto the desk, put the other end in his mouth, and used Mondo's matches to fire it up. The captain took a long, deep drag, then leaned back in his chair, eyes closed, held the smoke inside his diseased lungs for a long time, then let the smoke sift out through his nose with a satisfied expression.

Without opening his eyes, Royal said, "Agnes is going to kill me." His body shook with inner mirth. "No, she's not." The last was said in a near whisper, as if he were speaking to himself. Captain Royal opened his eyes and looked directly at Mondo. "Go ahead and smoke," he said, then closed his eyes once more. Mondo followed instructions. When he began speaking this time, Royal did so in a gentle voice, and didn't bother to open his eyes.

"There are people within the upper levels of the department who are—let me just say they're not the type I'd ever socialize with. And I'm not talking about the politicians, the networkers, or the ass kissers." Mondo nodded, even though the captain couldn't see it. He knew that the captain was talking about upper-level corruption.

"It's even in IAD. I've been fighting it my whole career, so I feel like a hypocrite, ordering you to give Phillips a break. No unit, no bureau's immune. They all got their share of snakes. And any unit that can't handle one of their own getting caught, well, it couldn't have been a very strong unit to begin with, now, could it?"

That look was back in the captain's eye, the look that Mondo couldn't figure out. He was getting a message here, obviously, but he didn't know what it was; the message was weak, the signal distorted. "I told you I know how to play the game, and now you and me, we're playing it: I'm telling you to put Jake Phillips back in the unit.

"*And* I'm telling you that Special Victims can have the Jimmy Duette homicide back. But only if you make Jake Phillips the primary investigator in the case."

"You *what*?"

"You got a problem with that, Lieutenant?"

Mondo felt the rage boil up inside him, rose half out of his chair, and spoke before he could think. "You son of a bitch." The captain sat back, shocked. Mondo knew that he was swimming dangerously close to an old, battle-weary shark, a shark with nothing to lose. Mondo didn't care. He stood up and stared down at the captain.

"That's what all this was about in the first place, wasn't it, Royal? The bullshit about the old days, how much your work meant to the department, that 'safety' you wanted to guarantee every citizen." Mondo paused. "It was an apology to me, wasn't it? All bullshit, right? All you care about is getting those precious retirement papers signed and turned in before some filthy, corrupt coppers can pull the rug out from under you. But what about me? What about the bureau and everyone on it who've worked their asses off to—"

"Shut your *mouth!*" The captain leaped to his feet, slammed a hand down on the desk as he shouted. Mondo was stunned into silence for only a moment.

"IAD wasn't in here checking up on Jake, were they, Royal? *Were they, Royal!* They were in here checking up on *you!*" Mondo's expression filled with his sudden insight. He repeated himself, softly. "They were in here checking up on you . . . What did they tell you—pull the pin, or they'd go to the press? Let you die while they tied up your pension in the courts for the next ten years . . . ?"

The captain, who'd been trembling with anger, now exploded.

"SHUT THE FUCK *UP!*"

The captain pointed his finger at Mondo. "You do what the fuck I tell you, and you do it this *minute,* or you're suspended right here and now, and Special Victims goes to whoever I *give* it to!"

"And who might that be, Captain—Jake Phillips?"

"You don't want to say one more fucking word, Lieutenant." The captain's tone held even more of a warning than his words. He glared for a moment, then repeated himself. "Not *one* more goddamn word."

Mondo opened his mouth, and the captain actually moved, as if he were about to come around the desk and engage Mondo in a fistfight. Mondo relaxed himself and stood his ground, giving the man his chance, but the captain caught himself, stepped back, then threw what was left of the cigarette into the ashtray. Sparks flew onto the desk. Both men ignored them. The cigarette bounced out of the ashtray and fell onto the carpet, smoldering. Mondo nodded several times, biting his lower lip, then spun and left the room.

The captain stomped out the cigarette, grinding it into the carpet, then sat down in his chair, breathing heavily, and grabbed for Mondo's cigarettes. He lit one and smoked it through, made sure he was calm and breathing normally before he reached for his phone.

Mondo slammed the captain's door on his way out of the office, ignoring the glares and surprised looks of the Homicide detectives in the room, and headed for the stairs, intending to blast through the doorway of his office, get on the phone, and shake things up. He didn't care what he had to do, how many favors he had to use up, or how many enemies he had to make; he wasn't going to live with this; he didn't *have* to live with this.

There was no doubt in his mind now: Jake was dirty, and the captain was, too. And if Mondo followed the man's orders, Special Victims would go down in flames.

Mondo was still thinking clearly enough to not let his people see him in this state. Particularly Jake Phillips. He walked swiftly toward the men's room, closed and locked the door behind him, then stood there for a full minute, leaning his back against the door, letting it hold him up. He heard someone rattle the knob; Mondo ignored it. He walked away from the door, leaned heavily on the sink, and looked at himself in the mirror.

He had to calm himself down, think this thing through, and then take the appropriate actions to save his bureau, whatever those actions might be. Mondo closed his eyes, leaned over, and allowed his forehead to rest on the mirror. It didn't cool his brow. He pushed away, stood up, adjusted his tie, his jacket. Although the captain's office was as clean as Mondo had ever seen it, he still washed his hands to get a filthy feeling off them.

At last, calm, he unlocked the door and left the bathroom, turned without acknowledging the Homicide bull who was standing there glaring at him. The man made no remark. Mondo walked to the stairway, and climbed the steps slowly.

He stepped into his office, closed the door behind him, still incensed and hoping that the captain would die before he could bring further shame to the department. He looked through the glass door, saw that everyone in the bureau was watching him, except for Jake Phillips, who was nowhere to be seen.

"A little upset, are we, Lieutenant?"

Mondo jumped, turned to the source of the words.

Sitting calmly on the sofa in the corner, legs crossed, hands folded over one knee, sat the IAD officer, Thompson.

The highly polished open-topped red Toyota all-terrain vehicle squealed to the curb in front of him without warning, and Ingram Pleasant, looking at the two men in the vehicle, at their expressions, thought he was about to become the victim of a drive-by homicide. The men were looking at him crazy, eyes wide, mouths shut tight, jaws firm. Ingram had seen that look before, right before somebody died.

He knew who these boys were, too, knew that and who had sent them. They weren't the polices. Ingram had a moment of pure terror as he wondered if these were the two who had come to his door earlier, shouting they were the polices when all they really wanted was to kill him.

"Hey, neutron," the man on the passenger side called out to him. He spoke the word as if Ingram's gang neutrality was something to be scorned. Ingram took his hands out of his pockets, slowly, so that neither man would get it into their heads that he was armed. He was certain that weapons were being held beneath the vehicle's thin metal doors.

"Hunh?" Ingram said.

"Get in, nigger; get in the back; come on, let's go; move your ugly black ass!"

Ingram quickly thought this over. He knew who they were, and who had sent them. He knew, too, that if he got into the vehicle he might never get out.

What would happen if he ran? Ingram briefly wondered about this, then immediately rejected the premise. These boys wouldn't be shooting at him with revolvers; they'd have automatics, Uzis, sophisticated shit like that. They close their eyes, then spray and pray, and Ingram wouldn't have a chance.

Ingram saw the impatience on the passenger's face. His order hadn't been immediately followed; he suspected Ingram was dissing him. With such people, Ingram knew, his instincts honed in the street, their perception of respect, coupled with their need for instant gratification, was enough to get a man killed if they even *thought* that the man was insulting them.

Ingram shrugged, as if he had nothing to hide or to lose, then grabbed the roll bar and hefted himself up and into the back. There was hardly enough room for him to even kneel down back there. The young man in the passenger seat turned as Ingram settled in, moved his body partially around so he could keep an eye on Ingram. Ingram kept his hands on the roll bar, to keep his hands in plain sight as much as to keep his body balanced.

This close up, Ingram could see that the passenger seemed to be in his midteens. The worst kind of killer of them all. The gangbanger lifted his weapon just enough so that Ingram could see the barrel. All Ingram could see was that it was round, long, and vented. That was enough for him.

"You don't want to do nothin' *stu*-pid," the young man with the gun said to Ingram. Ingram started to nod, then thought better of it. He shook his head from side to side. The barrel disappeared. The driver pulled away from the curb so quickly that Ingram nearly was thrown from the back. He hung on tightly, his face grim. The passenger laughed at him, never taking his eyes off Ingram. Ingram wondered if he would ever see Rasheed again in this life.

The vehicle squealed to the curb less than four blocks away, in front of a two-story house with cheap, faded, green shingle siding. All the windows that Ingram could see had been covered from top to bottom with aluminum foil, taped from the inside. The yard was dirt; the chain-link fence rusty. The gate hung off the fence, long forgotten as a point of entry. The front door had been painted black; gold gang symbols had been spray-painted in the center. A challenge to anyone of another gang who dared to enter this block, a sign to everyone else that the house was not to be harmed.

The driver got out and walked away from the vehicle without looking back. The passenger, now on his own protected turf, got out of the vehicle with the weapon hanging from his hand as openly, carelessly, and cavalierly as if it were a gallon of milk. He jerked his head toward the house.

"C'mon, motherfucker, what you want, an en-graved in-vite-a-tion?"

Ingram controlled the shaking in his legs, climbed out of the vehicle, and the gangbanger with the gun let Ingram precede him toward the house.

Jake sat alone in the computer room, staring at the monitor so he didn't have to think about anything else. He didn't want to think about his call from the captain—just as he'd been cleaning out his desk—didn't want to think about Anson even as he did the man's work.

Most of all, he did not want to think about going swimming with Pete Lemelli tomorrow morning.

Jake had accessed files that the average police officer didn't even know existed, had punched up Special Victims internal software, data that didn't officially exist, designed to be seen exclusively by members of the unit. In fact, the average police commander was not even aware of these files. Jake didn't know if the superintendent knew of their existence.

If the press ever got hold of this, Jake knew, the unit might wind up getting disbanded anyway, and this time, it would be forever. How many privacy rights were being violated here? Jake didn't know. But the press—and through them, the public—would recognize close parallels to the old, defunct Red Squad. The connections between the two groups, Jake knew, were closer than any of the officers of the unit would care, or dare, to admit.

Which was one of the reasons why Special Victims members

were so carefully scrutinized and handpicked. In fact, after logging on, Jake had been surprised to learn that he'd still had access to the files, that his identification number hadn't been deleted, which would deny him entry to the sensitive valuable personal information. He guessed that Mondo hadn't gotten around to locking him out yet. He knew that he soon would. Mondo didn't fool around. He sure hadn't in his office.

Jake had to fight the urge to remember his shame, to dwell on it. It was almost comforting sometimes, to wallow in his grief. He didn't know how long this had been going on, but he couldn't deal with it now, couldn't waste any more time thinking about it. Every day of his life, from here on out, had to be lived second to second, without thoughts of the future or of the past. He had to get through this without drinking, had to get his status back, had to get his position back, had to get his wife back.

He had to get his life back. Only then could he quit; only then could he walk away.

The information Jake was now pulling up had been pilfered from the Gang Crimes South files. A full half of all the information in the computer system had been taken from some other unit's database; the other half came from data punched in after each Special Victims arrest or when a bureau member working another, different case brought pertinent information that concerned one of the many criminals on file.

The database concerned criminal activity—conjectured or confirmed—of nearly every suspected felon who resided within the Chicago city limits or in the County of Cook.

Jake, under Anson's instructions, was now looking through the file on Kevin Wrisberg, and the file was as thick as any he had ever seen. What did he have here, eighteen, nineteen pages? But Jake didn't have to read every page, or print it out to look at it. He didn't care about the man's arrests, their number, or their resolution. He didn't even care about the crimes the man might be involved in now, at this moment. He hadn't been ordered to check up on the man; he'd been told to find his

location. Therefore all Jake cared about was the information at
the bottom of the screen: two long pages of internal, private
information that could never be used as evidence in a court of
law, personal opinions of officers who had worked on cases
against Wrisberg.

Opinions as to his living arrangements were of particular
value to Jake.

He wrote down the updates on Wrisberg's possible addresses, what vehicles he might be driving, the color, make, and
model of such vehicles, and whose names those vehicles might
be registered under. Intelligent crooks, those who lasted out
there, rarely had vehicles registered under their own names,
not unless they had legitimate sources of income that could
prove they could afford to own them.

All this information was gathered by officers who heard it on
the street, lucked into it in some way, or went out of their way to
find it out. Should Wrisberg ever be needed by anyone in
Special Victims—which seemed to be a logical guess—he
would be found, and the database would not be mentioned
should his lawyer wonder how. All that any lawyer or judge—
who for whatever reason was interested enough to ask—would
be told was that the infamous "unnamed informant" had given
the unit the information. The informant's name? Sorry, that
simply couldn't be given out, for the informant's own safety
and protection. The Supreme Court had already ruled that a
cop had the right to keep the names of such informants to
himself. Which also meant that there didn't have to be any such
informant to begin with.

Jake, always a bright student, had been learning. Was learning more every day.

Jake skimmed through the two pages at the bottom of the file,
writing down addresses, phone numbers, and the all-important
names of Wrisberg's known criminal associates. The KCA list
took up an entire page by itself; it seemed as if this Wrisberg guy
was connected to nearly every major gangster in the city of
Chicago.

Jake understood that he was doing what Anson had ordered him to do, but he knew that he was actually in the employ of Pete Lemelli.

Jake sat back in the chair, blew out a breath, closed his notebook a little guiltily, then impulsively reached out and shut down the computer. He leaned back in the computer chair, a stricken look on his face, and stared blankly at the ceiling for a long, long time.

Patrol officer Billy Wozak rode shotgun in the squad, his clipboard on his knee, held balanced there by his right hand. His left was free to grab the microphone should their unit number be called across the airwaves. He could also use it to operate the MDT—the mobile data terminal—a laptop-sized computer that gave him instant access to the Department of Motor Vehicles. Punch in the license plate number, wait a second, and *wham*, the information was right there in front of you. It saved a fortune in time and trouble and did away with a number of jobs for useless people who used to sit in front of big, fat computers and type in the same information, then relay it to whatever police vehicle had requested it.

Progress. In some ways, it had made Wozak's life infinitely better. CDs and Walkmans, large-screen television sets and VCRs. Things he could never have convinced his own father would ever be accessible to the average American when the elder Wozak had been Billy's age, were now a part of everyday life. In other ways, progress had, in Wozak's opinion, fucked nearly everything up. It could have gotten him killed.

At the moment, Wozak's partner, Zack Glendennon, was driving the squad slowly through their Southwest Side patrol area, holding a large foam cup of Dunkin' Donuts coffee in one hand, a coffee roll in the other, while he drove and shared with Billy the details of his failed marriage, which Wozak, today of all days, could have honestly lived without.

"I'd be with my *wife,* in bed, fucking my own wife, and

thinking about her, about my girlfriend, Estell. Jesus. Fantasizing about one when I was doing it with the other. That's when I knew it was over."

"Uh-hunh," Wozak said, distractedly. The light at the corner turned red. He braced himself as he thought that Zack was not going to notice, that he was in fact going to race right through the intersection, causing a major accident.

At the last moment, Zack hit the brakes. He slid to a stop without spilling a drop of coffee.

"She was all I could think about, every minute of every day! The kids, the old lady—man, nothing else mattered." Wozak could smell booze oozing out of the man's pores. He hadn't been drinking yet today, but he'd been bombed last night; there was no doubt about that.

Wozak wished that he'd pulled some of that special duty over at the Taste of Chicago. If he had lucked into that, he'd be ogling the babes right now, collecting phone numbers, rather than sitting here listening to this asshole's sob story. What good did it do to have an uncle with clout? His big shot Uncle Mike couldn't get him away from this drunken loser. Wozak had already asked, and been told to be grateful he even had a job in these hard times. Wozak fought a momentary guilt. He couldn't think about Uncle Mike right now.

"So what do I do? How stupid could I be?" Glendennon sipped his coffee, then wiped his mouth with the back of his forearm. Wozak saw little beads of coffee on the hairs of his partner's arm.

"Genius that I am, I decide to leave my wife. My wife, my kids, my dog, my house, everything I'd spent the past ten years of my life putting together, I walk away from." Ten years ago, Wozak had been a freshman in high school. At St. Rita's, not far from where they now were driving around. Did he need this shit? Hell no, he didn't need it. But he didn't have any choice. Senior detectives at crime scenes knew better than to tell Zack Glendennon to shut up; a two-year man like Wozak would get eaten alive if he tried.

Glendennon was a huge man, topping off at nearly three hundred pounds. At his last physical, they'd estimated that only nine percent of that weight was body fat.

The man was naturally solid, muscular, one of those freaks of nature who, if caught early enough and trained properly, became heavyweight champion of the world, or a starting nose-guard for the Bears. Glendennon didn't care about sports; all he'd ever wanted to be was a cop. He'd told Wozak that as often as he'd told him about his marital problems.

"Move in with the bitch, and what happens? Month later she dumps me for some bastard who works at the Board of Trade."

"Maybe it was the yacht that stole her heart," Wozak said, and Zack turned on him, incensed.

"What did you say? What did you say?"

Wozak sat staring straight ahead through the windshield, as if he hadn't heard the man. Zack waited a while. Wozak could hear him chewing his roll, sipping at his coffee. He heard the flick of his partner's lighter, smelled the smoke of Glendennon's cigarette. Wozak powered his window down an inch. It let out some of the blessed air conditioning, but it might also save his life; he took the secondhand-smoke studies seriously, Billy Wozak did.

At last Glendennon seemed to figure out that Wozak wasn't making fun of him. He asked, "So what happened to you last night, Billy? What was so important that the lieutenant called you in?"

"I had to guard an informant." Wozak gave the excuse he'd worked out with his uncle in advance.

"No shit?" Zack seemed impressed. "State changing his ID, or what?"

"Sooner or later. The guy was testifying this morning, and he told the ASA straight out, they put him in protective custody, he'd wake up with amnesia."

"Smart move. They got that special unit for them at the county. I wouldn't want to see the inside of it."

"Me neither."

"So what do you do with a slob like that? Was he a nigger? A white guy? What?"

Wozak automatically compounded the lie. "A nigger."

"What did you talk about with a *nigger* all night?"

"We played Scrabble."

"You *what*?" Billy felt Glendennon's eyes boring into the side of his head. He felt the man's weight pulling down the springs of the front seat. He did not look over at him. He thought that Glendennon might be trying to figure out if Wozak was busting his balls. Wozak did not want to embellish on what he'd said; he'd never been a good liar; most people could see right through him. The priests at St. Rita's, they'd been experts at seeing through him.

Glendennon said, "I can see it now. Some shithead trying to spell out 'motherfucker' on a Scrabble board." Glendennon smiled at the idea. " 'Ho.' " Glendennon now laughed aloud and ran down a quick list. " 'Honky,' 'shee-it,' 'hunh,' 'gud-d*aaa*mn,' 'lick-a-dick.' " Glendennon laughed again, then said, "White oh-preth-ah."

" 'Ho's' in the dictionary," Wozak pointed out.

There was a soft, brief blare of a siren behind them, someone wanting to get their attention. Wozak turned around, looked through the rear window.

A new Chevy Cavalier was following close behind them. Wozak could make out four men, at least, in suits, inside the car.

"What the fuck do *they* want?" Glendennon said wearily. He'd never had any use for detectives. Wozak, feeling a rising panic, thought he knew the answer.

Glendennon pulled to the curb and waited. Wozak powered his window the rest of the way down. All four detectives came at the squad car, two from each side, until there was a detective standing at all four bumpers. The one who'd taken the bumper behind Billy took a few steps forward. The man had his hand on his hip, resting on the butt of his pistol.

"William Wozak?" the detective demanded.

"What the fuck is going *on!*" Glendennon shouted and was ignored. Wozak nodded his head.

"Internal Affairs, Wozak. Get out of the car, and keep both hands where I can clearly see them."

Tommy Malardi walked north on Dearborn Avenue, looking for the First National Bank of Chicago's main downtown building, the check in his pocket, the cash right next to it. It was the best thing for him to think about right now, the money and nothing more, because if he didn't think about that and that alone, he might wind up killing somebody in this shithouse part of the city.

The truth of the matter was that Tommy hated to come downtown at all, unless he was already drunk and looking to get drunker still, and was looking to raise a little hell. At such times, it was good for him to cabaret in a large but still anonymous neighborhood, one where he wasn't known, one where hardly anybody really knew anybody else. As Tommy hadn't been drinking yet today, he had no use for the downtown area.

And when he *did* come down here, it was never at this time of day. Down here, nobody knew how to act.

At least five cars disregarded the lights, ran through every one of them after they'd already turned red, while horns blared wildly on the streets that had the green light but were now prohibited from moving because the mopes who had the *red* light were stuck in the middle of the intersection. Tommy couldn't understand this, because most of the main streets had traffic cops stationed at them, supposedly directing traffic, cops who weren't doing shit to stop the vehicular transgressions. The early rush hour crowd was clogging not only the streets but the sidewalks as well. The Iranian cabdrivers had learned their rules of the road from the shah's secret police, and if all that wasn't bad enough, the area, the entire goddamn downtown *area,* was crawling with nothing but niggers.

Everywhere Tommy looked, there they were, the jigs, either panhandling in hundred-dollar running shoes or trying to get him to buy some bullshit newspaper that they kept shoving right into his face.

Tommy had stayed flexed since he'd parked Rick's Buick in the indoor lot that had a huge advertisement on its wall that said it *only* charged seven dollars an hour for the privilege of parking your car there. Excluding city tax.

Think of the money, Tommy reminded himself yet again, as three high-school-age jigaboos swaggered past him, glaring at him, not giving up ground. Tommy didn't play into their power game; he let his shoulder bump into one of them, gave it a little extra for emphasis, then turned and walked backward, glaring at them right back. "You want something?" Tommy said. He opened his hands and held them out, pleadingly. "You punks want something?" The boys turned away from him and sniggered amongst themselves. Tommy became enraged at the insult, turned so he could see where he was going, then made himself think about the money; he had to keep thinking about the money.

Twenty-two thousand dollars. He'd have it in his pocket in a matter of minutes now. If the bank wasn't closed. What day was it, Tuesday? Wednesday? Tommy wasn't sure. He knew that banks kept weird hours; they didn't stay open as late as, say, your average Walgreen did, and they took certain days off altogether, right in the middle of the week.

Tommy saw the curving skyscraper from a block away, right there on the corner, across the street, the building starting out real big at the bottom, then bending upward into almost a point. He smiled. The name of the bank was plastered all over the building. There it was, straight ahead. He would make it; they had to be open.

He wouldn't endorse the check until he was safely inside the bank; he knew the sort of thieves that were running around this city—they could snatch the money right out of your pocket without your even knowing you'd been touched. He'd heard about guys like that, had even known a few guys who'd bragged in bars late at night that they could do it themselves.

Tommy personally had never been known for crimes that called for craftiness or manual dexterity. Brute force and muscle, he saw these as his strengths.

It was hot out today, even though it was getting late. Tommy swaggered down the wide sidewalk, knowing he looked good, that he looked confident as well as strong. With the bank in sight, even the niggers couldn't bother him now. Well, at least not too much.

All he had to worry about now was if the fat-boy radio talk show geek had stopped payment on the check. He decided that it wouldn't be an embarrassment for Tommy, even if he had. He would slap his forehead, shake his head, and tell anyone within the sound of his voice that Ray McCauley was a dead-beat son of a bitch who refused to pay his debts. What debts they were would remain his private business. Then he'd leave in a huff and go and take his frustrations out on Ray McCauley in person.

The bank was directly across the street from Tommy now. He stood on the corner waiting for the light, looking at it, his heart racing. The building seemed to take up the entire block. He could see the sign that announced that the place was open until six, and he managed to hide his excitement, although he did smile. Tommy stood on the corner and waited for the light to turn green, and when it did, he stepped off the curb, his eyes on the building, on the bank, looking at all the glass, which looked to have the longest, widest set of curtains he had ever seen in his entire life. Tommy stepped into the street, thinking about the money . . .

The car slammed on its brakes, squealed in front of him, and Tommy leaped back and to the side, shouting a curse in terror. He felt something hit his left side, hit it hard, and he fell to the pavement, flipped, then rolled, landed on his back and literally *watched* the car's bumper leap over his head, then move backward, as the brakes caught and held.

Tommy reached up, grabbed the bumper, and pushed himself away from the car, as if he were on one of those garage creepers. Only his back didn't have wheels, and all he was wearing was a light summer shirt.

"Mister . . . !" Small hands reached out and grabbed at him. Tommy pushed them away.

"Don't touch me."

"Are you all right? I didn't even see you!" It was a black chick, in her early twenties.

"You see the red light, did you manage to see that, when you weren't seeing me?" Tommy hadn't gotten up off the pavement yet. He was testing his body, moving this, flexing that, trying to find out if anything was broken. Everything seemed okay, except for his hip, which hurt like hell. And he'd scraped a bunch of skin off his back, pushing himself out from under the front of the car. He fleetingly wondered about his shirt, the back of his pants, knew that they would have been wrecked beyond repair.

"Red light? What you talking about with that red light bullshit, ofay? That light was *green!*" A black man was shouting now. From the sidewalk, though, not from the street. He hadn't been in the car; he was just one man in the crowd of pedestrians that had stopped on the sidewalk to watch the unusual drama play itself out. He shouted out, "I seen it all, sister; so did all these other people. I'll go to court with you, too, tell the judge ex*act*ly what I seen."

The young woman who'd hit Tommy with her car was ignoring the screaming man. She crouched down beside him. "I've got a car phone," she said. "Would you like me to call for an ambulance?"

Tommy saw hundreds of people lined up on the sidewalk now, watching. He heard car horns blaring and realized they were blocking the street. He sat up.

"You at least put your car in park? It ain't gonna run me over?"

The man on the sidewalk shouted, "You walked right in *front* of it! You lucky that girl's a good driver, dummy, or she'd have run you over already!" He turned his attention to the other pedestrians now. "You all see that? Who else witness for the sister?"

The woman whispered to Tommy, "I hate Malcolm X pretenders like that!"

Tommy used the car's bumper to get up, rose to his feet, then took a tentative step. He felt all right. The young woman took his arm to try and help steady him. The man on the sidewalk shouted out, "Shee-it!" in disgust. Tommy watched the man wave his arm, spit on the sidewalk, then turn his back in disgust and walk away from the crowd. There was some sort of plaza in back of them, the man was walking through it now, and Tommy could see him maneuver around five young, out-of-shape kids wearing red berets and cheap T-shirts with some sort of stenciling on them heading toward him officiously. What the fuck were they called? Guardian Angels. Just what he needed.

Cars were now driving around the woman's vehicle. The horns had stopped honking. Now that they realized that they weren't going to see blood or a fight, the crowd had mostly dispersed. Tommy turned to the woman.

"Sir?" She was still next to tears. Tommy looked at her shaking hands, thought about moving his groin into them. The only thing that stopped him was there were still some people watching them.

Tommy heard the sound of a siren blasting shortly somewhere behind him. Shit!

The woman said, "If you don't want to go to the hospital, I'll give you all my insurance information . . . I'll take full responsibility, it was *my* fault, I admit that . . . " She looked at Tommy. Tommy glared down at her. "My purse is in the car," she said, as if she'd suddenly discerned his character. She began to slowly edge away from him.

The Guardian Angels were closing in. Tommy ignored the

woman now, stepped back onto the curb and watched these stupid kids approach him. These were punks whose goal in life was to grow up and be security guards. Rent-a-cop wanna-bes. They didn't come any lower than that.

The squad was now at the far corner, only a block away. It blasted its siren in second-long bleeps, trying to get the other cars to allow it right-of-way.

The woman touched Tommy's arm; he looked at her again. "Mister? Sir? I'm so sorry about running into you."

The siren was closing in. It would be here in a few seconds. Security guards from the bank were gathered on the sidewalk across the street, watching. Tommy would have to think of the money later; tomorrow, maybe. Or maybe he'd come back. Or find another branch of the bank. As soon as he changed his shirt and pants and got the filth off his hands, then he could come back. Nobody would remember him then.

Tommy looked at the kids, flexed his muscles, made fists, and sneered. He saw that traffic was flowing west. He had the green light again. The Guardian Angels hesitated as Tommy glared at them, not so officious anymore. Without looking at the woman, Tommy said, "Get the fuck away from me, you stupid nigger bitch." He turned away from the bank and walked through the plaza, pushing right through the group of Guardian Angels, who puffed out their chests as he passed, then turned and watched him, and none saw the look of anguish and pain that had set on the woman's face.

The gangbanger leader said to Ingram, "Where Wrisberg staying at."

Ingram immediately lied. "I ain't found that out yet. He call me last night, pick me and my brother up where we stay, and then he drop me off back there again when we through." Ingram paused.

"You told me Sunday you'd have him located for me by now. You been lying to me, neutron?"

"No, I ain't." Ingram saw that the man didn't believe him. He said, "I know what he driving."

"That right?" The leader, who called himself King Youngy—Ingram didn't know his last name—did not seem impressed. Ingram was used to dealing with stupid people, so he wasn't upset when the man didn't understand Ingram's attempt at subtlety. King Youngy swiveled around in a black leather chair that had his initials stamped in the back in gold lettering—KYP—the letters placed inside a gold crown.

Ingram said, "He's driving a big black Mitsu 3K."

"They a million of them in this city. You know the license plate number?"

"I could find out."

"That man owe me a lot of money."

"I heard he ripped you off."

"He brag about that to you?" There was a rumbling from the dozen armed men in the room. Most of them wore their weapons openly, in shoulder holsters or stuck down the front of their pants. Most of them had only undershirts on. There was no air conditioning in the house; the air in here was dead, stifling, and rank.

The outside of the house was dilapidated, but the inside, though filthy, was lavishly—and tastelessly—furnished. A lot of money had been spent on velvet furnishings that the average person would look at once, then want to throw into the trash. Everything was stained, looked greasy. And the place stunk to high heaven. Ingram had to breathe through his mouth so he wouldn't puke. There was a large washtub set in one corner of the room. The plasterboard wall behind it was streaked and stained. The tub was half filled with piss; Ingram had smelled it as he'd walked over to the chair.

Why didn't people with money do more with it than this? What was the *point*? he wondered. Say what you wanted about Wrisberg, the man knew how to live good.

Ingram caught himself, then looked back at King Youngy and said, "I heard it on the street."

"You hear that he kill Ray McCauley, that white radio dick-head you all the time braggin' about knowin'?''

That stunned Ingram. "He kill *my* account . . . ?'' He didn't finish the thought, at least not out loud. But he wondered why Wrisberg had them dispose of some white punk's body without giving them a reason. What had he told Ingram about Mc-Cauley? Don't take action from the guy, that was all. He'd never even mentioned that he'd killed McCauley, too.

It crossed Ingram's mind for just one instant: tell this man where Wrisberg was hiding, give it to him, tell him everything else he knew, then let King Youngy and his boys handle all of it. Ingram closed his eyes and waited until the moment of weakness passed.

"You want to live to see nightfall?'' Some of the young men in the room laughed; others just glared, ready to follow their leader's command and kill Ingram on the spot. Ingram indeed did want to see nightfall, wanted suddenly, desperately to see it, but he would not share that information with someone like King Youngy. He would only take advantage of Ingram's fears, his hopes and dreams.

Instead, he told him, "Cocksucker never tell me nothin'. He did, I'da stay loyal to him.''

"You'da stayed loyal to him, I'da wound up killing you my-self.''

"I don't owe him nothin'; he put a pistol to my head last night and threaten to waste me.''

"He suspect we doing business, you and me? That we been talking?''

Ingram held up his hand—he knew how close he was to dying. He hurriedly said, "King Youngy, no, honest to God, he'd never suspect me. He thought I was getting out of line behind a collection I didn't make. He took it over hisself. I wanted my ten percent.''

"From McCauley, we talking about?''

"Yeah, from McCauley.''

"And you question your boss, then he didn't shoot you?''

King Youngy turned his head and spoke to his underlings. "See? What'd I tell you? That old man ain't nothing but a pussy." He turned back to Ingram.

"That bitch think he bad because he kill a few people. I kill more people in my lifetime than he ever even *meet*. Man drive around in his big fancy cars, talking shit about he in a al*li*ance with me and all my boys. I ain't in no alliance with shit!"

"He owe you a lot of money."

"Man makin' deals in my neighborhood and not givin' me my end? He know how I look at that."

"It's like I said, he rippin' you off, King Youngy."

"I want my money and his ass, both."

"I can't give you your money, but I can deliver you his ass."

"Then why you not take it last night, when you had your chance?" Ingram thought up the lie and spoke it without the chance to think it over.

"Man didn't have his gun out of his hand for a *second*. He was driving with it, King Youngy, with it resting on his leg, pointed right at me. Rasheed woulda jumped him from behind, in the street or in the car? I'd be dead."

"I suspect he plannin' on leaving the city directly."

"Wouldn't surprise me none."

There was a sudden, loud pounding on the outer door. Ingram jumped at the sound, but King Youngy just turned his head and looked at his men. Several of them moved toward it, to defend it rather than answer it. They took up combat positions on either side of the door, their weapons out, cocked and ready, up at shoulder height. If it was the polices, Ingram knew, they were all about to die.

"Who there?" one of them yelled, and a familiar voice came back, strong and hard.

"This be Rasheed Moore, and I wants my brother! I wants my brother right *now*!"

Ingram, relieved, looked over at King Youngy, who was shaking his head and laughing, showing gold front teeth that had diamonds set inside them.

"That boy too dumb to kill. Loyal, but truly dumb." He called out to his boys. "Don't hurt him."

He turned to Ingram, laughing out loud now. "Go ahead on to your brother. I just wanted to make sure, in my head, that you weren't dicking me around. But you call me now, Ingram; you call me every day. You ain't got the balls to do him in yourself, I do it for you, soon as you find out where he staying at. If I don't hear from you, I gonna send for you again. You and the retard both." King Youngy didn't have to finish the statement; Ingram knew what he meant.

"King Youngy, I get his ass for you," Ingram promised.

"Before he leave town. He leave town, I blame you, Ingram."

"Before he leave town," Ingram said. "I heard that."

Mondo had listened to Thompson's well-rehearsed line of bullshit for as long as he could without responding; he had just sat there patiently, staring blankly at the man, as Thompson laid it on him, the guy going on and on about how important a role the Special Victims Bureau played in the police department of the nineties; how every member of the unit was above reproach; how he and his division wished that every cop in the city had the ethical and moral standards of the Special Victims Bureau; how, if they did (when he said this, Thompson flashed that horrid, superior smile), he would be out of a damned job!

Mondo didn't reply, just sat there giving the man absolutely nothing, staring absently at him as if he weren't even there, lighting one cigarette from the butt of the last in the hopes of smoking the sanctimonious bastard out of his office. The pack of cigarettes was in the middle of Mondo's desk, and Thompson's eyes were drawn to it every time Mondo reached

over to shake one out. Three times Mondo had watched
Thompson watch his hand, Mondo silently manipulating,
Thompson biting every time.

The Internal Affairs detective had attempted his own subtle
manipulations as well.

Thompson would sometimes pause hopefully after a statement, inviting response, but Mondo remained silent, giving
Thompson no more significance than he would a painting on
the wall or a dirty window. His silence was calculated to make
Thompson squirm. It had about as much effect on the man as
rain does on a rock.

At last, Thompson sat back, crossed his arms, and shut his
mouth. Did he view Mondo as stupid? It was an old detective's
trick that Mondo almost smiled at, a trick Mondo had himself
learned twenty years earlier, and one he had used thousands of
times during the course of a suspect interview. If Mondo allowed it to, it would now become a game of chicken, a contest
of nerves; two little boys playing out a dare, and whoever spoke
first was the loser.

It was not a game Mondo was willing to play.

He said, "Detective Thompson, I wonder—if you can tell me
without kissing my ass for another hour—just what exactly do
you want from me?"

Thompson shook his head sadly, as if he'd been through this
many times before with lesser officers and had expected better
from Mondo. He pretended to be hurt, as if Mondo had bruised
his feelings.

He said, "We're not in an adversarial position here, Mondo.
Or would you prefer that I call you 'lieutenant'?" Mondo waved
a hand dismissively; he didn't care either way what this asshole called him; he just wanted him to say what he'd come here
to say, then get the hell out of his office. Thompson raised his
eyebrows at the slight, then frowned, as if he'd just had a deep
thought.

"Or *are* we?" He paused, staring back at Mondo.

"I have work to do, Thompson. If you want to chat, you

should go back to your own unit, or call and I'll let you know when I'm free for a working lunch."

Thompson raised his hands, then let them drop into his lap in a show of frustration. "What *is* it with you? I can accept your officers' dislike—I have come to not expect any more from the average detective than I do from the average traffic cop. All they can think of is their job security, their pension." Thompson flashed his small smile, and Mondo had to fight the urge to slap it off his face. Didn't the man have a clue as to how that smile grated on people's nerves? He had to. He probably got stiff flashing it, knowing that nobody could stop him from doing it.

Thompson said, "Where else can a high school graduate wind up making fifty big ones a year, *and* legally carry a gun and have the authority to use it—the post office?" Mondo let Thompson's smile sail over his head this time, along with the man's somewhat sick attempt at humor.

Thompson said, "They get to worrying about their position, and nothing else matters to them, not even—or especially—the truth." Thompson paused and stared at Mondo for a second for emphasis. Then he said, "Every word you say to them, they think it's calculated to entrap them, as if we *want* to investigate them, as if it's our choice."

"And you don't and it's not, is that what you're saying, Detective?"

"Hey, Mondo, you have to understand, we don't go *looking* for cops to investigate. Their own conduct brings us to them. Nothing would please me more than for the CPD not to have an IAD."

"Thank you for sharing that with me." Mondo lifted a pile of reports off his desk, waved them once, then put them back down. "Now, Detective Thompson, as you can see, I'm really busy today. So, I have to ask you again: is there something specific that you wanted from me?"

Thompson ignored him. "I thought, with a commander who'd been around a little in his time, who knew what was going on, that we'd be able to operate on a—I don't know—I guess a 'higher plane' is the phrase I'm searching for. It's becoming more and more obvious to me that I was wrong."

Mondo crushed out his cigarette, leaned over and shook out another one, then picked up one of the reports from his desk and began to study it as he lit up, now ignoring Thompson completely.

"Obstinate son of a bitch, aren't you?"

Mondo didn't respond. He reached for his phone, and Thompson cleared his throat. He punched in a three-digit number, and Thompson said, "You want to hang that up, Lieutenant," with a hint of threat in his tone. Mondo waited until Lynch picked up the phone. He said, "Kenny? Did you get any action yet on this Malardi character yet?" He paused and listened.

Thompson said, "I've got two words for you."

Mondo said, "Rick's live-in's worried?" then grunted. "Why, because he usually comes home the second he punches out at the factory?"

Thompson said, "Elaine Hoffman."

Mondo said, "Have the girlfriend fill out a missing person's report. I'll call down and have a copy sent up—wait." Mondo shut his eyes for a second and shook his head at his own stupidity. This IAD investigation was causing everyone to screw up, to forget fundamentals.

He said, "Did anyone from TAC bother to ask the girlfriend where Tommy lives? Have them go back—no, better yet, you and Hoffman go over there yourselves. Play on her emotions; act like you give a shit. Worm Tommy's address out of her. She doesn't have to know you're not there to fill out a missing person's. Get at least his phone number; she's got to have that. And, Kenny? This is heavily media-involved; let's pick this guy up before the six o'clock news has to remind the city again about what incompetent idiots all us cops are, okay?" He hung up.

"Special Victims panders to the media now, does it?"

"And Internal Affairs doesn't. I strongly suggest that you get out of my office, Thompson, right now. Before I throw you out."

"Elaine Hoffman," Thompson said again, as if the name were a password that Mondo hadn't heard the first time.

"You have some evidence against Detective Hoffman, bring it on. You want her transferred, pull your strings. You want to bring me up on charges, here I am. But you're going to have to do that shit in your own office, at your own desk." Mondo stood up and pushed his chair back with the back of his knees, for effect more than anything else.

He said, "But you *will* get your ass out of my office right this minute, Thompson."

Thompson didn't move; he seemed to be studying Mondo. He didn't seem worried or afraid; he seemed, rather, to be calculating, sizing Mondo up.

He said, "Jake Phillips is dirty, Mondo. He's filthy as a fucking sewer."

Mondo reached back without losing eye contact with the man, pulled his chair to him, then slowly sat back down. He pushed his cigarettes away from him and watched a look of relief pass across Thompson's face. He said, "You finally got around to what you came here to tell me in the first place. The 'higher plane.' " Mondo made sure that an attentive look was on his face when he said, "Tell me about it, if you would, please, Detective Thompson."

Jake walked out of the station house without checking back in with the bureau. He did this purposely, and for two specific reasons: so he could get his newfound information out to Anson as quickly as he could, and to avoid another confrontation with Mondo, not to mention the rest of the unit.

Jake didn't know how long he'd last with Special Victims now, nor did he know how much longer he really *wanted* to be a part of it. Everyone would know what had happened by now; the entire bureau would be united against him, would see him as a potential threat to their—and their unit's—status. What with the IAD investigation that had been going on for weeks now, and with the memory of Tony Tulio still fresh in their minds, the entire bureau had become keenly aware of how one loose cannon could sink the entire ship.

Jake, who at one time had been the heart and soul of the unit, was now seen as being that loose cannon.

Unbidden, Jake's thoughts retreated back to a scene that had occurred just a couple of years before, when on his very first night as a Homicide bull, he'd stormed into Captain Merlin Royal's office and demanded that he be transferred out of the Homicide department entirely. Because he refused to work with a lazy, drunken, hate-filled bigot by the name of Moore. Captain Royal had convinced him, in his not-so-subtle manner, that Homicide needed more men like Jake and less like Moore. Because of their conversation, Jake had stayed.

Now Jake tried to force the thoughts of that night out of his mind entirely; it was too much input for him to absorb; too much had changed, none of it for the good. He knew he had to stop thinking about it or, he knew, he'd break down.

Marsha had been right, of course. Jake had known it all along. He had joined the department to try and prove that a Phillips was worthy, to prove that one member of the family could wipe out another's sins. Two years ago, he'd have laughed at the suggestion that he'd give up Marsha, give up his daughter. He would have vowed to resign before losing all that.

And now look at him. Marsha was gone, his daughter too, and he was disgraced and dishonored in the eyes of his best friend.

Jake was walking through the alley that divided State Street from Wabash, suddenly noticing the strange looks he was getting from other officers. Jake pulled himself from his thoughts and headed for the parking lot when a familiar voice stopped him from behind.

"Sergeant?"

Jake turned and saw Dabney Delaney-Hinckle standing on

the other side of the alley, watching him closely and giving him plenty of space, as if she suspected she might need to flee for her life at any time.

Feeling much the same thing himself, Jake turned and hurried away from her.

"Sergeant?" she said again, her voice behind him now. There was a surprised quality to it that Jake couldn't figure out. What did *she* have to be surprised about? Jake didn't know; he just knew that he had to get away from her.

Other officers, mostly in uniform, were walking through the alley, heading from or into work. How did it get to be so late? Jake had blown the day. He felt himself shivering a little in spite of the intense heat. He looked up at the sun as he walked, as if wondering how it could make him so miserable. He felt an urge to vomit. The back of his legs were weak again; he was afraid they'd fold on him before he could reach his car.

He had his hand on his car door handle when Delaney-Hinckle covered it with her own. Jake stopped, shocked at her audacity, and turned his head to glare at her. She moved back a few inches, but her hand stayed where it was.

"That's battery, young lady. You want to try for assault as well?" Jake spoke the words, but without conviction. His voice was shaking; he feared a nervous breakdown.

Delaney-Hinckle removed her hand but stood so that he couldn't open the door without hitting her.

"The public has a right—" Jake tried to bluff his way through this by cutting her off. The last thing he needed in his life was this reporter stepping into it again.

"You see that big, ugly white building over there? That's the one, right next to the parking lot. It's called police headquarters. There's a press office somewhere inside there; the guard at the door'll tell you what floor it's on, as soon as you prove to his satisfaction that you're actually a reporter. The public can get its rights covered from in there. Now, you want to step out of my way, lady, or do I have to ask one of these officers to pinch you?"

"For what?"

"Officer! Hey, Officer!" Jake shouted it at one of the uniformed cops who was passing through the lot. The cop was at
least twenty years older than Jake, overweight and bald, and
now, at the end of a long shift on a hot day, he appeared tired, as
well as angry. There were large round wet spots under the arms
of his blue short-sleeve shirt. The officer paused, looked at Jake
with a "What the fuck do *you* want?" expression on his face,
then took a small step forward. Jake impatiently waved him
toward the car.

Delaney-Hinckle said, "Do you really want a witness when I
ask you what you were doing having a secret meeting with Al
Genco and Mike Anson this afternoon?" Jake looked at her,
stunned. He felt every last ounce of his energy evaporate. He
leaned, almost fell, against the side of the car, held on to it for
support. Delaney-Hinckle held her ground, a strange look
working its way onto her face. Jake lifted a feeble hand and
weakly waved the officer away. The officer shook his head,
grunted something, then turned and walked away. The reporter
stepped back, and Jake opened his door.

"Get away from me, right now." He could barely speak the
words.

"Right. I'm scared." She stopped and waited until Jake had
turned his head, was looking at her. "You promised me an
interview last night at the bar. I understand you'd really rather
not speak with me. The truth is, with all I've found out, I really
can't blame you. You want to tell me your side of the story,
Sergeant? The story's gonna go, one way or another."

Jake thought about this for a time, terror mounting within
him. If the two crooked cops had seen this woman snapping
pictures . . .

He made himself stop thinking about it; they hadn't seen her,
that was all there was to it. They couldn't have, and he could
prove it.

If they had seen her, he'd be dead by now; it was as simple as
that.

The only thing he had going for him was that one had nothing to do with the other; Genco and Anson had nothing to do with his divorce action or with his wife at all or with this woman's article for *Chicago Alive!* magazine. Jake almost grunted at the thought. The only thing he had going for him? He had absolutely nothing going for him. And he hadn't for some time. He'd been operating on instinct alone, trying to salvage something, and now, for the first time, it finally sunk in: he'd lost.

Trying to buy some time to think, Jake said, "You strike a hard bargain."

Delaney-Hinckle ignored him. She looked across the lot. "See that guy over there, on the other side of State Street?" Jake stepped back, as if she might strike out at him if he turned his back on her, then looked across the street, lifting a hand to his eyes to hide the bright sun. A man was standing in front of one of the cookie-cutter houses that had been put up a couple of years ago to house the yuppies who believed that living across from police headquarters would make them safer than the rest of the city. They bought into that without knowing that headquarters would be moving to the West Side before the end of this very year, before they found out that the subway would crack their foundations, causing their basements to flood.

The man across the street waved at Jake, then lifted a camera to his face and clicked away. The man was wearing a vest, despite the heat. The camera had a long, thick round lens attached to it; Jake could see that the camera was hanging from the man's neck by a long strap. The man lowered the camera and waved again. Jake, resigned, looked away.

He looked back at the reporter, at a complete loss for words. The sun seemed suddenly brighter, hotter; Jake was aware of the sweat pouring out of him. He wiped his brow, then shook his head, closed his eyes as he tried to think of a way out of this. Nothing came to him.

When the reporter spoke to him again, her voice, not at all unkind, came to him as if through a long, tin tunnel.

"I've got you in a box, Jake. He's got pictures of us together, with a time/date stamp on the film. If, God forbid, anything happens to me, those pictures wind up on the cover of *Chicago Alive!*"

Jake looked at her, shaking his head in disbelief.

"You think you're in *danger*? You think I'd . . . ?" Jake's voice trailed off. What did this woman believe him to be, some kind of monster? What had she been told? "You think . . . ?" he said again.

"You want to know what I think? I'll tell you what I think. I think it's time we talked."

"I don't," Jake said, and got into his car, slammed the door before she could grab at it, and locked the door.

Tommy Malardi stalked out of the elevator when it got to the floor where he'd parked the Buick—he'd remembered where he'd been by the little symbol of the Chicago Bears on the button, other floors having symbols from the White Sox, the Cubs, the Black Hawks, and the Bulls—and walked angrily toward the spot where he'd parked his car.

The car wasn't there. Tommy cursed aloud. His keys were in his hand and he thought, for just a second, about throwing them at the wall, then thought better of it and stood there, thinking.

Had he been on the Bears floor? Or the Cubs? Jesus Christ. Tommy shook his head, feeling pain in his hip, in his back. On the walk back here to the parking garage it seemed that everyone had been laughing at him, even the nigger derelicts. He had two grand in his pockets, *cash,* and a check for twenty thousand more. Why did what other people thought bother him so much?

Tommy felt a stabbing pain in his knee and winced. He cursed again and limped up the curving drive to the next level, to the Cubs level. He stopped and listened for the sound of a car coming down the ramp before he turned the corner, having been run down by enough cars for one day, and immediately heard the unmistakable sound of a police car radio coming from around the bend.

Tommy leaned against the wall in panic, then stuck his head cautiously around the bend.

There were two police cars parked on the level, blocking Rick's car completely. Tommy pulled his head back and breathed through his mouth. If he'd been hiding in the car with the damn thing running, he couldn't escape. Was it the window that had caught their attention? he wondered, then immediately rejected the notion. There were more cars with broken windows in this city, and too many twenty-four-hour coffee shops, for the coppers to be out paying any attention to a new Buick in a private lot with a single window missing.

That meant they were looking for him, specifically.

No, that meant they were looking for *Rick*!

Tommy didn't care one way or another if they were looking for Rick; it wasn't his problem; he had his money in his pocket. But he also had a torn-up shirt and pants and hands that were filthy and easily recognized. And he didn't need to be answering questions right now, not with the cash and the check in his pocket.

Tommy realized that if the cops left, they'd be coming down this ramp. By the same token, if another squad car came up, it would come up this same ramp and see him leaning against the wall like some kind of guilty asshole.

Tommy hurried away from the ramp, skipping the elevator completely and taking the stairs down to street level. By the time he hit the street, he was winded from fear as much as he was from the unaccustomed exertion. Tommy turned left on the street, away from the window to the parking garage. God knew what kind of camera hookups they might have watching the street. When he understood that he was home free, Tommy Malardi smiled.

He'd tell Rick where his car was parked and not tell him that the cops were watching it. Let that son of a bitch get pinched; see how he liked it, all the time looking down at Tommy. What did Tommy have to lose?

His gun, that's what. The thought intruded on his happy musings, and he stopped dead still on the street. His gun was in the trunk. He felt a surge of great relief when he realized that the gun couldn't be traced back to him. He was aware that the FBI couldn't get a good set of prints off a pebbled pistol grip, so the Chicago coppers probably wouldn't even check it. Probably one of the crooked bastards would just put it in his pocket, if they even found it.

Anyway, that was Rick's problem, not Tommy's, and he was smiling again as he walked down the street, then actually shook his head with mirth when he remembered that he'd fired a shot from the gun into the TV set at the fat guy's house last night. Seeing Rick get nailed for that would be worth the two-hundred-and-fifty bucks he'd paid for the gun on the street.

"The whole house of cards is collapsing around them, Mondo, and Phillips is going to be blown away with all of the other jokers."

"You have evidence of what you just told me, or is it just conjecture?"

"When I told you about the meet?" Thompson puffed out his cheeks and looked up at the ceiling, probably wondering how far he could go. "We've got sound and pictures. The coffee table was monitored from two angles, and there were three separate wires running."

"One, no doubt, attached to a man."

"No doubt." Mondo had to once more hide his anger at Thompson's little bitchy smile. The window air conditioner seemed to be working too hard for the room; Mondo had a chill he couldn't get rid of.

He watched Thompson carefully as he said, "You certain that Jake wasn't the guy wearing the wire?" He held his hand up to stop Thompson's expected argument. "I'm not calling you a liar or questioning your ethics. But it wouldn't be the first time one of your units didn't know what a different one was up to. As close as you guys play your cards to your vests. Jake might have called a—"

"Stop grasping at straws, Mondo. Phillips is dirty, and I think we both know it."

"So why are you telling me this? What purpose could it serve?"

"Just one. We know all about your conversation with Merlin Royal—"

"How did you . . . ?" Mondo shut his mouth hard when he understood how they could know; the captain's room had been wired. Mondo sat perfectly still and had to physically force himself not to glare at the man. The captain's office was police department property; they could do anything they wanted to it, wire it, monitor it for video and sound, give it to somebody else if they wanted to; there were no reasonable expectations for privacy. What bothered him most was the fact that they'd more than likely put their surveillance together while the captain had been trapped inside an MRI machine; tiny coffins had been encircling him, in fact as well as metaphor.

"We knew, too, that you wouldn't put Phillips on the Duette case, that you'd resign rather than do something you were absolutely convinced was against the best interest of your bureau."

"And you came in here to try and convince me to do the right thing."

"I wanted to, in a different manner. You made that somewhat difficult."

"You've got Genco and Anson for murder, what more do you need?"

"We're not Homicide, Mondo; we don't actually give a shit if Genco and Anson whacked Duette, except for the fact that it's more evidence to hang them with."

"What *do* you care about?"

"This department, goddamnit, that's what I care about!"

Thompson's sudden flash of anger surprised Mondo; he couldn't keep the shock off his face, and he knew it, and knew that Thompson saw it.

"What do you think, we join IAD for the hell of it, because we en*joy* investigating and sometimes arresting other officers? There're officers like that, of course there are; I wouldn't pretend otherwise. The same way there are guys like Phillips in the Special Victims Bureau."

"Phillips was a good cop, Thompson, one of the best I'd ever known in my career."

"But he's not anymore, is he, Mondo? And if we don't stop him, who will?" Thompson leaned forward and made a reflexive gesture toward the desk. It took Mondo a moment to understand what the man had done: he had been reaching for the cigarettes. Thompson looked at Mondo guiltily.

"I quit last March. Sometimes it's hard."

"I'd imagine."

"You can put all the irony you want into your voice, Mondo, but let me ask you one question: if I hadn't told you about Jake, if the captain hadn't said what he did, what would you have done? What would you have wound up doing about the kid?"

Mondo averted his eyes, then looked quickly back at Thompson. "What are you, afraid that your body language is giving you away? Answer my question, please, Mondo. What would you have done?" Thompson didn't know it, but his words had eased Mondo's mind; he hadn't known what had been discussed in this office earlier; Mondo's office wasn't wired.

Mondo said, "I'd have transferred him out of the unit."

"Phillips is a risk to more than your bureau, Mondo!"

"How many other coppers could you make a case against if

you wanted to, Thompson? I don't mean for drinking; I mean for anything at all. If you taped their phone conversations, followed them around the clock, checked their backgrounds, talked to extended family, neighbors, kids they went to school with? How many could you set up and throw off the force?"

"Probably five-eighths."

Mondo didn't say a word.

"But this isn't some bullshit setup, is it, Mondo? This is a guy we *know* is dirty, a guy we *know* meets with other dirty cops."

Mondo said the only thing that came to mind. "Is the captain—?" Mondo raised his hands, palms open. He couldn't bring himself to voice his suspicions.

"That's not a topic of conversation."

Mondo changed his tack. "How badly is Special Victims going to get bruised?"

"Not at all. We know you're clean, and there's nothing against any of the other members in your squad. Believe me, we checked."

"Pretty thoroughly."

Thompson got it right away. "What goes on between you and Hoffman after hours is not our concern here."

"But you'd use it as a wedge if you had to."

"I'd have used it as a hammer, if I'd had no other choice."

"Then what *is* the concern here?"

"When the . . . time comes . . . Phillips won't be identified by us as a member of anything other than Homicide—as far as we're concerned, that's what he is, and that's *all* he is. You're doing good work here, you and your team. There's no reason to try and put a stop to that."

"But all that's subject to change if I don't put Phillips on the Duette case, exclusively."

"We want all the evidence we can get against him and his newfound pals. Listen, Mondo, why do you think I'm here? We don't *need* Phillips on the Duette case; we've got a deathbed confession, on tape! Poor copies, yeah, but we got Phillips saying he's keeping the tape, more than likely to play for Lemelli, to jack up his price. We've got an accomplice, an inside guy. We've *got* them, cold! And Phillips along with them. At the very least, he conspired to conceal evidence of a homicide; whether he was once a good cop or not is immaterial, after he crossed that line."

"How long before you drop the net?"

"One day. I can't tell you what we're waiting for; that's privileged. But tomorrow morning, tomorrow afternoon at the latest, we close it down. We'd like to wait longer, but the publicity on this thing . . ." Thompson made a gesture, as if Mondo should understand such things.

Mondo shook his head. What he was hearing made sense, but it didn't lessen the pain. When Thompson spoke this time, his voice was low, with a hint of concern. Mondo would have rather had the guy be cold and hard.

"It's over for Phillips, Mondo; you have to understand that. Like I said, the house of cards is collapsing. The noose is gonna tighten quick, and a lot of dirty cops are going to feel the squeeze."

"What tightens the noose?"

"We have a—someone on the inside. We've got two cops with direct links to the head of the Chicago outfit, one of whom will soon be under twenty-four-hour surveillance; the other one we're picking up"—Thompson looked at his watch— "right about now. We need them, one of them, on tape, taking orders from the guy, explaining things to him. To Lemelli, I'm talking about. We've got someone else—let's just say that someone's about to go into protective custody, as soon as we're ready. That could work for us or against us. He—or she—came to us, so it'll go easier for . . . him or her. If it's a double play, if he's working both sides of the street, we'll know about it, the second Genco's scooped up." Thompson shrugged.

"It's in their hands, not ours. Personally, I'd like to wait a month, two months, see what swims into the net." Thompson sighed, as if he were about to give up more information than he'd prefer. He said, "There's going to be a meet tomorrow. Early. As soon as it's over, we make our move."

"And Jake goes to Stateville."

"Not for very long, I wouldn't think. It was his choice, Mondo." Thompson was warming up to him, Mondo could tell. He also knew that the man wouldn't even be here if they thought for a second that Mondo would tell Jake he was in trouble or was otherwise dirty in any way at all. So they trusted him. Big deal. He'd worked for twenty years to be trusted by men like this? He knew he should be flattered, maybe even relieved, but the only emotion he could work up at the moment was anger, tinged with disgust.

"It's a game, Mondo, and you know that as well as I do; you're as media savvy as we are; you know about the show. The six o'clock news, remember? We don't want them spreading bad stories about us; it's all got to be positive, or as positive as we can make it. We have to show the public how well we can police ourselves. If we don't, they'll demand that others do it, and nobody wants that."

"And some mixed-up kid who got in over his head goes down as hard as the guys who killed Duette."

"Oh, not at all. They're going down for first-degree *murder*, Mondo. Jake'll get his ass tainted with the same brush, absolutely, but he should come out of this with an agreement, with a plea. Listen, Mondo, look at it this way. The guy just turned out to be more like his father than anyone could ever have guessed."

Mondo looked at Thompson, at last understanding the reason for this meeting.

"You want me to convince Jake to come over with you guys."

"When the time's right. It's the only way he can avoid doing time, Mondo."

"How about disgrace?"

"He brought that on himself when he went over to the other side."

"And the guy . . . inside? He might be one of the killers, but you'll pretend that he came to you, turn him into a hero."

"Hey, what can I tell you? You know as well as I do that problems like this don't get solved without a snitch you have to look out for."

Mondo began to smile as he figured out what Thompson was saying. "Your snitch won't be able to tape Lemelli, will he? You need Jake for corroboration, don't you, Thompson?"

Thompson didn't seemed upset that Mondo had figured him out. He probably thought he'd orchestrated the entire thing. He said, "We have to have him, Mondo. Our intelligence tells us that there will be a meeting with Lemelli tomorrow morning, in the swimming pool in Lemelli's basement. We can't get in there, the feds can't get in there, the Organized Crime Task Force can't get in there. We'll have our . . . man . . . somewhere on the premises, but we'll need Jake for the corroboration, yes." Thompson flashed his grin. "Maybe for more than that."

"Do two things for me, Thompson," Mondo said, and the detective raised his eyebrows at the soft tone of voice, the sincerity in Mondo's tone. He nodded.

"First, save your bullshit for the press conference, and second, got out of my office."

Thompson's beeper went off as Mondo spoke his final word. He tore it from his belt, looked at it, made a disgusted face, walked over to the desk, grabbed Mondo's phone, and turned it toward him without bothering to ask for permission. He punched in a four-digit number, calling somewhere in the building. Mondo heard only his side of the conversation, with appropriate pauses between his words.

Thompson identified himself curtly, then asked what was wrong. Then he got all surprised, shook his head in disbelief. He said, "He did *what*? Goddamnit, you were supposed to pick him up at the station!" Thompson called someone a dirty cocksucker, a stupid motherfucker. Then he told whoever he was talking to to pick the kid's ass up, to get the nephew into protective custody, right this second. And to get the—

Thompson paused briefly to look at Mondo, then said to grab the *other* guy off the street, right now. As careful as he was to watch what he'd said, his next sentence betrayed the topic of conversation.

"Shoot Anson down, if you have to," Thompson said. "He's the one who's the brains; he's more dangerous than Genco, for God's sake!" Thompson paused. "What? We *got* the nephew? Thank God. All right, start debriefing him." Then Thompson said he'd be right there to coordinate it, then slammed Mondo's phone down and stalked out of the room without a backward glance.

A lfonse Genco walked into the station house ten minutes before the start of his tour and was instinctively aware of two things right away: something heavy was going down, and its objective was to destroy him. He kept getting all these mean, obvious looks from people, not the usual furtive glances he'd sometimes get, looks that shifted away when Genco met them with his own probing, steady gaze; this time the observers were glaring, and they didn't care if he noticed them.

Oh, Jesus.

Who knew how much? Did anyone know *any*thing? Or was it all just speculation due to somebody in IAD asking around about him again? Genco had had plenty of *that* before.

Something in the way all these coppers were glaring at him told Genco that it went deeper than that this time. A whole lot deeper.

How deep? Genco didn't know and couldn't tell. He hadn't had his ear to the ground all day, before he'd even met with Anson, before he'd fucked up with Lemelli listening, and he knew now that that had been a mistake. He'd talked on the phone too much.

Genco absently flexed his bruised knuckles. There were cuts on several of them. Would there be DNA evidence linking him to the murder?

Dear God in heaven, Genco wondered now, how could be have been so stupid as to go off on Lemelli like that in front of Anson? He'd been trying to put the guy in his place, that's all, show him who was boss. He hadn't ever thought in a million years that Anson was the sort of slick operator who could outthink a man like himself.

And how could he have been so stupid as to bring Duette into this building? He hadn't intended to kill the kid, had only wanted to beat a confession out of him, and what better place was there to do that than in the basement of a police district building? How was he to know that Duette wouldn't crack? Hell, when he'd still been a detective, he'd gotten hundreds of confessions out of thieves, rapists, and killers without expending half the energy that he had with this guy, Duette. It was the man's own fault. If he'd gone along with the program, he'd be alive today. In horrific pain, probably, with Lemelli's men removing his skin inch by inch, but still, alive.

And he wouldn't be Genco's problem. Genco wouldn't have had to dump the body; he wouldn't have had to worry about a couple of winos seeing him; he wouldn't have had to worry about front-page headlines wondering if the police had tortured some poor son of a bitch of a thief. Why had he done it? What had caused him to be so dense?

Genco knew that greed had caused him to do it. Greed and the fact that he'd been left alone for so long now by his superiors that he'd once again grown arrogant.

Genco wandered over to the pay phone attached to the wall, next to the double front doors, dropped in his thirty cents, and checked for messages on his private voice mail line. There were none, which caused him concern. Usually, by this time of day, there'd be *something,* from any number of connections, people who wanted things from him, who wanted to do things for him. Now, suddenly, all was quiet. This did not bode well for him, particularly in light of what had happened last night. He'd been hoping against hope that at least Anson would have left a message, trying to set up a meet, looking to reconcile with him.

All right. It was all over for him. It wasn't as if he hadn't seen it coming.

Genco hung up the phone, looked at his feet, and thought with a ferocity that no one who had ever known him would ever have suspected him of possessing. How bad would it be this time? If he was indeed under suspicion, how bad could it possibly be?

Genco had been investigated a great number of times over the course of his long career. He'd been officially suspended twice, and even fired on one occasion, back in the early seventies, when the first Mayor Daley had brought in yet a new police superintendent from out of state, a superintendent who'd been authorized to pursue a thorough cleaning of the department's house. It had taken three long years of court battles, but Genco had at last been reinstated, with full back pay, after a federal judge had thrown his firing out on an obscure but important technicality.

After that, Genco, having learned his lesson, became far more cautious. At least, he had been until last night. And this afternoon, Jesus Christ, what had he been thinking? Up until the time he'd been fired he'd been blatant, abusing his power and authority with abandon, with the knowledge that certain high-ranking members of the department—in collaboration with the outfit—were looking out for his best interests. Since then, until last night, he'd been far more careful.

Which didn't mean that they'd stopped watching him, waiting for him to fuck up.

He'd been investigated when he'd been promoted to sergeant—and not all that much later to lieutenant—above other candidates who'd been far more educated and better qualified, and he had again and again wound up being cleared of any impropriety, because of lack of proof that strings had been pulled to ensure his career success. He knew that none of the other dirty police officers in the department—some of whom held very high rank—would ever do anything to stop him; they needed all the loyal and trustworthy help they could get if they were to make all the money that was available to them. And back in those days, the outfit had had a lot more power than it did now, and none of its leaders had ever been known for speaking freely and openly with investigative deputies from any federal or local police agencies, let alone Chicago's.

Not that it never happened, but it never happened the way the straight, untainted officers might have wished; more than one crook had curried favor with certain members of the department by dropping tidbits that couldn't hurt them into the ears of favored detectives. Usually this happened when someone was muscling into their turf; a call would be made, a raid approved, and the outfit honcho's competition was removed without savagery or bloodshed.

The older outfit leaders had learned, through the eight decades of their dominance over the citizens of Chicago, that they could operate more efficiently and profitably without attention from the press or the public. The old-timers had learned to get their way quietly, using legitimate operatives as their surrogates.

Genco had often been the copper who'd been used in such a manner. It had made him, throughout the years, a very rich and powerful man. He knew that there were others far above him whose character and belief in the law was above any taint of reproach. They had been the ones who had pushed for Genco's removal and, once stymied, had done everything in their power to render him otherwise ineffective.

But they'd never gotten him out of Homicide, and he knew how that had to irk them. Now they'd seen their chance, and they were taking it, as Anson had.

He had to close his eyes a minute to clear his mind of

thoughts of Anson. If it took him forever, he would kill that man. Genco opened his eyes.

On the positive side, as far as he was concerned, after serving two suspensions (with pay) and being reinstated after his firing, Genco had come to something of an agreement with the hierarchy of the department. He wouldn't embarrass it, and they wouldn't keep trying to fire him.

And, geniuses that they were, they'd thought that making him an administrator would somehow stifle his larcenous urges, or at least the opportunities to capitalize on them.

As usual, they'd been wrong.

Nor had they—or the passage of time—subsumed his keen survival instincts. Genco felt them turned all the way on now, knew without doubt that something vicious was in the wind, something that stunk horribly and had his name attached to its toe.

He realized that he'd been staring at the floor long enough to have attracted even more attention than he'd been getting. Genco looked up, around, then walked through the lobby past the sergeant's desk and over to the old stairway, feeling a great number of eyes on his back, feeling the hair on his neck sticking out, giving him warning. He had a nearly violent urge to defecate.

He knew without doubt that someone was waiting for him upstairs in the Homicide squad room, more than likely behind his desk. He knew it without having to think. IAD, the Office of Professional Standards, maybe even a couple of Homicide bulls, Genco didn't know who, but he knew, he *knew*, that someone was up there, and they were up there with handcuffs, maybe even a signed warrant.

His ass had not only been caught this time, but caught in a trap from which there might be no escape. God*damn* Duette. Why had he had to spit on him?

Genco put his hand on the stairway railing, put his foot on the first step, as if preparing to climb them up to his office. He suddenly removed his hand and foot, snapped his fingers, then turned around and began to walk back the way he'd come, as if heading back to his car, as if he'd forgotten something important that he'd left inside his vehicle and was now going back to get it. He shook his head at his own stupidity and even smiled ruefully, his head down, his hands in his pockets. A nonthreatening, middle-aged police officer just heading out of the building for a minute. Or two.

Or maybe for the rest of his life.

He shouldn't have brought Duette here. He shouldn't have trusted Anson's word that the man was dead. He shouldn't have taken the body out of the station house basement without making sure that there was no life left within it.

Genco wasn't the type to make foolish mistakes, and he cursed himself for them now as, sweating even more profusely than the midafternoon heat called for, he hurried down the sidewalk, over to the manned parking lot across the street from the station.

He should have made good and damn sure that the man was dead. He should have—should have nothing.

Now that he thought about it, he realized that he shouldn't have done any of it. How badly did they have him? How tight was their net? Could he beat it again? Did he have one more victory in him? Genco thought about these things as he waved casually to the uniformed guard who was stationed inside a small air-conditioned booth to watch the cars of police officers, in a lot where the cars had been vandalized so often that the guard's hiring had been mandated. Genco made sure there was a smile on his face as he walked slowly to his car, got in, started it up, and drove off without undue delay.

The outfit, which he'd served throughout his career, was nowhere near as powerful as it used to be; the old guys had either died off or been shipped to various federal penitentiaries. They left guys like Lemelli in charge, guys who didn't have the intelligence, the wisdom, the experience, or the patience to think things through before acting on them, guys who let their egos dictate their conduct.

As Lemelli had done after somebody had robbed him.

Nobody knew who had done it, but there were grave suspicions about Jimmy Duette; suspicions, and that was all. Strong enough to get him alone and ask him a few questions, that's all. Who'd have thought that he'd refuse to answer any questions? That Genco would have to do what he had done? The kid had wasted the whole ride to the station demanding to speak to his lawyer. By the time he'd understood what was probably going to happen to him, he'd dried up, lost his voice.

The cat had got his tongue, and Genco, try as he might, couldn't manage to pry it loose.

And now this. Over what? Over who? What was Duette? A nobody, that's what he was.

The world wouldn't miss Duette; world, hell, Genco thought as he drove the speed limit down Ninety-fifth Street, heading for the expressway. Duette's own wife more than likely wouldn't miss him. A wave of self-pity engulfed Genco now as he thought of everything he was giving up and what he was losing it over. He sniffed back tears as he pulled onto the entrance ramp, then waited impatiently for the red merge light to change to green.

A horn honked behind him. Genco looked in his rearview mirror, then looked back at the light, saw that it had switched to green without his even having noticed. He took his foot off the brake and drove carefully down the ramp, merged into the dense early rush-hour traffic, heading north, aware of his ultimate destination, and knowing he'd probably have to be very lucky to get there.

What was he supposed to have done? What else *could* he have done, not accept the ten percent fee for finding and returning Lemelli's money? The hundred thousand *dollars* that somebody had stolen from Lemelli's vault? It was an open contract, for Christ's sake; anyone could have collected it. And how many people, how many cops, even, would have been honorable enough to turn the money in, if they found it? Hell, Genco might even be the only one left with that sort of honesty inside him. He'd settle for ten percent and return the rest, and Lemelli knew it, which was why he'd personally sent for Genco in the first place.

No matter how Lemelli might be feeling about him now, the man had known that for ten percent of a hundred thousand dollars, Genco would kill, gut, clean, cook, and eat one of his own grandchildren. But he'd give back the rest of the money; and Lemelli, even a lowlife, small-time, hateful dummy like Lemelli would have to respect that.

Even with the windows up and the air conditioning blasting, Genco heard the symphonic car horn, and it shocked him enough to look over. A Lexus had pulled up alongside him, the driver shouting something at him, waving his hand around in Genco's direction. What the fuck was *his* problem? Genco looked over again, and the guy was still shouting to himself and waving his hand around.

No white man could be this stupid. Genco thought he knew what was going on, and shook his head in dismay. He must have cut the guy off. Jesus, some people just couldn't wait to die. But no, that couldn't be. Genco had done nothing to cause the man's ire. He'd been in the middle lane since merging into traffic; he was driving the speed limit. He briefly flirted with the idea of pulling his gun and pointing it at the guy, and would have if everyone and his brother didn't have a car phone hooked up these days.

Genco ignored the man; he didn't have time for this. The expressway was ending and his Cermak Road exit was right around the next turn. Genco flicked on his right blinker, got over into the far right lane. He had to wait at the stoplight dividing Chinatown for a couple of minutes, until he got the arrow. When he turned onto Twenty-second Street, he heard a horn honk again. Genco looked into his rearview mirror and saw that the Lexus had stayed with him, was now almost kissing his bumper.

J ake pulled over to the curb in front of the Metropolitan Building and waved casually to George, the doorman, who was
standing just inside the air-conditioned lobby, carefully watching the street. He left the car running so the air conditioner
would keep him cool, then unfastened his belt, wondering how
long he had left to operate.

He ignored the passersby, the rush-hour walkers, hurrying
down Dearborn. He jumped when one of them tapped on his
passenger-side window.

Jake sat looking at Marsha. She looked at him. He somehow
managed to nod.

Jake unclipped his holster and shield from his belt, placed
them under the seat. There was an immediate sense of relief
when he removed the two items that used to lift him up but
now seemed only to be dragging him down.

He was feeling a near calmness, a relaxed sense that came
with this loss of control. Marsha was there, watching him. Jake
shut off the car.

It was all out of his hands now; he knew what he had to do.
He looked over at his wife, stepped out of the car.

"Hi." Marsha seemed bashful, timid. Jake walked around to
where she was, stood on the curb, wanting to grab her, wanting
to hold her.

She said, "I got a little upset this afternoon."

"It was my fault."

"No."

They looked at each other for a moment.

"You want to come upstairs?"

"I was thinking more of a walk?"

Jake asked Marsha if she was hungry, and she looked at him so strangely that he couldn't help but smile.

Genco waited until he was on Wabash, then pulled over to the curb in front of the liquor store, pulled his weapon, and waited. He watched in his rearview mirror as the man in the Lexus got out of the car, both hands held out in front of him in some sort of *take it easy* gesture. The man took off his sunglasses, stopped, then took a small, hesitant step toward Genco's car. Genco shook his head, put his pistol away, and got out of the car.

"I thought you guineas all drove Lincolns," he said, and the man winced but controlled himself quickly.

"I didn't think you recognized me." He flashed a quick guinea smile. "What's the matter, you don't remember your own people anymore?"

"You ain't my people."

The man ignored the insult. Genco had recognized him as one of Lemelli's sycophants the second the guy had taken off his sunglasses, but for the life of him, he couldn't remember the guy's name. What Genco wanted to know was, why was he following him, and when had he gotten onto him?

"You insult your own people, too. What's this 'guinea' shit? You ain't Italian no more?"

Genco pushed for a confrontation; he might not have been able to say anything to Lemelli, but he could take his anger out on this small-level hood in front of him. What did he have to lose? It was all over for him, anyway, with Lemelli, with the department. He said, "I got about as much in common with you as I do with all 'a these niggers walking up and down this sidewalk."

The man winced again as he seemed to notice for the first time the hordes of black people heading into, from, and hanging around the liquor store. He made a cutting gesture with his hand, which Genco ignored.

Genco said, "What were you, waiting for me back at the station?"

"I was heading toward the station house at the same time you were leaving, I was coming to see you."

"You forget about phones, beepers?"

"I forgot about a lot of stuff since early this afternoon. Listen, you should be fucking grateful I went to all the trouble I did."

"Tell me why."

"On account of even though you're out, the Man wants to look out for you. You met today with two men in a restaurant; one of them was wired, audio and video, and it wasn't the first time they got you on tape. That's what I was told to tell you."

Genco took an involuntary step back. As soon as he did, he knew he'd lost whatever advantage he'd had over this man, but he couldn't stop himself. The words had struck him like a hammer.

"You sure of this?"

"Absolutely certain."

Genco shook his head bitterly. "That fuckin' kid, that fuckin' *punk*! It was that Phillips kid, wasn't it? Jackie's kid was the rat."

"That I couldn't tell you. All I know for sure, Al, is that the Man himself took a phone call this afternoon." He paused for effect, and when Genco didn't respond, he said, "The Man, he don't take phone calls, from nobody, never. You ever talk to him on the phone? No. *He* calls *you;* he don't *never* let you call him. So's, anyways, he takes *this* call, like he's expecting it? Next thing you know, he's having a coronary, making other calls, setting things up, and then he sends me out to warn you."

"Warn me about *what*?" Genco said. Although he knew, he still had to ask.

"You're caught, Al. IAD's onto you; they know everything, and the trap's sprung. They got the kid that played lookout for you last night, too; he's getting sweated right now, down at the Fourth District."

"You got to be shitting me!"

"I wish I was. They got the insider, and the kid, and now they're coming after you."

"I knew it."

"But I got a way out for you."

Genco's eyes narrowed. He'd just bet this guy did. He looked around the street again, as if shocked. He shook his head. He said, "Come on. I was going over to my storage box. You come along with me and tell me all about it in there."

The man seemed relieved. "Jesus, I thought you'd never ask. I get nervous around all these *tuitsoons,* you know? You want to take the Lexus? No offense, but it's a better ride all the way around, Al."

Kevin Wrisberg sat in the chair, his weapon in his hand, wondering how everything could get so fucked up. Hadn't he been the Man just a few short years ago? He shook his head bitterly. Young niggers come up, they got no respect for nothing or nobody. Don't care what you organized, what you put together. They see *Scarface* one time, and they all want to take over.

He couldn't believe the run of bad luck he'd been having lately.

First, the barely teenaged gangbangers had taken over the South Side after the old-timers got political and put their operations undercover while they tried to win hearts, minds, and paroles by convincing everybody they were legitimate voters' organizations now, rather than drug-dealing killers. When this had first happened, Wrisberg had been in his glory. The less they took for themselves, the more there was for him.

What none of them had counted on was the kids, who didn't give a fuck.

He knew all about them now; now he had big trouble with them; they were going to kill him, if they could. Wrisberg's once-powerful organization was in shambles, his men either joining up with the newly enlightened 'politicians' or joining forces with the kids, who were too dumb to stop them from stealing them blind as long as they kissed the leaders' asses and called them "king" or "prince." Either way, no matter how you looked at it, Wrisberg came out on the short end.

Even the deal, the peace he himself had helped to negotiate years ago with the dagos, that was dead now, history. One of the men he'd gotten to know back then, a man he had still been paying money to every other week so that the dagos would leave him alone, had told him how the old man kept a half a million dollars, cash, in a vault in his basement. Man swore he'd seen the money counted, knew how much was there. Wrisberg grunted at the memory. Half a million, his black ass.

He'd organized the robbery, set it up, had negotiated a four-way split, and what happens? They get lucky enough to pull it off because the old man, in his arrogance, let his security go to hell, and it winds up there's only a hundred grand in the safe. A lousy hundred grand. His connection within the outfit had disappeared, and Wrisberg had assumed that he was dead or in hiding, one, so where had that left him? Wondering if the dude had given him up, that's where.

He goes to ground and minds his own business, keeps his eyes and ears open, and the next thing you know, his man Duette turns up dead on a golf course. Well, that's what the damn media said, but as usual, they'd gotten it all wrong. Duette hadn't been dead, at least not at the time the radio had said he was. And Duette damn sure hadn't been dead when Wrisberg had told Rick that he was.

But still, the radio report had given Wrisberg ideas. With the dago gone, dead, or in hiding, and Duette dead as well, there were only two of them left, he and Rick. Rick and Duette, together or alone—it would have been impossible to kill either or both of them. They weren't friends, asshole buddies, but they had the old-timer's code. Kill or rob one, and the other comes looking for you, and if one of them had turned up dead in any other way, shit, Wrisberg would have been a candidate to join the dead one right quick.

But with the crazy hillbilly gone, with Duette out of the picture? What did he have to lose? Nothing, that's what. Killing Rick had left him with the entire hundred grand for himself. And the chance to get a fifth of that amount back again, if Rick's cuz had come through.

Big, ugly, dumb, but strong. That's how Rick had described his cousin. A stand-up guy. Well, he'd soon see. Ingram couldn't have come up with the money if you'd handed the punk an Uzi; he just didn't have it in him to go out and hurt somebody. Tommy, on the other hand, if you let him get the drop on you? Wrisberg had known men like Tommy before, and he winced as he thought of what they could do when given their head, some authority.

He heard a key in the lock and stood up, his weapon in his hand, ready. About time, he thought. Spent the morning calling the motherfucker and being ignored for the effort. When Tommy walked into his apartment, Kevin lifted the gun and waited.

Genco had left his car on the corner in front of the liquor store—it was also directly across the street from the Harold Ickes public housing project. When the cops found it—if they found it—they would think that some nigger from the projects had stolen it. If he got real lucky, they might even put it together that Genco was dead, had been killed in a carjacking. At least he hoped they would draw that inference. It would give Genco more time to set his long-term plan into motion.

But that was for later. At the moment, he had a short-term plan to work on.

The mob underling had finally figured out that Genco didn't

know his name, and had made sure that Genco knew it. He'd told Genco that Lemelli had told him, "Joey, go and talk to the guy; tell him the plan, how we're going to look out for him." The son of a bitch probably thought he was being diplomatic.

As for Lemelli's plan, Genco by far preferred his own. But he didn't interrupt Joey as the man steered his Lexus down Wabash Avenue, listened but didn't pay much attention to his words or his ingratiating manner; Joey was here to kill him, or at the very least he'd been sent to set Genco up for a hit. That wasn't the sort of behavior that Genco looked for in a man when seeking a pal.

So Genco said nothing as he took off his tie and slipped out of his sport coat, took his time turning around in the seat, then tossed them casually onto the backseat of the Lexus. He wanted this man at ease, wanted him relaxed, thinking Genco believed him.

"Look less like a cop that way. Christ," Genco said, "they're probably scouring the city for me right now."

Genco didn't turn to face Joey, just looked through the windshield, wearing his short-sleeve sport shirt, knowing he had some time. If this Joey had been sent to murder him, he wouldn't do it in his own car; he would wait for a better opportunity.

Such as inside the storage warehouse.

Joey would now likely believe that Genco trusted him; if he didn't, Genco would never have turned his back on him, as he had when he'd put his tie and jacket in back. To make Joey feel even more at ease, Genco unclipped his weapon and shield, held them in one hand as he leaned forward and snatched his handcuffs off the back of his belt. He turned his back on Joey again, climbed up onto his knees, then leaned over and placed the items on the floor in the back, covering them carefully with the sport coat.

"We got a boat going out of the Series terminal on Ninety-fifth Street, leaving for Corona at midnight."

"Corona?"

"Ever been there?" Joey seemed truly interested. Genco

shook his head. "You don't know what you're missing; you'll love it, believe me."

"See that building up ahead?"

"Uh—the one that has STORAGE written in gigantic letters on the side? The only fucking building on the block, Al?"

Genco grunted a laugh. "That's the one." Joey drove up to it, parked right in front of the place. "Hard to believe all the parking spaces they got on the South Side, huh?"

"Yeah, well," Joey said, looking around a little nervously, "it don't exactly look like a residential area."

"Kind of desolate, ain't it? Wait here; I'll just be in there a couple of minutes."

"Al, wait a second, can I talk to you before you go in there?"

Genco tensed. Had he been wrong? Jesus Christ, maybe they all *did* drive Lincolns, and this Lexus was stolen, a hit car that Joey would leave his body in as a public warning to others. He tried to keep the fear off his face as he let go of the door handle and turned to face Joey.

But Joey didn't have a gun in his hands. If fact, he looked a little uncomfortable, somewhat sheepish, when he said, "Al, this deal, well, the thing of it is, let me just blurt this out. Before . . . what happened today . . . you were always good to us, to Mr. Lemelli, you know what I'm saying? Which is why he's doing this for you, in spite of everything. And I don't want to insult you, but he told me, I mean, he *ordered* me, Al, to stick with you like a second cock, to not leave your side until you're safe on the boat to Corona."

"What if I got to go to the bathroom?"

"Al, he even addressed that issue, honest to God. You want me to tell you what he said?"

"Nah," Genco said, vastly relieved, as he turned to the door again and added, "I appreciate his concern." He closed his eyes as he opened the door; if it was going to happen, it would happen now. He said, "Come on, let's get in there. It'll only take a minute."

* * *

Genco was stepping over a huge slab of broken sidewalk, checking carefully to make sure no snakes were hiding under it, when he heard the beep which signified that Joey had set the car's alarm. Which meant that it more than likely *was* Joey's car. Hell, who'd go to all the trouble of stealing a Lexus to go out on a hit? You'd use a Ford or a Chevy, a car that fit in, something no one would look at twice. He had his keys in his hand, ready, and he kept his back to Joey. He wondered if this Corona deal was legit. He wondered where the hell Corona was, what country it was in. He couldn't take the chance that it was; he couldn't consider that for a minute.

"I didn't believe there was this much empty space *left* in this city!" Genco put the key in the lock of the heavy steel fire door, turned it, leaned on the handle, and stepped inside. He turned to see Joey standing on the sidewalk with his hands on his hips, his suit coat pushed back, looking around in wonder at the empty garbage-strewn lots, the block of prairie that surrounded them. Genco took the moment to see if he could spot a weapon anywhere on the man. He didn't see one, which didn't mean Joey wasn't packing.

He said, "The garboons don't take over until dark. You want to come inside, or you gonna wait out here?"

"I'm comin', I'm comin'."

Joey stepped inside. Genco made him hold the door open so he could see what he was doing when he unlocked the second, inner, steel security door.

"Got enough protection in here, you think?"

"Not enough to keep the cheapskates who keep their shit in here from stealing the fuckin' lightbulbs." Genco pushed the second door open and told Joey to lock the first door behind him, then waited as Joey did so. Joey came through the second door, and Genco locked this one, too, as soon as Joey cleared it.

"Nobody's here?"

"They sell space, not attentive service. And they got no heat or cooling except for what seeps in through the bricks from the outside. You want it, you got to provide it yourself. And good luck putting an air conditioner in a room that ain't got no windows or electrical outlets. Keeps people from moving in, I guess is their reasoning."

"Moving in *here*?" Joey said, as he followed Genco down a hallway that had steel doors on either side, set only a few feet apart. There were bare lightbulbs hanging from wires in front of every door. Maybe half of them hadn't been stolen. If the door had little glass windows, the place would have looked like the underground solitary confinement area at Marion penitentiary, only a lot dirtier. "Where would you piss?"

Genco shook his head as he walked ahead of Joey, feeling the hairs on the back of his head stand up. It was crucial that the man think Genco trusted him for a few more seconds, but still, he hated having his back turned to a guy like Joey. At last, Genco stopped at a door that was midway down the hall, squinted as he looked for the right key. He said, "Where would you comb your hair, brush your teeth?" He turned the key in the lock, pulled the heavy door toward him. "Where would you keep your bottle of Aramis?"

"You takin' a cheap shot at me?" Joey said, and Genco came at him with the baseball bat that he kept just inside the door, swung from the floor with one hand and hit Joey as hard as he could in the kneecap, then stepped back, breathing heavily, as Joey fell to the floor, his screams echoing against steel and brick, unheard by anyone but Genco.

"No." Genco said, when Joey had stopped screaming. He took a two-handed grip on the bat and hit Joey in the other kneecap. "*That's* a cheap shot." Joey didn't respond. Joey had passed out.

Genco patted him down quickly, took the little .380 out of the belt holster that was shoved down his pants in back, then left him there, walked into the storage space, the gun in one hand, the baseball bat in the other.

Over the years, Genco had stashed three-quarters of a million dollars in here, along with a passport, a driver's license, a Social Security card, and various other forms of identification, all under the same assumed name. It was his getaway money, a way for him to escape the country if the heat ever came down, give him a chance to get away and wait for his wife to come and join him, and not in Corona, either.

Three-quarters of a million dollars, in a safe inside a burglar-proof storage space, surrounded by emptiness in the ugly part of the South Side. No bank security boxes for him, for the feds to find. A lifetime of stealing was all in here.

Or had been; it sure wasn't now.

Genco realized with mounting terror that his safe was open, the money gone. Genco walked over to the safe, dropped his weapons, knelt down in front of it, and felt around inside, not believing his own eyes. All that was left inside were nonnegotiable, unimportant papers: his will, his insurance policy, his copy of the police department address book, his old copy of the union agreement . . .

His money was gone. Who could have taken his money? *Who the fuck could have taken his money?*

Genco turned and looked back at Joey. He was still unconscious. He turned back to the safe. There was nothing for him now, nowhere he could go and nothing he could do. He'd been ripped off; they were onto him.

He realized he was trapped.

Genco's scream, when it finally came, was as loud as and even longer than Joey's.

Elaine Hoffman and Kenny Lunch parked in front of the building and walked around to the side stairway. In this neighborhood, such a stairway was considered the front door. "You want to cover the back?" Elaine said, because she knew if she didn't, he would, and she knew, too, that he didn't want to make the suggestion to Elaine. He wouldn't want her to go back there. He was enlightened, but still old-fashioned; he'd want her in front, where witnesses were more likely to be watching if anything untoward should occur.

"I'll go back there," Kenny said, as if he hadn't even thought about the back until she'd mentioned it.

Though they were here to arrest a killer, they hadn't called for any backup. They weren't at all certain that their information had been right; they knew for sure their informant wasn't.

The woman they'd spoken to, Richard Malardi's fiancée, Marie, had given them this address, but she'd lied to them about everything else, so she might be lying about this, too. Kenny wanted to take his time, to check it out first before coming over and taking it down, and they had a number of ways at their disposal that would enable them to do just that, such as through the gas, phone, or electric companies, but Elaine had somehow convinced him that they shouldn't waste the time. She told Kenny that they had to wrap this up as quickly as they could; it would make the Special Victims Bureau look good, solving a high-profile, celebrity murder so quickly. Kenny had finally, somewhat reluctantly, agreed.

Elaine gave Kenny a full minute to get back there before she mounted the stairs, her weapon out and down at her side. Slowly, she climbed the stairs to what Marie had told them was Tommy Malardi's apartment.

The one thing she hated about this sort of apartment was, there was no place to stand when you knocked. Just the little platform in front of the door, the landing. The door was right there, in front of her, and there was no other space to stand but in front of it, on the little wooden landing. A dead target, if whoever was inside didn't want to come out peacefully.

Then again, if it was safety and security you were after, you should be driving a bus.

Elaine swallowed her fear and knocked, hard, three times, then called out Tommy's name. This close, with no cover to protect her anyway, Elaine didn't feel foolish by putting her ear to the door. She heard nothing. She leaned against the railing, just in case, and kicked the door this time. Waited. Again, there was no response.

There was no window in the door itself, probably so people walking up and down the steps couldn't violate your privacy by looking into your apartment every time they came in or went out.

But there was a window built into the wall, maybe two feet past the landing.

Elaine could step over the railing, onto the tiny little piece of wood that jutted out under the bottom of the guardrail, hold on to the railing with one hand, lean over, and, if she really stretched out, see inside the apartment. If she was lucky, she could do that.

Kenny would kill her if he knew she was going to do that. But Kenny was around back; Elaine could hear him pounding on the other door and announcing his presence.

Elaine holstered her weapon, held on to the guardrail, straddled it, then stepped over it carefully, foot by foot. Her toes were now supported only by an inch or so of landing; the arches of her feet were pressed in tight against the bottom of the guardrail, as if that would do her any good if she slipped. Elaine shook the railing once, just to make sure it was sturdy. She pressed one hand against the wall and inched herself out and over. She grabbed onto the windowsill, still holding the railing with her other hand, and forced herself to lean out further still, so she could see inside.

Elaine gasped, closed her eyes, and forced herself to hang on.

There was a body lying in a pool of blood inside the apartment, the body half in the kitchen, the other half hidden from view by the wall that separated the kitchen from the rest of the apartment.

Elaine looked again, just to make sure, then pushed off hard with the hand that was on the windowsill. She grabbed the railing and flipped herself over and stood on the platform until she caught her breath. Then she reached for the radio on her belt, and called Kenny.

*   *   *

"We're fine with a forcible entry," Kenny said, sizing up the situation in his precise, by-the-book manner. He was a lot calmer than Elaine was, standing there relaxed, thinking about what they should do, while Elaine, flushed and sweating, leaned against the door. "Hell, we might get sued if we *don't* go in there." Kenny looked at the small back porch, then looked over at the window. He looked over at Elaine. "How tall are you?"

"Let's say it was a stretch."

Elaine moved away from the door and Kenny said, "Want to call for—"

"No. If there was anybody in there, the knocking would have flushed him."

Kenny shrugged and, without pause, lifted his foot, kicked the door, and stepped back and pulled his weapon as Elaine, already armed, went in, low and ready, through the door ahead of him.

Tommy Malardi was lying facedown, his head and shoulders in his living room, the rest of him in his kitchen. Elaine touched nothing as she walked around the corpse, was extremely careful not to step into the blood, just as careful to preserve the integrity of the crime scene. She wasn't supposed to touch anything until pictures had been taken, the lab crew was finished, and the medical examiner's representative had declared the body officially dead.

Kenny came out of the bedroom, his weapon holstered, calm and relaxed. Elaine looked at him; he shook his head. She looked back at the corpse. Tommy Malardi's pockets had been turned inside out. A slim piece of paper had been torn in half and thrown on his back. It took Elaine a second to recognize it as a check. Both pieces of the check were lying facedown on Tommy's back.

"You want to go call the crew, Kenny?" Elaine said, and Kenny looked at her suspiciously. Elaine put as innocent a look as she could muster on her face, and raised her eyebrows.

"What?"

"What, what? You've got something going; I can smell the noodles cooking."

Okay. So he knew. How was he going to stop her? Elaine crouched down carefully, as close to the body as she could get without touching it.

Kenny said, "Elaine, stop it; come on, get out of the apartment, right now."

Elaine looked at the back of both pieces of the check, saw which half had the thin line for endorsement. This would be the half that would have at least part of the payee's name on the front. It would also have the check owner's name, address, and, with any luck, phone number printed in the upper left-hand corner.

"Goddamnit, Elaine, I mean it!"

Using the tip of her pen, Elaine lifted the half of the check up, squinted, cursed, then flipped it over so she could read it.

Still squatting, not looking up, carefully maintaining her balance, Elaine said, "The check's McCauley's. It's made out for twenty thousand dollars. It's made out to Thomas G.—I can't see the rest of the name, that's all that's on this side. What do you want to bet the other half of the check says Malardi?" Elaine left the turned-over half of the check right where it was, and stood up very carefully. Kenny was glaring at her, no longer calm and relaxed.

"He was stupid enough to take a check for a gambling debt, Kenny. These ain't brain surgeons we're dealing with here. We got a bookie without the courage to collect his own bets; he turns to a muscle-bound leg breaker, who takes a check, thereby pissing the bookie off to no end." Kenny didn't answer. He was too busy glaring at Elaine.

Who said, "What do you want to bet we find the smoking gun at Ingram Pleasant's apartment, tossed under the bed, like we won't bother to look there?"

Controlling himself, ignoring Elaine's smile, Kenny Lynch said, "I think we better get a warrant this time, first."

There was a middle-aged man standing on the corner of Congress Parkway and Michigan, right there at the entrance to the Taste of Chicago. What was left of his hair was grown out long, tied in a ponytail in the back with a bright pink bow. His tie-dyed T-shirt was sweat stained and filthy. He was holding a bunch of clean T-shirts in his hand, holding them far away from his body; there was a joint dangling out of the side of his mouth, and he probably didn't want to burn the shirts. The T-shirts were stenciled with the words NATIONAL ORGANIZATION TO CHANGE THE MARIJUANA LAWS. The man was shouting out at passersby in a froggy, California-surfer-dude voice that the shirts were going for twenty dollars. The man looked at Jake and Marsha and wanted to know if the dude wanted to buy one—he looked at Jake again more closely, squinting at the square. "For the chick, maybe?" he asked.

"Smoking weed sure did *you* a lot of good," Jake said, and Marsha, surprisingly, laughed.

"Do you want a beer, Jake?"

"Is that a trick question?"

"Marijuana's better for you all the way around, did you know that?"

"Bite your tongue. It's a gateway drug."

"Yeah," Marsha said. "It might even lead to drinking."

The midafternoon crowd was huge, people packed elbow-to-elbow. Jake and Marsha moved into the flow, bounding against each other every now and again, with Rollerbladers inching through the crowd, people who were pushing bicycles blocking the rare paths, gangbangers and millionaires all eating, mingling, and listening to the music as if they didn't have a care in the world.

They had the anonymity that huge crowds afford. Jake felt himself loosen up, not much, but enough to talk. Marsha wanted trust? She had no idea what she was going to wind up with. Jake didn't know where to begin, but he knew that sooner or later, mixed in with this crowd, he would tell his wife everything.

It was important that she be told.

He said, "You want a rib sandwich?" Marsha was playing along with him, as if she, too, were afraid to speak, in case she said the wrong thing. Or maybe she was giving him time; Jake couldn't tell.

"From where? There's forty places to buy them."

"Can't go wrong with Robinson's."

"You wait right here; I'll get the tickets."

Jake stood by the garbage can, watching as Marsha walked over to the ticket booth to purchase the tickets you had to use in order to buy anything at Taste; cash was forbidden. Everything cost a set amount of tickets; it was a gastronomical amusement park.

Jake watched the crowd in amazement, so many people, so many of them seemingly happy.

There were people, hordes of people, and different kinds of music everywhere, from the regular sound stages the city had set up to the street musicians with boxes in front of them for donations. There were plenty of beggars, too, hoping to con some suburbanite into giving them some of the fifty-cent meal tickets, which they could then sell to somebody else for a quarter. Jake didn't even bother to acknowledge them when they approached. There were others in more obvious, desperate need. A heavyset man in a wheelchair sat not far from where Jake was standing, holding out a tin can; the crowd flowed around him, as if he weren't even there. He had a hand-painted sign attached to the back of his wheelchair, extending out and over his head, like a hood. WW II VET, the sign said.

Jake wondered how you could live fifty years like that, what the man's life had been like.

A group of five stone-faced, nut-skinned, ageless South Americans were setting up speakers on the grass. Jake watched them, his spirits rising. They would play mandolin and pan flute music that was breathtaking in its simple, artistic composition. They'd spent the last few summers working the city, usually a little north of here, on State Street or in front of Water Tower Place. A crowd was already forming around them, waiting happily for them to begin. Jake watched a young man lift his laughing little daughter up onto his shoulders. The little girl was licking an ice cream cone. The ice cream was dripping onto her father's head, but the man didn't seem to mind. A young woman in a halter top and cutoff jeans had her arm wrapped around the man's waist, her head leaning on his shoulder. She was swaying to some inner music, in a rhythm only she herself could hear.

Jake felt a lump rising in his throat, and had to look away.

It was almost impossible for him to believe that the brutally beaten body of Jimmy Duette had been laid down on the grass of a golf course just a few blocks from this spot. It was hard to believe that there were nine hundred people killed every year in a city whose citizens seemed to get along so well at this kind of party. The hardest thing of all for him to believe was what had happened to him in the year since this party had last occurred. He couldn't look at it straight on, had to sneak a peek from the side, come up on it from the back, or the thought might drive him insane.

Jake, trying not to think about it, looked around but couldn't spot Dabney or the man with the camera, her backup. He saw a lot of cops he knew, both in uniform and plain clothes.

He felt Marsha's closeness before he saw her, felt her warmth and smelled her perfume. He turned to face her, and she handed him a thick rib sandwich.

"Can't go wrong with Robinson's, right?"

"You should have let me wait in the food line, at least . . ."

"Chivalrous, Jake, but I handled it."

It was almost as if they were dating again. Jake thought of old

Comiskey Park, of chairs with numbers on the arms. Baseball games and hot dogs, being young, smart, with your future in front of you; Jake thought about being in love.

Jake held the sandwich in his hand, looked down at it as if he didn't quite understand what it was he was supposed to do with the thing. Marsha chewed a mouthful of ribs, then seemed to notice what Jake was doing. She seemed suddenly shy, as if remembering who they really were.

Jake looked up at her. "I've been working undercover," he said to her, and Marsha stopped chewing and looked at him.

Jake said, "I guess it's time, Marsha."

"Time? Time for what?"

Jake shook his head. "Time to tell somebody. It's been building up for a while. A *long* time, I think."

"Tell somebody?" Marsha was thinking, making connections. She seemed almost fearful, now that the trust she'd demanded was being given her. Still, she said, "You can tell me, Jake."

"It started six months ago, started out slow, but in the last few days, everything escalated quickly." Jake shrugged. "And it didn't get really ugly until the end, until last night."

Jake's tone was soft and sad, his eyes wet, his bottom lip quivering. His hands were shaking, too. Marsha had seen the sandwich shaking before he'd handed it to a heavyset old man in a wheelchair who had some sort of homemade sign sticking out of the back of the chair. All of that could have been symptoms of a bad hangover, but Marsha didn't think so; she didn't think he was trying to con her, either.

Marsha kept silent as they stood there looking at each other. Her expression was solemn. Jake's was shameful.

At last, he said, "It just went all to hell. I've got IAD breathing down my neck; I've got that reporter in the middle of things, taking pictures that could get me killed. You're gone, Jesus, Marsha. And now I'm an accomplice to murder."

"You're *what*?"

"That guy they found in the park last night. I set him up. I didn't know what they were going to do with him, but I gave them his name, his address, his known associates, his hang-outs. I feel responsible."

"Who'd you give it *to*?"

"A pair of crooked Homicide cops. I've been trying to build a case against them for the past six months."

"But you said IAD was breathing down your neck. If you're undercover, aren't you working with them?"

Jake shook his head. "It was all between me, the captain, and the superintendent. We cleared it through him, and I've got the only copy of the tape recording of the meeting, in case something goes wrong. IAD doesn't know about it; Mondo doesn't even know about it." Jake shook his head. The crowd was suddenly making him feel very sad.

"Come on, Marsha, let's get out of here."

They began walking down Congress Parkway again now, past throngs of people heading into Taste, laughing, cheerful people. No one paid the somber man and woman any attention at all.

"That reporter was making me crazy. She blew it all open before it was time."

"It's a crusade with her, Jake, did she tell you her story? Her father was a cop. He wound up killing her mother."

"Oh, dear Jesus."

"I decided not to do the story because she wouldn't even write down any of the good things I told her about you, about how happy we used to be." Marsha took his arm and squeezed it. Jake heard her catch her breath. "Oh, God, where did it all go wrong?"

"With me, that's where, Marsha. You left me before I went undercover. I think that's one of the reasons Royal chose me for the job."

"And because he knew you were honest, incorruptible, brave, and loyal."

"I wish I could believe that."

Marsha quickly changed the subject. "Jake, why didn't you tell Mondo? How could you go about your daily life and just carry this all inside you?"

"It wasn't easy."

"Tell me, Jake, tell me what happened. How it started, how you got involved."

Jake, in a halting voice, began to tell Marsha everything.

Wrisberg couldn't believe it; he just couldn't fucking be*lieve* it! What kind of asshole took a check for a gambling debt? He was glad he'd shot Malardi, glad he'd killed his dumb-ass cousin, too. Kevin Wrisberg knew that if he didn't have to move on, and move on right away, he would look up everybody in the city named Malardi, look them up in the phone book and kill the rest of them, too. Wipe out the genetic line, for the betterment of society.

That's how mad he was when he parked his car in front of the building where he kept his safe apartment. Though God only knew for how much longer the place could be considered safe. With King Youngy and who knew who else on his ass, wanting to kill it, there was no telling. Anyone could see him coming or going; anyone would turn him in, especially if there was a reward on his head.

Which was why he was just going to go up there and get his clothes, get his money, then get his ass into his car, head south, and never come back. Maybe he'd even look up Duette's old lady, down in Louisiana someplace; she was probably lonely after all this time. No, he'd stay away from the white folk for the time being, none of them were reliable; they were all stupid and dumb and hateful.

He was thinking such thoughts when he stepped through the door of his apartment and saw two stupid, dumb people looking at him hatefully, but they weren't white folk.

They were Ingram and Rasheed.

Ingram was holding the small suitcase that held Wrisberg's money. Rasheed was holding a pistol.

"What it be like?" Wrisberg said, the last words he ever spoke.

Thompson said, "We don't know where he went, we were waiting upstairs; we didn't want to make a scene downstairs, where the civilians could see us."

"Yeah, the press, too. Wanted to keep everything in house until the press conference, right, Thompson?" Mondo was glad they were talking on the phone. He was afraid of what he might do to the man if Thompson had been standing in front of him.

"You know where Phillips is? We checked his apartment; he's not in."

"You think Genco might be after *Phillips*? What for?"

"He'll know that somebody turned him in by now; he'll suspect the new guy, Phillips. We want to have a little talk with Phillips before we put a warrant out on him, you know what I mean, Mondo?"

"You prick!" Mondo was thinking on his feet, shouting into the phone. "You organized this!"

"What? You give me too much credit."

"You have people at his apartment?"

"We're stretched too thin for that. We're out searching for Genco, you know. He's the rogue elephant, not Phillips."

Mondo looked out at the squad room; he'd sent all six available members out to serve the warrant with Lynch and Elaine. He hung up the phone without another word, grabbed his coat, and was out the door.

Ingram and Rasheed could not believe their good fortune; they laughed and sang and played the radio as loud as it would go, all the way back to their mother's apartment. It wouldn't be her apartment for long, though. They would now be moving up in the world.

Ingram said that they should rent their mama a Gold Coast apartment, a three-bedroom place, where the two of them wouldn't have to share a bedroom, where they could even have their own toilets. Rasheed said fuck that, he wasn't renting shit; they could buy a high-rise condo. Or maybe one of them pretty houses on Elm Street, as he personally wasn't real fond of heights.

There was a suitcase right there, on the front seat between them, that had more money inside it than they'd ever seen in their lives. And King Youngy wouldn't have to know anything about it.

King Youngy? The king himself? "He nothin' but a asshole," Rasheed said. "He can kiss *bofe* of our asses." Ingram couldn't see a hole in his brother's plan. King Youngy wouldn't know anything about the money; he'd be so happy that they'd killed Wrisberg that he might even make them lieutenants in his gang.

"You call mama as soon as we get home, go down the drugstore and call her, Ingram. She ain't working in that hospital kitchen for one more *minute*!" Rasheed said. Ingram said he would do just that.

He pulled the old, battered Cadillac to the curb a few houses down from their own and shut it off. There were a bunch of cars on the street today, but he didn't pay them any attention. A lot of people in this neighborhood did not have day jobs; the curbs were almost always filled.

The two of them got out of the car and played catch with the little suitcase.

Ingram ran ahead, up the cement steps, arms outstretched. "I'm Jerry Rice; hit me, Steve Young!" Rasheed threw the case, and it landed squarely in Ingram's chest. Ingram, laughing, opened the door to the building, and walked into the barrels of a whole bunch of guns.

"DOWN! NOW! HIT THE STREET, ON YOUR FACE, MOTHERFUCKER!"

Rasheed still had the gun, and Ingram turned to him, disregarding the officer's command. "RashEED!" Ingram felt something hit him hard in the back, and he tumbled down the steps, smacking his head a good one on the concrete, hearing gunfire, shots he knew were coming from several different weapons. There were hands all over him, roughly searching him, holding him down. His arms were twisted up around his back; he felt something snap in his arm, shouted out a scream, but it wasn't a scream of pain, it was a name.

"RAAAAASHEEEEEEEEE*EEEEEEED DDDDDDDD*!" Ingram shouted, before one of the cops slapped him in the head and told him to shut the fuck up before he shot him.

"They came at me because they thought I was like my father. Tested me, asked for favors, and I did them. Anson came to me, not Genco. Genco's the crazy one, but he's the weaker of the two. As soon as Anson came to me, I went to the captain."

They were walking again, passing Wabash now. A group of people were waiting for the bus up on State. Jake looked at them, thinking about it.

"At first Anson acted as if he just wanted to be my friend. He played it very carefully, made sure I was compromised before he started giving me money."

"And what did you do with it?"

"Every dime of it's in a lockbox at Citibank. Along with about forty videotapes. I have had no contact with the superintendent since the meeting. I've only talked to the captain when I had to. But I had to a lot. As for the money, the times it was handed over, who gave it to me, why, everything was written down in a ledger."

"And pictures? Tapes? You mentioned videotapes. So you have supporting evidence, Jake? My God, if Dabney runs the pictures she has of you . . ."

"The recorder, believe it or not, was hidden in my weapon. No cop would ever touch another cop's weapon. They'd frisk his balls, they'd touch his ass to look for a wire, but they'd never touch his weapon."

"And the pictures?"

Jake grunted a laugh. "Hell, I almost *told* them where the camera was, just today. It's inside the Rolex. You tap the stem, it starts working. It's closed circuit. Tape machine's in the trunk of the car."

"Police equipment?"

"No." Jake smiled cheerlessly. "I got it all at the Spy Warehouse; everything. You believe it?"

"My God, when I saw the Rolex . . ." Marsha looked at Jake peculiarly. "You know what I thought?" Jake didn't answer. He knew. In a softer voice, Marsha said, "You could have gotten *killed*."

"You want to know something, Marsha? That was part of the attraction. You'd left; I'd been drinking. I wasn't seeing Lynne every day. I'd lie in bed at night and fantasize about dying, about them killing me, about what I did coming out in the papers and on TV." Jake stopped speaking for a second. "I thought you'd understand me, if that happened. Thought you'd know that I was a good cop, a good man."

"I always *knew* that, Jake!"

"Maybe it was me who didn't always know it."

They walked slowly past the Harold Washington Library, Jake dodging around a group of happy young people who were coming out of the place all at once, Jake looking ahead to Plymouth Court. After that, Dearborn and home.

"When I told you this afternoon that I needed some time?" Jake took a deep breath and let it out. "It all came to a head a little later. I'm meeting with Pete Lemelli tomorrow morning. I understand we're going swimming."

"Pete Lemelli, the gangster?"

"The one and only."

Marsha stopped him right on the corner. There was a new Lexus parked in the bus tow zone, directly behind Jake's car. A van was double-parked next to the police vehicle. Jake watched as the cameraman in the passenger side of the van lifted his camera up and began to snap their picture.

"Jesus Christ, just what we need!"

Jake looked back at Marsha as she said, "You're not meeting with him, Jake. This is it. This is decision time." Over Marsha's shoulder, Jake saw Dabney Delaney-Hinckle walk around the side of the van and begin to approach them.

Marsha said, "You make up your mind once and for all what you want in your life. If it's me and Lynne, you quit, right now, today. You've got your captain—and God knows who else—manipulating you. You're in over your head with men you *know* have killed at least one man, and now you're going off to a meeting with a mobster? No. I forbid it." Marsha reached out and grabbed Jake's biceps, held him tightly, an arm's length away. Dabney would be able to hear her in just a second.

"I mean it, Jake, we don't need the money! You don't need the excitement! We can be a family again."

Jake said, "Watch it," as Delaney-Hinckle came up to them, smiling.

Somewhere in his cop's brain, Jake registered the fact that the door to the Lexus was now wide open.

Jake's line of sight was obscured by the reporter, but he still noticed a somewhat familiar figure walking rapidly toward them, a heavy man in a short-sleeved shirt, who was now breaking into a run.

Jesus Christ, it was Genco. And he was lifting his hand up from his side now, a hand that was holding a gun. He pointed the gun at Jake, and there was nothing that Jake could do.

Genco was right there now, in front of him, and Jake had two choices—slap at the gun with his right hand, or slap at it with his left. He didn't have time to think about it, processed this information in a microsecond while Genco was sticking the gun barrel into Jake's stomach. Genco held the gun in his right hand; it was on Jake's left side.

If he hit the weapon with his right hand, the shot might hit one of the women.

Jake slapped clumsily at the gun with his left hand, and the first bullet hit him in the center of his stomach. He felt the force of the blow drive him back, over the planter, onto his back in the gravel. He heard men shouting, heard a woman's long scream.

Jake thought that his father was hitting him again, had given him a good shot to the belly, where he usually hit Jake, in a spot where it wouldn't leave any marks for the nuns to see, or the gym teacher. His father had hit him in the belly, only this time, his fist was on fire.

The second bullet hit Jake in the shoulder, and he barely felt it, just registered a jolt somewhere in his upper body.

The third bullet hit him in the neck. It felt, to Jake, like a mosquito bite.

He heard several more shots, and then there was the sound of scuffling. Jake was on his back, staring up into the sun. The woman wouldn't stop screaming. Ma? Was that his mother? Jake heard his name shouted, shouted over and over again. He thought that if he kept looking at the sun, he might go blind. But he feared that if he closed his eyes, he would die.

His father was leaning over him now, looking down at him, and Jake tried to smile, tried to tell him that he forgave him. It seemed important for Jake to finally say that to his father. He felt something wet flowing out of his mouth. Had daddy punched him in the mouth? Odd. He'd never done that before. Jake thought that he must have been a very bad boy this time.

"Jake! *Jake!*" He felt his father slapping his face, and he closed his eyes, squeezed them tight. He tried to not cry, but felt the tears flowing out of the corners of his eyes.

"Jake, *goddamnit,* look at me, Jake!" Jake did.

It wasn't his father after all; it was Mondo looking down at him.

"*Jake!* Can you hear me, Jake!" The terror in Mondo's voice forced Jake to open his eyes wider still. There was a sudden, intense, hot pain, deep within him. He tried to clutch his stomach, but his hands wouldn't move.

Jake came back to reality for a time then, remembered that he'd been shot. He panicked, knowing he was gut-shot, and that he was more than likely dying.

"Marsha!" He tried to shout the name, but it came out barely a whisper.

"Jake, hang in there, son, hang in there; the ambulance's on the way."

Jake felt Mondo squeezing his hand. Where was Marsha! He could hear her screaming. He wanted to talk to her, to tell her that everything was going to be fine.

His shoulder was burning; his neck, too. Three times? He'd been shot three times? He'd never make it. He started sobbing, shouting.

Mondo said, "It's all right, Jake, it's all right; you're going to be okay."

"Good . . . *cop!*" Jake shouted.

"What?"

"Good . . . COP!" Jake said again. Tears were rolling down his cheeks; he was hyperventilating. He knew if he didn't stop it, he'd pass out, and if he passed out, he would die, but he couldn't control himself; he didn't have any choice. The pain was so bad, so bad!

Jake Phillips didn't want to die. Not at thirty. Not alone. Not without Marsha holding his hand. Where was Marsha?

"Good?" Mondo's face was close. Jake could smell his breath. "Kid, you were the fucking best I ever saw." Jake nodded, and felt himself drifting. Mondo's hand was squeezing his, but Jake felt only a dull, receding pressure.

The pain was going now, too, fading away. That was a good thing. He didn't know how much of *that* he could have taken!

Jake was a good cop; sure he was, the best. Mondo had said so himself.

And there Marsha was, swimming into his vision. Jake heard

the sirens closing in. The sun was obscured by Marsha's hair. She was leaning over him, crying.

Jake Phillips felt a brief flash of sadness that Marsha had witnessed this, was there to watch him die. It would have been better if she'd seen it on TV. The feeling passed, and he closed his eyes, let go of Mondo's hand, and gave himself over to the darkness that attached itself to him with as much intensity as the hot pain had just moments before. As he swam into it, Jake heard his name loudly shouted, knew that the voice was Marsha's, and he tried to smile.

He would never know if the smile reached his lips.

The funeral was held on the coldest day of the year, just one full week before Christmas, seven shopping days left.

He'd hung on in the coma a lot longer than the doctors had thought he would. But then again, doctors didn't know everything, now, did they? They didn't know about heart, about courage, about the will to live. You couldn't quantify such things, so they couldn't be taught in medical school.

Mondo thought about this as he walked into the funeral parlor, escorting Elaine in ahead of him. The two of them were no longer sneaking around. She had transferred out of Special Victims after killing Rasheed Moore, on the same day Jake Phillips had been—on the day that Jake had been shot. My God, almost six months ago now. Had it been that long? Where did the time go?

The funeral parlor was filled with people, mostly police officers, come to the wake of their fallen comrade. There was a festive mood in the air; Mondo could smell alcohol. He saw Thompson making a beeline toward him, tried to avoid him, but there he was.

Mondo couldn't hit him here, not in front of all these witnesses. The two men hadn't spoken since the day—well, since that day.

"Lieutenant Mondello, good to see you." Mondo nodded at Thompson.

"Mrs. Mondello, congratulations."

"It's still Hoffman, but I appreciate the sentiment." Thompson's face fell.

"I thought you two got married . . . ?"

"We did," Elaine explained, "but I didn't change my name."

Mondo watched Thompson act as if he didn't understand, as if Elaine had tried to briefly explain quantum physics. He himself still didn't say a word.

"Well, that was one tough son of a bitch, wasn't he? Hanging in there all these months?"

"Some people just have a stronger will to live," Elaine said, and Thompson, feeling a part of the group now, actually beamed.

"The wife's just destroyed; I mean, she's really taking it hard."

"The daughter?" Elaine asked, and Thompson pretended to be sad.

"She's not taking it real well, either," he said.

Mondo felt no anger, no resentment, no hatred. He just wanted to look at this man for a minute, that's all. He felt Elaine squeeze his arm.

Heard her say, "Well, we better go pay our respects." People were passing them now, nodding, lowering their eyes when they saw Mondo, their smiles fading as they passed the lieutenant; it could have been because they knew that Mondo and the deceased had once had a strong, nearly unbreakable bond, or it could have been because of who Thompson was, what he did; Mondo didn't know.

"I hear Marsha's in medical school now."

"Yes," Mondo said, the first word he'd spoken, and Thompson took to them like a shark to chum.

"She's at the U of C?"

"We better go pay our respects," Elaine said again, and Mondo touched her hand. He wasn't ready yet.

"And . . . ?" He left the question hanging. Thompson could figure it out or play dumb, it was up to him.

"Listen, I blew it, all right? I'm sorry. Turned out, all things being even, we didn't even really need Jake's testimony; there was nothing he could have told us that we didn't already know from Wozak and Mrs. Genco. Jake's tapes, they were icing on the cake." Thompson must have seen the look that passed across Mondo's face. He hurriedly said, "Genco—the stupid bastard—he'll spend the rest of his life in a wheelchair, behind bars." Thompson paused. "Nice shooting."

Mondo had to close his eyes for a moment. He felt Elaine holding tightly to his arm.

"He probably can't even *think* about what his wife did to him." Thompson shrugged. "It helped that we didn't go after the money. That's between her and the IRS."

"Wasn't for a few small details like the captain and the superintendent's sworn testimony, the tapes, the ledgers we found in Jake's box at Citibank, not to mention the pictures the reporter took, showing Jake taking a bullet on purpose, you'd have been right about him, huh?"

"Mondo, honest to God, who could have known?"

"*I* should have known."

"Well, at least he went out a hero, what with the blow-job story that reporter wrote, the pictures . . ."

Mondo nodded his head, bit his lower lip. Anyone watching would think he was grieving over the expected but horrible death of his friend.

Mondo said, "Excuse me," and lowered his head, took his wife's hand and squeezed it, then walked with her through the crowded viewing room and over to the casket, where Mondo nodded at Jake Phillips, who was seated in his wheelchair, still recovering from his wounds, seeming uncomfortable with all the attention he was getting from the officers in the room who hadn't seen him in a while.

Marsha was at Jake's side, her hand resting on Jake's shoulder.

Mondo and Elaine would be going back to the Phillips household for a Christmas celebration as soon as they got out of here. But first they knelt together and said a prayer for the repose of Captain Merlin Royal's soul.